UNABASHEDLY CHOSEN

1

CULEBRA CHRONICLES

HALF-PAST 2 PUBLICATIONS

This book is a work of fiction. Names, characters, places, and incidents are the product of the author's imagination or are used fictitiously. Any resemblance to actual events, locales, or persons, living or dead, is coincidental.

Copyright © 2024 by Chrissy Chicory

Cover Design: Caroline Marques
Illustrations: Canva.com
Editing: Enchanted Ink Publishing
Book Design and Typesetting: Enchanted Ink Publishing

ISBN: 978-1-963402-07-0 (E-book)
ISBN: 978-1-963402-04-9 (Paperback)

Library of Congress Control Number: 2024900137

Thank you for your support of the author's rights.

W W W . C H R I S S Y C H I C O R Y . C O M

Dedicated to my mom, Aunt Debbie, and
both of my grandmothers, whose memories
and lessons remain a guiding light.

UNABASHEDLY CHOSEN

1

CULEBRA CHRONICLES

CHRISSY CHICORY

CHAPTER 1

CRICKET

The chilly air wrapped around Cricket, her fair skin crawling. Darkness hung heavy like a blanket of gloom. She was used to this subterranean world but had to steel herself against its oppressive atmosphere. This place below her family's antique shop resembled a dungeon from a medieval fairytale. The stone walls were scrawled with ancient paintings of the fae, drawn centuries before the city above was built.

The room was lit by torches, long wooden poles with pitch-soaked rags that burned bright and hot. The scent of burning wood filled the stale air. Cricket glanced around the vast space. The place was littered with crumbling books, odd trinkets, and pieces of decaying furniture. Her vintage yellow dress and youthful frame made her stand out amongst the darkness.

The area hummed with the vibrations of the ley lines, pathways that ran between two worlds like a secret river.

Cricket was dual-natured, born between two planes—part fae and part human. Her mother had given up much of her power when she chose to bond with a mortal man. Although Cricket had inherited fae gifts from the Culebra line, her mother's line, she was unable to access them fully because of her mortal father. This left her feeling lost. It was a heavy burden for her to carry, yet she bore it gracefully. Despite doubting herself, Cricket would courageously take on the mantle her aunt Habina had left behind when she died nearly a decade ago. She would become an embodiment of both realms—one who could traverse both planes with ease.

Gingerly, she traversed the cavernous room, her eyes fixed on the cold, dark fireplace before her. Caressing the yellow sapphire set high in her bronze ring, she cleared her mind. "Illuminar," she quickly whispered. Vibrant orange flames flickered atop the torches, casting animated shadows on the stone walls, as a roaring fire leaped to life in the fireplace. A faint glow illuminated the eyes of the many canine guardians carved in the smooth black onyx mantel. Their fur undulated, and their heads moved, as though they were living creatures, alert and ready to hear her words. For centuries, these mythical guardians had kept the Culebra line safe from harm.

She ran her fingers through her thick flaxen locks. Drawing a few stray strands from her temple and then kneeling on the worn-out Persian rug, she tossed them into the blue-green flames. The fire's warmth kissed her face as her hands instinctively rose to invoke the power of the air. Chanting softly, she could feel its invisible currents brushing against her skin, infusing her with its essence. She opened her eyes slowly, basking in its ethereal beauty and elemental magic.

A rumble beyond the thick wall to her right gave her a start. She and her sisters had been forbidden by Gran and Mama from ever entering the mysterious tunnels. Their aunt Habina's disappearance further confirmed the danger that lurked beyond the entrance. The story of what happened had never been fully explained to them—Cricket had been eighteen years old at the time, plenty old enough to be brought in the loop—but it was awful enough for the adults in their family to seal off all access points to the Sub from beyond their guarded space. Although the occasional rumbles were still audible even after all these years, she paid no attention to them and continued her chant.

Energy began swirling like a vortex around her body. Sparkling blue light, an electric blend of purples, pinks, and blues, shot from her hands. It spiraled upward to heat the room; the fire was stoked into crackling life. The energy twisted around her until it looked like nothing more than a shimmery streamer floating in the air. Submitting to the protection spell that heated the room, the energy quickly faded to almost nothing. Only the sizzling of the fire could be heard.

Her eyes fluttered open, and she felt a familiar wet sensation on her cheek. Tikaboo, her beloved Cavalier King Charles spaniel, was standing there with those deep chocolate-brown eyes. The pup had been a present from her friend Bash her first year of university, to help with homesickness. After a gentle peck on the head, the pooch joyfully pranced off, as she did every morning—a sweet reminder of their unspoken bond.

Cricket stood up, the warmth of the fire still lingering on her skin. The rumble beyond the wall had grown louder, and she could feel the vibrations under her feet. She walked over to the wall, placing her hand on the uneven surface. The vibrations were coming from the other side. Her curiosity piqued, she closed her eyes and focused her energy on the wall, trying to sense what was on the other side. Images of dark, twisted creatures began flooding her mind, their mouths viciously snapping at her. She could feel their hot breath on her skin, their sharp teeth tearing into her flesh. She gasped, breaking the connection, and stumbled back, her heart racing. Even though she was half fae, she knew her powers were no match for whatever dwelled behind the wall.

She took a deep breath, trying to calm her racing heart and steady her trembling hands. Part of her morning routine was to check in on and reinforce the protection spell. She needed to reinforce it before starting her day. She reached for the yellow sapphire in her ring and channeled her energy into it. The gemstone glowed brightly, and a surge of power coursed through her body. She closed her eyes and concentrated, the images of the creatures still fresh in her mind.

"Protectors of the Culebra line,
hear my call once more.
Strengthen the wall that keeps evil at bay,
and protect the mortal realm from harm forevermore."

The wall trembled, and for a moment, she thought it would crumble, but then it steadied. She could feel the energy of the spell pulsing through the stones, reinforcing them and making them stronger.

She took a deep breath, trying to center herself, and then reached for her light cashmere sweater hanging on a nearby hook. As she slipped into it, the images continued to swirl in her mind.

"Cricket!" her grandmother's voice rang from upstairs. "I need your help up here!"

Cricket leaped around the circular iron staircase, her feet nimbly bouncing off each step. She shouted back to her grandmother as she rounded the last bend of the spiral staircase, gliding gracefully into view. She stood tall with a beaming smile, slightly out of breath but otherwise triumphant. "Coming, Gran!"

"Can you help me fit all these boxes in here?" Gran spread her arms, showcasing the piles of boxes that created an obstacle course around the myriad of antiques. Cricket scanned the floor of Baubles and Whatnots, their family antique shop. The scent of leather was heady but not unpleasant. The dust was less offensive than she expected with a haul of this size. Boxes and totes were stacked four high, forming a precarious mountain range running the length of the store. The amount of merchandise was more than she'd anticipated. Cringing at her miscalculation, she shot an apologetic look at Gran.

"I didn't think there would be so many boxes," she muttered, the immense pile of items on the shop floor looming in front of her. She was determined to make a success out of this shop and prove to Gran that she could handle it on her own. But Cricket knew how difficult it was for fae to let go and move on from their mortal lives, especially when they were so deeply connected with them like Gran was. She wanted nothing more than for Gran to rejoin the fairy realm and claim her eternal youth. But until she was certain that her granddaughters had grown powerful enough, Gran wasn't willing to leave them in this realm unprotected.

Gran waved her hand dismissively. "Don't worry about it, child. We'll manage." She gave Cricket a reassuring smile.

Through the front window, Cricket could see the quaint cobblestone streets of Old Town bustling with activity. Families leisurely walked beneath the flowers of the Spanish moss trees, while merchants hawked their wares from small shops along the sidewalks. The movers' truck was blocking the street, creating a traffic jam. She had to think fast for a quick solution.

"Gran, I think we should have the movers bring the boxes to the Sub." She held her breath, expecting a negative response.

Gran's icy-blue eyes bore into Cricket's. Her tiny frame gave no clues to the power behind those eyes, but Cricket stayed strong and held her gaze, waiting for an answer. The rule was that only members of the family were allowed to descend the steps. Gran referred to it as the Law, and until now, no one had challenged her on it. Gran pushed her spectacles up her nose with a bony finger, setting the gold chain swaying. A frown creased her forehead as she stared at the staircase behind Cricket. Cricket knew what she was thinking. Her eldest daughter had disappeared down there. The Law was there for a reason. "Not a good idea," she said curtly, her eyes narrowing.

Cricket heaved an exasperated sigh. "Then we'll have to close up shop. We can't let people come in here the way it is. It's a lawsuit waiting to happen. If we move all the boxes to the Sub, I can do the inventory down there tonight. Then I can gradually bring up the collection for sale and take the stuff we want to donate directly to the car."

Cricket watched as Gran shifted her weight from foot to foot, knowing how heavy this decision was for her.

"Maybe . . ." she said hesitantly. "I'll need to be down there with them to make sure nothing happens." She moved toward the stairs.

"Gran, it's just boxes. I won't let them wander. I'll send them right back up. I can handle it." Cricket held her by the elbow and guided her back to the desk. Gran didn't need to navigate those steep steps or be in a space that made her so sad. "I'll head downstairs and start clearing an area for the boxes. Just send the guys down."

Gran let out a deep sigh. "All right," she said. "Otis is picking me up for bingo soon anyway." Otis had been Gran's companion for a few years now, and Cricket was glad he was able to bring some joy into her life after the loss of Aunt Habina. Otis had managed to pull Gran out of her deep depression gently and gradually during their time together. He was a good distraction. Her eyes lit up at the sight of him. Though, obviously he was oblivious to the fact that Gran was fae. No one knew that the women of Cricket's family communed with the elements.

"Ah, so that's why you're so dressed up," Cricket remarked.

Gran blushed and spun around to show off her white jeans, red flower-print blouse, and white flats. Her eyes sparkled in the light.

"You look beautiful," Cricket said with a smile.

Gran's eyes shifted to the window, where the movers were outside stacking boxes on a hand trolly. "Thank you, Cricket. You might want to step into the ladies' room and freshen up before the movers come back in." There was a hint of mischief in her tone, but Cricket couldn't imagine why her appearance would be so important to Mr. Henderson. He'd helped them on many moves and was old enough to be her father. "You look like you rolled out of bed and skipped your morning routine. Very uncharacteristic of you," she continued, her red lips forming a frown.

"I thought I would get by on charm today," Cricket shot back over her shoulder. She'd been so immersed in a book last night, she couldn't put it down until she'd finished it, which happened to be at four a.m. *Worth it.* She had still managed to make her bed, have a cappuccino, and perform the morning protection ritual before opening the store.

"Run a brush through that rat's nest of hair," Gran yelled after Cricket as she began descending the stairs. "As charming as you may be, no one's going to get past the sloppy to see it."

Cricket rolled her eyes and pulled the hairband out, combed her hair with her fingers, and twisted the strands into a messy bun at the nape of her neck while taking the stairs two at a time. She lifted her arm and took a whiff and frowned.

"This will have to do for now, Gran," she mumbled.

The Sub had become a nice, cozy temperature with the fire burning. As Cricket glanced around the room, wondering where she should stack the boxes, a cold wind blew against her neck. Turning toward the sealed wall, she noticed tiny specks of light penetrating the edges of the cement around the bricks. She began cautiously walking toward it but was startled by voices and commotion at the stairs.

"Cricket? You down here?" Mr. Henderson's voice rained down into the Sub.

"Yep!" she shouted back, heading toward his voice.

A pair of well-weathered boots descended into sight, followed by a face that had seen years of sun. Mr. Henderson's muscular, stout frame was crowned with a kind, fatherly face that peeked around the stack of boxes he carried.

"Where would you like these?" he asked, taking a moment to catch his breath.

The sound of something sharp and jagged scraping against the stone wall echoed through the Sub. Mr. Henderson, confused and startled, looked toward the direction of the noise with a furrowed brow. Cricket, always alert, quickly sensed his concern and pulled his gaze toward her.

"Um," she said loudly.

The scratching continued. It was impossible to tell what sort of creature could make such a sound, but whatever it was had clearly taken an unhealthy interest in their presence. She needed to make this quick. As she looked past Mr. Henderson to the other mover, she was delighted to see a young man. His tousled blond hair was slightly damp with sweat at the temples, and his tanned, muscular body sent a smile to her face. *So that's why Gran told me to brush my hair,* she thought. Gran was always trying to fix her up.

"Over here, if you could," she said, pointing to the wall farthest from the scratching noise.

Tikaboo, eager to make a new friend, sped up the stairs in a flash and got wrapped around the man's legs. She rose on her back legs, brushing her front paws against his trousers. He almost lost his footing and tumbled down the steps, yet he maintained his balance enough to not step on the pup.

"Cricket, this is my son, Alex." Mr. Henderson gestured toward the younger man as he set the boxes down.

He gave a slight nod, and she returned the gesture with her own. His smile grew wider. It was apparent that he had inherited his father's kind, blue eyes.

"So, let's head back upstairs." Cricket waved a hand toward the stairs.

Alex's eyes roamed over the room. "Man, your insurance must be insane . . . Does this flood every hurricane season?"

"Oh, we're fortunate," she replied with a shrug. "Must be in an unusual spot; it's never flooded to my knowledge." She winked at him for emphasis. "And a little protective shield doesn't hurt either."

He cocked his head to one side, amused at her response. "Interesting decor style," he said with a grin. "I like all the swords on the wall coming down the stairs." His laughter echoed through the large space as his eyes scanned the wall of ancient books surrounding the ornate fireplace.

Cricket was charmed by his curiosity, smiling despite herself. "This is where we keep our family heirlooms," she explained patiently. "They've been passed down for centuries." Her gaze followed him as he approached the crystal skull resting on the desk.

Alex nodded in appreciation before turning back to face her. "I've never seen such an eclectic stockpile of items, and being a mover, I've seen quite a bit." He gestured around him with wide arms.

She gave a small nod of affirmation before heading up the stairs. "I'm sure you have; let's head upstairs."

"Cool skull!" Alex exclaimed. "I heard these have some kind of special powers." He reached for it, but she quickly snatched it away, a flush of panic racing into her cheeks.

"Sorry," she said, seeing the wide-eyed look on his face. "It's extremely fragile and belongs to my sister." She breathed heavily, returning the skull to its metal stand. Legend had it that these crystal skulls were believed to possess powerful healing and spiritual energies — Babs knew this firsthand. Her conduit to earth's ley lines was a silver skull earring, granting her access to their magical properties no matter how far away she traveled. With just a slight thought from Babs, the ancient energy could be drawn upon, allowing her to tap into its power and manifest whatever she desired.

"Son, leave things alone, now," Mr. Henderson hissed as he pushed boxes against the wall. Let's grab some more "boxes," Mr. Henderson headed for the stairs.

Alex turned to follow him. Their heavy boots created low thuds as they trudged back up the stairs. Cricket's eyes softened, and her heart filled with the warmth that came off the two of them. It made her think of Babs working with Mom on the farm. Their fae powers drew from the earth. They could grow anything. Their knowledge of nature was vast and powerful. She'd never thought about how nice it must be to do this together. Aunt Habina had been the only other person in their family who'd communed with air, like her. Gran was trying to teach her, but it was frustrating to both, since she couldn't do it herself. The truth was, it was on her to figure it out for herself. Not an easy thing to do as a halfling. Cricket was different from her mom and Gran. She wouldn't accept the limitations they had endured, both by choice and in sacrifice. She would never settle to be a mere halfling, a shadow of what she could be. No, she'd figure out a way to take up the full mantle of her fae heritage and stay close with her family.

Thirty minutes passed, and at last all the boxes were stacked neatly in the Sub, ready to be explored. She walked Alex and Mr. Henderson upstairs for the final time and said goodbye. While she swept the shop floor, the doorbells made a light jingle sound.

Humidity from the afternoon heat rushed in from the outside as Otis strutted through the door. "Ladies, ladies. How lovely to see you on such a beautiful day." He flashed a broad smile of unnaturally white dentures toward Gran.

His silver locks were plastered in place. His dark caterpillar eyebrows framed his red-tinted glasses. An unlit cigar stuck out from the midst of his salt-and-pepper mustache and beard. He tapped his gilded cane on the pink granite floor three times. Grabbing his cigar, he placed it in the front pocket of his Hawaiian Santa surfing shirt. Anything went, as far as fashion was concerned in Florida.

Cricket looked from Otis to Gran, noticing a touch of pink coming to her grandmother's cheeks as she grinned up at the handsome gentleman. *Hmmm, he has his own magic.* It couldn't be the white tennis shoes with the tube socks and shorts combo, but it was something, by the looks of her smile.

"Hi, Otis. I hear it's bingo night," Cricket said.

"Yes, and I'm feeling lucky. How about you, honey bear?" he asked Gran. "Are you going to win us a bag of money so we can travel the world?"

"You bet I am!" Gran said. "Otis, do you want a glass of wine before we head out?"

"That would be just lovely." He stopped in his tracks and raised a hand to his ear. "Is that flamenco I hear? Are you feeling passionate today, my saucy girl?"

Things had been so crazy; Cricket hadn't paid any attention to the music Gran was playing. The soulful guitar wailed a passionate tune. Otis flourished his hands and stomped out a few flamenco steps and put his hand out to Gran in a dramatic fashion.

"Good ear!" Gran exclaimed. She looked pleased that he'd noticed. She used her hands to lift her light frame off the chair and walked elegantly out from behind the desk, taking her time, staring Otis down, enticing. Then she raised her arms along with the guitar while circling Otis with delicate steps. They were adorable.

Cricket imagined dancing with Bash that way. She'd been fighting off feelings for him for so long now, yet she still desired to be close to him. But she knew a fling between them would be too costly—Cricket's powers were at stake if she ever dared to fall in love with a mortal. As much as it broke her heart, she had seen what happened to her mother when she chose love over power, and Cricket refused to suffer the same fate.

For now, she needed to focus on running the family store and showing Gran that she could handle things here on her own. Take care of Gran first, then figure out her own life path.

"We'd better get going," Otis said, giving Gran one last dip.

"Cricket, are you sure you can handle all this?" Gran asked.

"Yes, I'll be fine. You two go on and enjoy your evening. Tikaboo will be here to keep me company. Won't you, cutie?"

As Cricket turned to head for the steps, she awkwardly bumped into a statue on the glass counter, sending it crashing down into the glass case filled with antique beer steins. Colorful ceramic shards littered the floor like leaves falling from a tree.

Cricket winced, looking at the filthy floor. "Sorry, Gran. I'll clean it up."

"Don't worry about it, Peanut. I can skip bingo if you need me to. Maybe this project is just a bit too big for you," Gran said while frowning at Otis.

"Yeah, hon, no big deal. We can do bingo anytime." Otis chuckled. "No use crying over broken glass, or something like that."

Cricket dropped her gaze to the ground in front of her,

feeling a flush spread across her face. "No, I got this. Enjoy your date," she mumbled as she grabbed the dustpan.

"If you're sure." Gran smiled. "I'll probably be back sometime tomorrow morning, before the shop opens."

Both of their quaint apartments were situated above the iconic shop in the heart of Old Town St. Augustine, Florida. Cricket had moved into Aunt Habina's old quarters right after finishing college, and her grandmother had resided in the other for as long as Cricket could remember. The walls of the centuries-old dwellings were thick with history and comfort.

"Gotcha, no worries. I can man the fort."

As Gran and Otis left, Cricket started sweeping up the shattered pieces of the statue, her mind still preoccupied with thoughts of Bash.

The romantic music enveloped her. She couldn't help but wonder what it would be like to dance with him, to feel his arms around her and his lips on hers. The image made her knees weak.

But she quickly pushed those thoughts aside. Love was not an option for her, not when her family's legacy depended on her staying in control of her powers. She couldn't risk everything for romance, no matter how strong her feelings were.

Once the mess was cleaned up, Cricket headed back downstairs. Exhaustion washed over her body, and she suddenly regretted staying up late to finish that book. She wanted to do this job correctly. She wanted Gran to be proud of her. But there was no way she was going to get through all these boxes.

Unless . . . She quickly pulled out her phone to text her sisters.

Cricket: SOS, exhausted and need to do inventory . . . come for backup? Bring pizza? I have wine.

Zadie: . . .

Babs: Not a good time. Mom's out of town for the week. I have way too much on my plate.

Zadie:

Cricket: Please!

Babs: Fine, what time?

Zadie: . . .

Cricket: Now-ish?

Zadie:

Babs: Zadie, am I ordering for you or not?

Zadie: Fine

Cricket: Okay, see you guys soon

CHAPTER 2
BABS

Babs strutted through the crowded Pizzeria with a cool, edgy demeanor that radiated vivaciousness. Everywhere she looked, people scurried about in chaotic bliss, clattering dishes and chattering voices carrying through the air. She spotted a green plastic chair tucked away in a corner of the outside seating area and quickly slinked into it. As she waited for her order, Babs scanned the tabletop littered with advertisements for the eatery, annoyed by their noise and commotion.

Finally, her usual waitress gave her a complimentary lemon water and assured her the order would be ready soon.

Babs stubbornly spiked her black Converse-clad feet onto the chair across from her and took a long, satisfying sip of her water with lemon, savoring it's tart flavor while running her thumb over the perspiration on the glass. Her fuchsia lipstick marks blotted one side of the glass as an act of defiance against straws. Her awareness landed on her aching feet; Mama had left the responsibilities of the farm to her while she was away. She knew it wouldn't be just a few weeks, like Mama had promised.

Babs's mother had been called to England more and more frequently over the last couple of years, by the leaders of the druids. Each time she went, they asked her to stay a while longer. What made her mom so important to their plans was beyond Babs's comprehension, and her mom wasn't giving away any clues. She sighed in frustration and crossed her arms.

Without Mama's cooking, especially coffee and breakfast every morning, everything felt wrong. Even worse were the gnomes in the garden; their presence was cold comfort. They were more work to her than help.

As Nadine's icy breath skimmed across Babs's neck, sending shivers down her spine, she heard soft words swirling around her: "Why are we dropping everything to do Cricket's job on top of ours? Farmers market day is so draining." With that, Nadine's sheer form materialized next to her.

Babs watched her twin sister, Nadine, who was transparently hovering beside her. She had a faraway expression that Babs recognized as a sign of a foul mood. Babs could feel the cool chill of the supernatural presence and resisted the urge to bite at the inside of her cheek as Nadine spoke in her calm, deep voice.

Babs had had a pleasant time that morning at the farmers market, accompanied by Nadine. She set up their booth with fresh produce and homemade goods while Nadine's dark figure danced around the customers. The market had been busier than usual, with baskets full of vegetables being snatched up by eager hands, and jars of honey and goat cheese disappeared too quickly for Babs to keep track. Thanks to her sister Zadie's spell on their booth, there were no products left for Babs to carry back to her truck. After the long day, she felt exhausted but content.

Her sister Zadie was fae of the sea. Everyone in the family seemed to admire her for the power and grace she exuded while manipulating the watery depths. Though jealousy gnawed at Babs's heart at times, it was overridden by unconditional love for her older sibling.

Babs was a creature of the earth. Nature waxed and waned over her; she easily took its power as her own. Plants bowed to her touch as if she were one of them. The farm was her home. Rain and sun alike beat upon her skin as she worked and labored. Her mother shared the same gifts, and there was plenty of room for the two of them; yet when Babs needed space, she always had the woods. She was never truly alone with Nadine; life was pleasingly good.

"We should be sprinting through the lush forest right now, not wasting away at this tedious table awaiting a pizza for our beloved sisters. You know you'd rather be home," Nadine huffed.

Nadine floated across the table with grace. She cracked a daring smile and blasted her breath on the dead candle in front of her. The lifeless wick sprung to life, reflecting in her stealthy silver eyes. They were the same in every way but one: their eyes. Nadine's gaze was as frigid as arctic ice, while Babs's eyes were like warm liquid chocolate.

Babs felt a freezing chill envelop her, wishing she could suddenly teleport back into the quiet embrace of home. The city felt so stifling with its chaotic masses, stifling air, and concrete barrier blanketing the ground. She would gladly never leave her land or venture beyond the woods. When she touched the soil, she could feel its throbbing heart-beat and clearly hear the trees whisper as bees hummed in melodic tunes around her. The vegetation surrounding her grounds was wild, thick, untamable. She had hacked through the bramble with steady hands until she reached a small pond only miles from her humble abode. Huge ancient trees with moss-covered trunks loomed like sentinels over an alligator-infested lake that pulsed with life when she drew near. They hissed in unison as they sensed her coming, then sniffed the air to pick up her scent. When recognition dawned on them, they had basked lazily in the sunbeams to let her sit peacefully and listen intently.

The sudden blare of a car horn shook her out of her musing.

"I would rather be home," said Babs with displeasure as she thought of Cricket, "but Cricket needs help." Babs sighed glumly.

"You just don't get it, do you? Zadie is a year older than us, and Cricket three. The only reason they even tolerate you is because of our father — the one we never knew. Pity is why they include you. And both only call when they need something. It's not like they want to just hang out with you," Nadine spat as she floated up higher, her transparent bare foot dragging across the chair next to her, knocking it over. Babs bent down to set it back up.

"You're wrong. Gran is aging and can barely handle running the store anymore, plus Cricket has had to explore her air magic without Aunt Habina's help over the last decade. The least we could do is bring her a pizza on days that she finds stressful. That is what sisters do." Babs sighed. "She does the same for me."

But Babs knew there was no way she could reason with the domineering Nadine. She could be so possessive when it came to spending time with Zadie and Cricket, especially since they refused to accept Nadine as their sister. They claimed not to know what she was and demanded she not commune with her. The topic of Nadine was strictly off-limits.

"Babs, you know you're not at home, right? You should put your feet on the ground." Nadine's voice was full of arrogance as it rang through the air. Babs felt her feet fly off the chair across from her and slam into the ground.

"Hey, no need to be so aggressive," Babs seethed through clenched teeth as Nadine jostled her.

"Don't be such a whiner," Nadine snarled viciously and dug her fingernails into Babs's arm as Babs twisted and yanked it away. A burning welt instantly appeared where Nadine had made contact.

Babs averted her gaze from Nadine's menacing stare, focusing instead on the vast concrete parking lot stretching out before her. The cars bustled about in rows like a colony of ants.

Ignore it. Best not to get her going, or there will be hell to pay.

Nadine's voice was a sinister whisper as she leaned into Babs's ear. "Look at that wretched family there, under that faded sign. Such an innocent babe! Look how it giggles when the fan swivels and tickles her with its breeze."

The baby's gaze seemed to be drawn to Nadine like iron filings to a magnet. Babs found it interesting that children could see so easily what adults could not. With a wicked tug of her will, Nadine pulled the baby closer to her malevolent face. Its eyes widened with terror, and its face grew bright red.

"Knock it off!" Babs bellowed, jarring everyone in the vicinity and making a waitress that was passing by shriek in shock.

Babs threw apologetic glances at the nearby table while Nadine innocently shrugged. "What? I'm not hurting anything," Nadine replied coyly as she drifted back to Babs's side, her silver eyes still locked on the baby's terrified form. "I'm just bored."

The toddler released a great breath before banging its toy on the table defiantly, as if challenging Nadine's menacing presence. The adults surrounding them returned to their conversations, though they tossed glances periodically at Babs out of the corner of their eyes.

The mahogany door swung open, and a waitress emerged, gracefully holding a serving tray with one hand and a breadbasket with the other. Her eyes darted around the space until they landed on the family with the baby. She placed a tray filled with red plastic glasses on the table. Babs gazed at the waitress's thigh, where a colorful David Bowie tattoo was peeking out from under her jean miniskirt.

Babs admired tattoos. She liked how they commemorated special events or periods in a life. She had celebrated her twenty-first birthday by getting her own tattoo of La Catrina, the Queen of Día de Muertos, which draped down her left arm. The Queen's index finger covered her mouth in warning, while a clock below ticked off the moments passing by. Every line and dot was done in purple — except for La Catrina's eyes, which were an exact match to Nadine's silver ones. She glanced at her G-SHOCK watch, desperate to leave soon. Nadine had already grown bored and was starting to become restless.

As the first waitress walked back into the restaurant, a second emerged through the door and walked towards her with two pizza boxes.

"Here you go; I have a Wonder Woman and a white pie, add mushrooms. Oh, and the other bag has your family-size salad." She smiled at Babs sweetly. "I'm guessing you go for the Wonder Woman."

Her blond ponytail swirled around her while she talked, her lips smacking and popping with a large piece of gum between her teeth. Babs watched intently as it flicked from one cheek to the other, fast in its movements.

"You called it."

Nadine wafted behind the waitress, tucking a loose strand of the blond's hair behind her ear. Then Nadine's gaze turned hard and cold as she leaned in closer and slowly licked her cheek.

The blond shivered and flinched. "Oh, I suddenly feel nauseous," she murmured, placing her hand on her stomach.

"Just as sweet as she looked." Nadine sighed deeply, licking her lips hungrily and wrapping her arms tightly around the waitress in an iron grip. The waitress's skin grew pale; her eyes went dull, unseeing.

Babs's eyes locked on Nadine's mocking stare. A knot formed in her stomach that seemed to grow larger. Babs stared Nadine down. She finally let go of the terrorized waitress and crossed her arms, saying nothing.

Victorious, Babs sprang to her feet. She felt the familiar weight of her wallet and phone in her cargo shorts pocket. She fingered the flask of rum in the other pocket, along with her trusty pocketknife for protection, as she firmly donned her aviator sunglasses.

In a small voice, the dazed waitress murmured, "Goodbye then."

"Yep," Babs replied curtly, leading Nadine off the patio.

After a long hike back to the truck, rivers of sweat ran down Babs's back. She slid into the driver's seat and glanced at Nadine in the passenger-side mirror. Nadine was sleek, as a cheetah.

The pizzas fit neatly in the back seat. The hard plastic of the visor felt cool enough, but Babs's sweaty hands left a mark. The steering wheel was too hot to hold as she turned on the ignition. The stiff leather seat stuck to her thighs, the same shorts she'd worn for the last week. She reapplied the fuchsia lipstick and ruffled her short purple hair. The sides of her hair were shaved close. The tiny studs in her ears felt mildly sharp against her fingertips. She lingered on her silver skull. She was never without it, for it held a deep connection to the full-sized crystal skull safely stored in the Sub—a place of powerful and magical energy. As she ran her fingers over its delicate carving, she felt a hit of energy enter her system.

The crackling static of the radio filled the space between.

As Nadine ran her hand through Babs's new do, her facial expressions softened.

"I thought you didn't like it," Babs responded. Nadine's shadowy dark hair seemed to move by itself, cascading over her like a living entity. Her dress clung to her form like an insubstantial shroud.

"It will do, I suppose. At least with your hair shorter, we can tell each other apart."

Babs shifted the truck into gear.

Nadine glanced out the window and smiled slyly. "Mama wouldn't be too happy to know we were leaving the house unattended for the night."

Babs rolled her eyes. "We will be back before sunrise. I don't want to stay in Old Town too long; it zaps my energy. There is too much concrete, and the 5G makes me feel numb all over and unable to sense my surroundings. I don't know how Cricket and Gran do it," Babs said warily.

"Well," Nadine purred, "the grounding spell you cast at Baubles and Whatnots makes it energetically clean inside. It just would be a real shame if something bad happened at the farm while we were gone," Nadine said sweetly.

"The gnomes are on watch, and I cast an invisibility spell

on the whole property before leaving. I did Mama's whole protocol," Babs grumbled. "It's ridiculous, you know. Nothing, human or otherwise, would be interested in our property. I don't see what the big deal is." She glanced down at her watch. The ethereal tick of the second hand filled the air; they had been in town for almost an hour. Nadine seemed almost oblivious to the sounds of the city—the electric hum of the streetlamp, the creaking of metal gates, and most notably, the absence of birdsong. Hundreds of years of human interference had dulled the magical vibes, and there was no hint of it in the air.

Nadine brushed a strand of dark hair out of her eyes and raised her hands above her head in a lazy stretch. "I'm sure Mama has her reasons. You don't think she is hiding something important on our property, do you?" she sneered, her laughter like tiny daggers piercing through Babs's skin. "There's got to be some reason she is so protective of the farm."

"It's in her nature to be cautious. There isn't a reason."

Nadine rolled her eyes and changed her focus to the middle-aged couple across the street wearing matching navy-and-white striped shirts and long white shorts. Black fanny packs seemed to hold up their middles, their arms weighed down by dozens of shopping bags. They were both looking at a map, brows furrowed in confusion.

"Are they heading to the winery or the brewery?" Nadine asked as she looked at Babs with disdainful amusement.

"Neither—the chocolatier!" Babs retorted nervously as she glanced away from Nadine's gaze.

Babs could imagine Cricket being like them—dressing up in matching outfits and finding theme parks fun—out of the three sisters, it would be Cricket who would live a normal life . . . but not Babs, never Babs.

Nadine's mouth curved into a sinister smirk. "Well, I know that is your favorite place here," she purred menacingly. "Of course, if you are going to indulge in chocolate — and we all should — it must be the highest quality," Nadine said placatingly.

Chocolate was Babs's guilty pleasure, a warm embrace of sweetness that she just couldn't avoid despite eating healthily on most days.

Babs rubbed at the welt on her arm that still ached with pain. "I hear you." Babs grinned, relieved Nadine's dark mood had passed. "Do you think we have time to grab some chocolates?"

Nadine grinned and nodded in the direction of the local chocolate shop. Babs followed her lead, like always.

CHAPTER 3

CRICKET

The inky night sky steadily wept its tears, obscuring the treacherous cobblestones. Zadie's lithe figure silently moved through the darkness, her small frame barely visible with each step. She hopped over a puddle, and her small feet skidded on the mud below, sending her fragile body crashing to the ground.

Babs, who had been nimbly keeping up behind her, effortlessly lifted her off the ground with a mighty heave, and they raced back into the family antique shop. Thunder boomed overhead as they shifted weighty boxes already sifted through by Cricket and sorted into keep-for-the-store or donate. The walls were lined with wooden shelves that bowed under the heft of old books, stacks and stacks of plates, vases, figurines, and all manner of knickknacks. Zadie and Babs shivered as a cool rush of humid air blanketed their skin. They heard Cricket calling them from the Sub. Their feet felt heavy as they slipped down the iron steps for what felt like the hundredth time this evening.

Cricket cast her gaze to her watch: three a.m. The hours had gone by with a blink, and yet she felt unsettled. Even the comfortable silk vintage-style pajamas draped on her body and satin slippers on her feet could do nothing to ease her foreboding. She had been blessed with an extraordinary power since childhood—when she laid her hands upon a trinket, it would magically transport her to the past. As if a dream, the object would unveil its secrets.

Aunt Habina had taught Cricket when she was growing up about the ancient wisdom of harnessing magic intentionally as a protective tool. Since then, she had been steadily honing her skills of siphoning negative energy from objects that had become harmful and releasing that energy into the ley line that would neutralize that energy, restoring it to good.

Cricket took a deep breath and closed her eyes, her senses alert to the foreign energy in the sub. The pungent smell of mothballs and the dry, brittle feel of old photographs filled her mind. She opened her eyes and saw Zadie standing beside her, radiating assurance and safety—her aquamarine gaze filled with concern.

"You doin' all right?" Zadie asked. She placed her tiny hand on Cricket's shoulder and gently squeezed it.

Cricket nodded and forced a smile. "Yeah, just feeling a little drained."

"I can only imagine," Zadie said sympathetically. Her voice was calm and soothing like the ocean waves on a summer day.

The boxes they'd gone through so far held mostly personal home items, from modern times back to the 1920's.

Zadie and Babs had thoughtfully piled up the boxes filled with miscellaneous objects that were older for Cricket to go through one by one at her own pace. With each ancient piece she touched, a strange energy pierced her soul—

memories that predated her own life experience. But so far this evening, all were normal and happy in origin. The artifacts were safe to be moved upstairs right away.

"What do you think causes objects to be vulnerable to gathering bad mojo?" Zadie queried, her fingers spinning a snow globe in her grasp. The flurries of snow inside the glass orb swayed gracefully with each revolution.

"The way Habina explained it, items — small as a thimble, large as a house — anything created by human imagination has the ability to collect and hold memories. If an item has collected too many dark memories over time, its resonance could turn malicious. It could form its own sentience — come alive, so to speak. If left unchecked, these items could influence the minds of unsuspecting individuals."

"Like haunted houses?" Babs asked.

"Sure, haunted houses, gravestones. The world is littered with items that have negatively influenced countless people, sometimes subtle yet other times explicit. There were knives that pestered the mind to kill in cold-blooded rage, dolls that hypnotized children into a profound sadness that left them listless and frail."

"Eww, your magic is so serious. I prefer mine." Zadie sprawled her lithe limbs across the woven rug. Her flaxen tresses cascaded across many grand cushions.

"Not everyone can be a siren, Zadie," Cricket retorted.

"Protection powers, being able to ground energy, these are important magics." Babs nodded at the wall concealing the tunnels. All had been quiet on the other side so far this evening.

Zadie yawned. The bottom of her turquoise tank top revealed a blue tattoo of an octopus that encircled her midriff, its tentacles extending outward from below her denim cut-off shorts. Tikaboo scratched at the slithering form.

"Zadie, don't bait Tikaboo," said Babs as she flopped onto the tremendous leather armchair and hooked one leg over the armrest. Her foot swayed back and forth in a hypnotizing manner. She pushed away the strands of lilac-hued hair that obscured her right eye. Torchlight twinkled off the jewelry that adorned her ears. "Zadie, did you hear me?" Babs questioned more firmly with a note of vexation in her voice as her fingers caressed her skull earring.

"Yeah, yeah. I just didn't want to have to chase around the little guy, all right? It's much simpler when we are in the water. I am the faster swimmer. If he goes missing down here, then you're finding him!" Zadie rotated her azure topaz ring on her index finger so that it faced inward and pressed it softly against her tummy. She closed her eyes and inhaled deeply. "Kraken, I release you," she muttered unceremoniously.

Babs and Cricket observed as the tattoo began wriggling, sliding down Zadie's side. Tentacles started protruding from beneath her leg until they fully formed and detached themselves into a two-foot-tall crawling octopus. It unfurled its arms and embraced Tikaboo, merging with her red-and-white colors, making it difficult to differentiate canine from cephalopod.

"Off they go," Cricket encouraged contentedly at the spectacle. She grabbed her mug of matcha tea. Her velvet slippers made a familiar soft noise across the stone floor.

Tikaboo bounded around the room, her paws pounding the floor with each step. The kraken clung to her back, its tentacles lashing behind them in a tangled mess. Zadie dodged and rolled between the duo, narrowly avoiding being trampled as Tikaboo charged past her. When she sat halfway up, she waved her arms wildly and shouted at Tikaboo to stop.

The frenzied dog scrambled to obey but got her legs tangled in Zadie's long hair instead. Tikaboo yelped as she was yanked from her feet and knocked into a pile of crates in the corner.

The firelight cast dancing shadows across the walls, and for a moment, Cricket could have sworn she saw a figure moving against the corner of the room with silver eyes. Babs stared off into the corner, transfixed by something unseen.

"Let's call it a night. I'm so tired I'm hallucinating," Cricket said.

"I call your bed." Zadie yawned. "I should be in my own, or in Tom's."

"Her couch is more comfortable anyway." Babs started to kick off her shoes.

Cricket's curiosity was piqued. "Still with Tom?" she asked Zadie, pulling her hair back and retying it in a ponytail. His name had been on Zadie's lips for quite a while now. She usually didn't stick with guys that long. She was more of a love-them-and-move-on type. But Tom wasn't her usual beach-bum fling. He seemed to be something else, like a trustworthy anchor holding her ship in place. Dangerous, for a fae.

Babs cut in, "She likes her men seaworn, and this one is well worn."

Zadie ignored them both. Typical, she never talked about her private life.

"Really, nothing? You're not gonna elaborate at all?" Cricket pressed.

"What is there to say? I like Tom. End of story."

Cricket's heart halted as Zadie burst into her siren song, summoning Kraken. Her hypnotic voice curled around the dark corners of the room. The air thickened with anticipation as she and Babs approached the boxes shrouded in shadow. Out of the darkness Tikaboo emerged, head bowed and ears lowered.

"Where's Kraken?" Cricket asked. Tikaboo turned back to the shadows, forcing Cricket to open her palm to the candelabra attached to the wall and whisper, "Illuminar." The candle wicks burst into flame, illuminating three unnoticed boxes, making it easier for Cricket to see.

She pulled away the top two boxes and saw a chest with several layers of paint on it that had a keyhole opening. It must have been how Kraken had squeezed into the box. Honestly, he could compress his body into anything. She tried lifting the top of the chest, but it wouldn't budge—until she uttered the command "abrir," causing an audible crack of the paint as the lid popped open. Underneath were some old linens—quilts and such. She mussed the pile of soft cotton blankets. There was no sign of Kraken.

The energy of the room changed in an instant. Cricket closed her eyes against the sudden vertigo.

She was no longer standing in the Sub with her sisters; she was on a white wooden porch with freshly painted white wicker furniture and colorful wildflowers brightening the landscape. Lost in a dreamlike trance, she watched as a woman wearing a long dress of yellow-and-blue gingham slowly rocked back and forth in the chair, humming an old tune. Her hands rested protectively on her stomach as she smiled down at the quilt draped over it; she was expecting a child.

White light surrounded Cricket as she returned to the present moment abruptly, jolting her shoulders to reorient herself. She shook the quilts out gently as she searched through the dim light for Kraken, but he was nowhere in sight. Tikaboo continued to paw at the trunk.

"Did you mean to do that?" Babs asked.

"Honestly, no. I'm just so drained. I should have gone to bed long ago."

Cricket and Babs peered into the trunk, only to find it empty. Annoyance flashed across Babs's face as she scanned the corners of the box in search of a clue. All of a sudden, her eyes sparkled with optimism when she noticed a small hole in the bottom. She wasted no time in producing her pocketknife and hastily scratched away at the paint until the false bottom cracked open. Inside was an agitated Kraken thrashing against its confines while an ancient book rested in another corner, its pages so worn that they seemed to have been read a thousand times over. Cricket slowly reached out her trembling hand and touched the spine of the book, every fiber of her being telling her to turn back—that this was the source of the unease she had felt throughout the evening. But there was something inexplicably irresistible about the book.

Zadie moved with mystical agility, summoning Kraken into her embrace as if he were a missing puzzle piece. His form coiled around her arm, and shockwaves crackled between them like electricity. Gently pressing her ring against the crown of his head, she whispered sweet assurances in his ear until he was absorbed completely into her body. Zadie's eyes closed in silent contemplation as an invisible force began to swirl around her.

"Kraken says the book isn't good," she declared, and for a moment the room seemed to breathe with their combined energy. "He must have felt some troubling magic within its pages."

Cricket instinctively grabbed the book and leafed through the pages, but Zadie warned her to stop. "Wait until Gran gets here tomorrow; I don't think we should handle it without her." Yet Cricket paid no attention—she was transfixed by the ancient book before her. Its mysteriousness beckoned her, teased her. She couldn't help herself; she had to touch it. The secrets of the book were calling to her, and she felt compelled to answer.

Cricket kept stroking her finger over the soft yellow sapphire ring on her right hand, willing herself to keep calm and focused. She placed the book on her lap. The leather felt warm in the palm of her hand; she longed to reach out and let those pages slip between her fingers. There was water damage and burned areas scattered throughout its twisted edges. She flipped a few pages. The edges frayed apart with each turn, revealing drawings of constellations, cargo lists, and journal entries. She flipped more until all faded but the book.

She stood in a dark corner of the catacombs, her skin prickling at the sight of bones entombed along the carved-out walls. Pyramids of skulls were guarded by crucifixes at the foot of the staircase leading up toward the single source of light that illuminated the room.

Towering above all was a tall man with a thin mustache, whose dark eyes scanned the area intently. He seemed to be looking for something as he bellowed out questions about how the intruders could have possibly entered. His fingers anxiously fiddled with the ends of his mustache as if searching for an answer to his own query.

The air was heavy with tension. A soldier nervously wiped sweat from his brow with a soiled handkerchief before responding, "Don't know, Captain. We had several men at the top and twenty stationed down here. There is no way in but from the top."

Cricket crept forward, craning her neck to get a better look. The place struck her as familiar. Something stirred behind her. She turned around and saw shadows moving, then felt something fall to the ground, which she quickly realized was a gold coin. Curious, she picked it up. Her attention returned to the men in front of her when she heard them discussing that all of the gold had been spirited away, along with extra artillery and ammunition.

The captain pulled at the lace at his neck; his life on the sea showed in his well-worn face as he spoke in disbelief: "You're telling me all of the gold is gone?"

The soldier's hands trembled as he spoke. "Yes, sir. It seems all the gold has been stolen away, and with it the extra artillery and ammunition, as I said before, sir." He kept his eyes downcast, fixed on the mud-caked boots that clung to his feet like a second skin.

The captain spun round and spat on the ground in fervent passion. "Our beloved Queen Elizabeth, may she reign forever, did not send us across the ocean for naught! We will not be defeated by those Spanish heathens!" His voice thundered through the air as he inclined his head toward his men and added in a low whisper, "Keep your wits about you, soldier. We are here to bring back her gold, no matter the cost." He paused for a moment before turning around to face them with fierce, beady eyes blazing like two burning stars. His face glowed brighter with feverish loyalty as he lifted up his book threateningly.

"Devil among us!" he roared. "Devil I say!"

He lumbered toward Cricket like an angry beast while spittle gathered at the corner of his mouth, ready to be unleashed. His icy fingers clasped onto her wrist like a vise, as his gaze settled on the coin gripped tightly in her hand.

"I fear you not, devil!" the captain barked out in defiance.

"How could you — " she asked in bewilderment, panic pooling in her gut.

He seemed oblivious to her words as two soldiers dropped to their knees and crossed themselves in prayer. The remaining men *followed suit soon after; all eyes turned to heaven in desperate supplication.*

In all her visions, no one had ever seen her before. Some had heard the lightness of her breath, sensed her presence, but never saw or touched her.

"Behold the demon who has stolen the queen's gold!" the captain roared as he thrust the book above his head with the gold coin he had taken from her fist.

"I didn't take your gold! I didn't do it!" she whimpered in desperation, but he took no heed.

"Wail for eternity, fiend." He opened the book to its last page and placed it on the ground before her. An iron knife glimmered in his right hand as he slashed across the palm of his left hand, letting blood drip down onto the center of the page. Her fear soon turned into terror when he grabbed her fist and sliced open her own flesh. Intense pain surged through her hand as the pain traveled up her arm as if her body was being set on fire. She lost control of herself and screamed in agony. The commander pressed his bloody hand onto the page and said, "By my lifeblood bound to this book, these bones lining the walls act as my witness. I curse thee, spawn of darkness!" With a single press of their bleeding hands against the book, she knew he held total power over her. "Return what is mine within four tides or wander between worlds forever!" His sour breath accosted her nostrils as he menacingly stood just inches away from her, searing fury radiating from him. His grip tightened around her hand like an iron chain as he pushed the book to her solar plexus and sneered. "Bring back the gold, to this place, or else your fate is sealed."

She felt the book fall from her hands as her vision cleared; Zadie and Babs were standing before her, their eyes wide with shock.

Zadie exclaimed, "We saw you go stiff and thought you might be having a heart attack!"

Tremors raced through Cricket's body as she remembered the scene—the curse, the blood, and the fear that had gripped her so suddenly. Clenching her fists until they shook, she looked down. She fought to steady herself, willing her heart to stop pounding against its cage.

"You must have bumped your hand. You're bleeding." Babs wrapped a cloth around her hand and continued gently, "Start slow, take some deep breaths. Tell us what happened."

Cricket took a few ragged breaths before beginning her story. Desperation crept into her voice as she explained the cave, the bones lining the walls, and how she'd been spotted by a captain who charged her with stealing his gold.

Fear coursed through Cricket's veins like an icy river, as she could still feel the captain's wrath directed toward her. Tears threatened to spill over as she told them about how he had cut both of their hands, smearing them together in a primitive blood pact on the page of the book that now lay open in front of them. Her eyes widened with dread as she finished with a quiet whisper: "He cursed me . . ."

"That sounds ominous," Babs said.

"I shouldn't have touched it! But it, it called to me."

Zadie grabbed the book out of Cricket's hands and stared hard at the brown stain on the center of the page. "What is this?" she asked, blinking rapidly.

"He cut his hand and mine; that's our blood. He shoved the book at me. I didn't get a chance to syphon the energy or transfer it to the ley line. I think, it's in *me*. I think the curse is in me."

Zadie's grip tightened around Cricket's hands, the color draining from her face. In the center of Cricket's left palm, a spidery web of purple-and-black streaks snaked out from the cut.

"No . . . no no no!" Zadie screeched, scrambling away from her and clapping her hand over her mouth as her wild eyes darted around the room.

"What? What do you know?" Cricket begged, her chin trembling as she fought to keep the tears brimming in her eyes at bay. Habina hadn't warned her about objects having this kind of power. All her syphoning attempts had been successful, until now.

"Cricket, it's the most powerful sea curse there is. Pirates are ruthless. Everyone knows that. But even they have their own code — one which if broken can result in a pirate being sentenced with the dreaded 'Black Spot.' This means that death herself has been unleashed upon you — in whatever form she may take: illness, accident, or even driving you to take your own life! It's impossible to avoid or prepare for her arrival, as she can strike from any angle." Zadie sighed, wiping a shaky hand across her forehead.

"Is there any way to break the curse? The merfolk must have some cure or something capable of fighting it?" Cricket leaned closer, desperately hoping for answers. If anyone knew of a cure, it would be the merfolk.

"No, unfortunately there isn't anything that can lift the Black Spot once it has been issued," Zadie murmured, turning her gaze downward towards Cricket's wounded hand.

"He said I had four tides."

A heavy silence fell upon the sisters as Zadie muttered, "Two days; we have two days."

Babs leaned into her sister Cricket; her eyes wide as she stared at the palm of her hand. She nervously chewed on her bottom lip before quietly asking if Cricket could go back inside the book and undo what happened.

"No," Cricket replied, shaking her head. "My magic doesn't work like that; I can only go back once. At least, that is all I have been able to do so far. Once the object shows me its nature, the connection is completely severed after the experience. But once is enough for me to know if it's bad news." Her gaze drifted away as she thought of her aunt. "I wish Habina was here!"

"Okay, I'll try!" Babs blurted out.

Zadie and Cricket looked to Babs. Her face had gone red. She was staring into the corner, as if she was seeing someone. Zadie lost her temper.

"Are you still seeing Nadine?" Zadie asked through gritted teeth.

"Let's stay on topic . . ." Babs tried to redirect the conversation, knowing full well what was at stake if they pursued that subject further.

Zadie continued, "Nadine isn't real, Babs. Grow up. We know it's hard that she died, but good grief, you are in your twenties. Accept reality; our sister is gone."

Oh my God, things were bad enough already without this turning into yet another fight night about Nadine. Hadn't they had enough of these already?

"I'm not discussing this with you." Babs's nostrils flared as her vision clouded with teardrops streaming down her face.

At that moment, the fireplace erupted in a bright blue flame that lit up the entire room. The crystal skull began to glow. Babs pulled at her earring.

"I'm not saying what you see isn't real; I'm saying it's not our sister," Zadie persisted. "Don't you think it's weird that only you can see and sense her?"

Cricket stood up and walked to the corner of the room, unable to bear witnessing them fighting any longer.

"No, I don't think that it's weird to be able to see and

sense my identical twin," Babs declared with unyielding conviction as her eyes burned fiercely with determination. "I've never known life without her; she may have passed, but she never left me." Babs balled her hands into fists. "I have always trusted and supported both of you whenever you needed me. Hell, Cricket, you just got cursed by an object, and I'm not standing here telling you it's all in your head or you are somehow misunderstanding the situation. I'm just trusting you and showing up. Why can't you reciprocate that trust and loyalty?" She pounded her fist against the floor as a deep rumble echoed through the ground, and the skull on the mantel began to glow brighter with an otherworldly light.

"Babs, I'm sorry," Cricket said with a hint of desperation in her voice, "but Nadine is gone, and you must accept it. Mama and Gran have been clear on this. I'm trusting their judgment. If you insist on speaking about seeing something that isn't our sister, then you are really putting us in a bad position. Zadie and I have kept your secrets so far, but this must stop. We can't keep going like this."

"Really. So glad you cleared that up." Babs spun around, her face turning to granite with fury, and glared at the fireplace.

"Hasn't Mama's heart been broken enough? Bringing up her dead child isn't going to help anyone," Zadie whispered woefully.

"Babs, you know I agree with Zadie," Cricket said as she shot a cautionary look at Zadie. "Enough of this conversation. Let's focus on what needs to be dealt with now."

Zadie breathed out heavily before reluctantly agreeing.

Suddenly, crackles of electricity burst from the skull, and sparks began to shoot wildly around the room.

"Babs! You need to get control of yourself!" Cricket screamed desperately. "We said we would stop taking about it."

"Shut up, I'm concentrating!" Babs grabbed Cricket's wounded hand, clearly tapping into the crystal skull's mysterious magic. The crystal lit up like a beacon of light, an orange blaze that promised hope. Electricity filled the air. Babs let out a frustrated yell.

"I can't, it won't," Babs stammered. "How is it possible that the curse is stronger than the skull? It's tapped into the power of the ley line directly. It can neutralize anything."

"I knew it wouldn't," Zadie said, rolling her eyes.

"No, you didn't," Babs shot back. She reached into her pocket and took a swig from her flask.

"It was a good idea though," Cricket said encouragingly. "Thanks for trying."

Babs shrugged. "Do you have any idea who the guy was that cursed you?"

"He mentioned something about Queen Elizabeth, and their clothing was like the costumes from the reenactments of . . ." Cricket trailed off, rubbing the palm of her hand.

"Reenactment of what?" Zadie chimed in.

"Drake. Sir Francis Drake." Cricket nodded. "They looked like the actors that reenact Sir Francis's raid every June."

"I missed this year's reenactment. I was out sailing," Zadie mused. "Are you sure it fits that time period? There have been a lot of privateers and pirates in our area's history."

"Positive," Cricket answered, still rubbing absently at her hand.

"Well" — Babs grimaced — "how do we find out about this guy?"

Cricket walked over to the bookshelf and began to browse through the books, hoping to find something on Sir Francis Drake. After a few minutes of searching, she pulled out a dusty old tome titled *The Life and Times of Sir Francis Drake*. She flipped through the pages, looking for any mention of the treasure.

"It says here that Drake was a famous pirate who sailed the seas in search of treasure on behalf of England," Cricket said, scanning the pages. "He was known for his cunning and bravery, and he amassed a great fortune during his lifetime."

Babs sighed, "That is a pretty vague description, not much to go off of. Cricket, why don't you hit up the historical society tomorrow to see if Bash can help you identify the diary as Drake's? Identifying the captain is the first piece of the puzzle. We are guessing Drake, but we need to be sure."

Zadie smirked. "Are you still crushing on Bash?"

Sisters could be so annoying. But at least they had stopped fighting. Cricket began to pace across the floor, feeling a mix of excitement and fear. She wanted to find out if she was right about Drake and the lost treasure. Her slipper stepped on a wayward book on the floor, causing her to stumble dangerously close to the fireplace. "I'm okay," she murmured, trying her best to ignore the idea that perhaps this was an early sign of the curse. But surely she had time to fulfill the task. The curse wouldn't just kill her right off the bat.

Babs and Zadie stood silently, eyes wide.

"I'm okay, I swear," Cricket muttered, trying to reassure them.

Zadie stepped forward and hugged her tightly, swaying slowly back and forth like seaweed in the surf. "The lost treasure," she whispered soothingly. "I'll ask around at the marina; sailors always know the old stories."

But Cricket still felt overwhelmed by worry. Though she wanted to believe that everything would work out in the end, deep down she was fearful that two days just wasn't enough time.

The moment was broken abruptly by Babs's loud voice. "We have to find the final piece of the puzzle," she said sharply. "You said something about a cave full of bones? I think I know who I can ask about it." Despite her attempt at calmness, her tone still held a hint of resentment.

Why did they have to talk about Nadine? Tonight, of all nights! Cricket anxiously rubbed her hands together and asked, "Are we good?" as she looked directly into Babs's eyes.

Babs didn't answer right away, hesitating with her gaze fixed near the wall. She absentmindedly touched her lip with a quivering finger, a telltale sign of her anxiousness. "Yeah," she finally said quietly. "We're good, and we are going to figure this out."

Cricket sighed and started flipping through the diary, taking pictures of every page with her phone's camera.

"Babs, let's be extra cautious. Tie the book to the skull!" Cricket encouraged. Its milky surface shone dully in response, pulsing with arcane power. The skull would protect the diary from magical detection and alert Babs if anyone tried to touch it.

"Done." Babs nodded, the tension slowly dissipating. She took the book and placed it on the fireplace mantel and set the skull on top of it, directly between the guardians. "I'll see what I can find out about the cave tomorrow."

"Sounds like a plan," Zadie said, flashing a smile.

Cricket watched as her sisters headed up the staircase, feeling the weight of the curse heavy on her shoulders. She knew she couldn't do this alone, but the thought of dragging her sisters further into this mess made her heart ache.

She glanced at the skull as it glowed dimly in the dark room. She knew it was safe. Her eyes glanced over the wall that hid the tunnels, all was quiet. For now, she had to rest and try to stay positive. Tomorrow they would find a way to break the curse.

She closed her eyes and took a deep breath, willing a sense of calm to wash over her, but as she exhaled, something sounded like the faint flapping of wings.

The words were inaudible. Light and lilt. Far away and foreign. She frowned, wondering if she was just imagining things. But then she heard it again, clearer this time.

She discerned the voice: the intimidation, the authority. It was unmistakable. "I'm coming for you." The ominous timbre whispered like the sound of fluttering wings. "You're mine." Cricket opened her eyes and looked around the room, but there was no one there.

CHAPTER 4
ZADIE

Stunning and resplendent, Zadie glided toward Tom's dock. Her luxurious blond locks billowed in the salty ocean breeze, a siren's tendrils on land. She shimmered in the sun, her tanned skin reflecting the midmorning heat, her navy bikini highlighting her tight curves with finesse. Her denim shorts were damp from carrying the local light pilsner cans, yet she seemed weightless and free. But inside, Zadie was burdened by the knowledge of her sister's curse—something that no Florida sunshine could ever hope to wash away.

The turbulent melody of the ocean surged through Zadie's soul, echoing a distant calling she had known since birth. Yet a quiet dread weighed heavy in her heart, for with each passing day came a reminder of what her fate did hold. Aunt Maj had left too soon after her sister Habina's death, leaving Gran two daughters to mourn. With every year that passed, Zadie understood Maj's deep longing for the embrace of salty waters.

She ached to feel the waves against her skin, but her loyalty kept her feet planted firmly on land. She wanted to enjoy living near her family in her own ship near Tom for as long as she could. But it wasn't easy — Tom had left for two months for his latest dive, and even though Zadie wasn't particularly clingy or the monogamous type, he met all her needs in ways no other had before. She was excited for his return but scared of bonding too deeply with someone who wasn't fae, realizing that the day of her departure was eventually going to come.

The St. Augustine Municipal Marina was a sight to behold. The countless boats moored alongside the docks radiated a quiet charm, especially in the presence of the majestic Bridge of Lions and the torch-lit martini lounge in the distance. It wasn't just an ordinary marina either, as many of the people who called it home had taken up full-time residence on their boats, including Zadie's own love interest, Tom. He was often away on business for extended periods of time, but that didn't stop her from being excited each time he returned.

His little haven was moored on the south end of the marina, just off the shore. His sixty-foot tugboat was brimming with diving and recording equipment. As for its captain, he was as rugged and sturdy as his vessel. Every modern contraption was aboard to assist him — the best of the basics to safeguard every adventure he embarked upon, into unknown depths, in search of history hidden under the waves.

Tom explored the fathoms of the ocean, always searching for obscure treasure beneath the surface. His skilled dives had earned him a storied portfolio of discoveries and significant finds. Museums everywhere grasped at all his generous donations of artifacts he'd ascertained over the decades, delighted to have them preserved in their collections. The riches he obtained were nothing compared to what he valued: the captivating thrill of discovery and adventure. Zadie was mesmerized by his enthusiasm and brilliance.

Last season, he'd escorted her on his tour of book talks in Miami, and the reaction to their age difference was palpable. Envy from the other older men and disdainful glances from their wives. But she knew that age was simply a number; for them, it had no bearing on their relationship. Their souls were intertwined, regardless of what the societal norms of the day dictated. And why should they let the judgment of others have any bearing whatsoever on their love?

"Permission to come aboard, Captain?" she called out, her voice loud enough to overpower the engine's rumble and the dull sound of Buffett's "It's Five O'clock Somewhere" coming from the restaurant across the street. It was five o'clock for sure in Zadie's book; she had already been drinking for a few hours now. A moment of relaxation would do her some good. Life was too short not to have a beer or two occasionally.

"Zadie?"

She heard his voice, deep and throaty, calling from the darkness inside the cabin.

"I come bearing afternoon refreshments." She smiled charmingly as she wiped away her still-damp eyes. Her sunglasses hid the puffiness from any onlookers.

"Then board me, love," he teased.

His bowline was tied with precision, and the wobbles of the big ship vibrated his rope. She climbed aboard gracefully, like a skilled sailor accustomed to the roll and pitch of the vessel. She could still make out the sounds of Tom banging away at something from below deck.

"So, what's the problem this time?" Zadie asked, taking a long pull of her cold beer. She felt the bubbles snake their way down her throat as she greedily chugged.

Tom's head peeked up from below deck, his thickly coated chest shimmering in silver fur. "I can't get to whatever is clogging the bilge, and I've been working on it all morning." His feet steadily moved across the well-maintained teakwood deck, and he settled into one of the chairs at the table. His rust-colored trunks were smudged with black oil smears. "Hey, Zadie, why the early celebration?" He flashed a smile of amusement as he asked.

Despair tightened her heart. Usually, she drank when she was happy; that always ended with at least one great story and a fun night. But now, she couldn't feel anything except fear. Her emotions were wild like a raging sea, unpredictable. She ignored his question. "Care to be my much-needed distraction?" She wanted nothing more than to forget about the impossibility of saving Cricket from her curse.

This was Zadie's fifth beer of the morning, and still the overwhelming ache in her stomach had not left. She needed to figure out how to help save Cricket. Tom was the pause button she was desperate to press. He gave her something she hadn't realized she wanted: security and comfort that felt like an emotional lifeline. She could hardly believe it, how quickly she had become addicted to his charm and ached for his touch.

Her eyes traced the contours of his sculpted body, searing each inch of his bronzed skin into her memory. The faint scars covering him were a testament to all he had been through and how resiliently he had kept going. She was captivated by his boldness and courage, living life on the edge and coming out the hero from countless harrowing ordeals. His strength and fearlessness awed her.

Zadie's fingers tenderly ran across his skin, tracing the faded white scar that bisected his abdomen. As her fingertips grazed him, a shudder of pleasure reverberated through her body. She was suddenly aware of the warmth radiating from him and could feel her heart racing. Her breath quickened as she got closer to him, overcome with intense longing for his protection and support. All at once, her worries melted away.

He wiped his hands on a cloth. "What's that look about?" he asked, lifting her chin till her eyes met his gaze.

Desire stirred in her belly. She brushed past his question, though his inquisitive eyes probed for an answer. Instead, she kept her focus on the gentle cascade of sweat dripping from his toned body.

"How did you get so sweaty this early in the day?" She shifted closer and breathed in his musky scent.

"Zadie, I'm a mess from all the work I've been doing!" He tried to move away, but she held him tight, her legs locked around his.

"I love it when you're like this." She encircled her arms around him and rose up on her toes. "You look so rugged," she purred.

Tom lowered himself down, embracing her tightly, and planted a passionate kiss on her lips, the taste of tobacco and saltiness flooding her senses. His moan ignited a spark inside of her, and she answered with one of her own. "You're driving me wild," he rasped.

She felt his arousal against her abdomen, and as she skirted her fingers under the waistband of his shorts, he caught them midair.

"Zadie . . ." His voice was trembling in her ear as he spoke deep and raspy. "Not now; the boat is literally sinking." Despite the urgency, they shared a playful smile between them.

All she wanted to do was feel his skin close to hers, desire radiating through her very being. Drawing a deep breath, she stepped closer to him, enjoying the heat of his gaze as it roamed over her body. She smiled coyly and yet with complete confidence.

"I tell you what," she said, her voice low and sultry. "I'll have your bilge cleared for you before you can finish that pilsner."

He let out an amused laugh. "I'd like to see you try," he said, taking a long sip from the can.

"Oh, don't worry," Zadie teased back, batting her eyelashes in anticipation. "I've got this."

She grabbed another can and held it up in a toast before turning away from him.

Tom called after her, his voice inviting and husky. "Hurry back to me, love. You've got me all warmed up."

She descended the wooden steps into the depths of the boat. His dishes were piled in the sink, and spicy fish stew bubbled in his crockpot; tools were strewn everywhere over the teak flooring; the carpet had been rolled up on the main table. His berth door hung ajar, inviting her to relive their passionate nights together. Even as the ankle-deep water lapped around her feet, all she could think about was how many times he had taken her into that room for passionate pleasure.

Looking at the several inches of water covering the floor, she realized he hadn't been exaggerating. This job couldn't wait.

The bilge was the lowest part of a boat's hull, collecting any leaks. She could feel the hum of its power as it worked tirelessly to remove the excess water. It was working but it wasn't keeping up. Tom knew this too.

Zadie placed her hands above the water, dipping her index finger in and swiveling and swirling, creating a tiny funnel in the water. "Give to me what doesn't belong," she commanded. Nothing happened. The bilge continued to suck weakly on the water that surrounded her feet. She glanced up the stairs; Tom was still seated at the table. Her head wasn't focused enough to do this; she couldn't even clear a bilge! It should have been an easy task, but the beer had set in, making it hard to concentrate. She gazed long-ingly at Tom's bed. All she wanted to do was crawl in it and fall asleep—but that was not an option.

Closing her eyes, Zadie murmured a single phrase that she had uttered countless times before—"Kraken, I release you!"—and the magical bond between the two of them was summoned. Kraken, her familiar, her absolute best friend, peeled away from her side and stood proudly in front of her, ready to take on any challenge.

"Kraken, something is blocking the drain." She motioned for him to approach with a wave of her hand. He wiggled in anticipation of adventure. Kraken didn't hesitate. He slith-ered into the murky water and swam around with increas-ing vigor. Within minutes, air bubbles rose to the surface as Kraken's movements churned the water violently. After several moments of searching, Kraken emerged with an old piece of plastic bag clutched in his tentacle. The sound of the bilge filled Zadie's ears as she watched Kraken proudly climb out of the water and back up her thigh. She could see the water begin to drain.

"Great job!" she praised him.

Kraken was positively glowing with joy as he melded back into her side. She walked to the sink and wiped off all the grime.

After turning on Tom's fan to help dry the space out, she climbed back out of the cabin, smiling, and presented to him the piece of plastic bag.

"Now, how did you manage that?" he uttered in amaze-ment.

She slowly straddled his lap; she stretched her delicate fingers over his nape. "With these tiny, nimble hands," she whispered ever so close to his ear.

Tom interjected with a seductive suggestion: "Why don't you show me what else those hands can do?"

A fleeting shudder took hold of her body as he kissed her neck hungrily. His touch was like an intoxicating elixir, and she wanted nothing more than to succumb to its power. She tenderly grazed her nails along his broad shoulders and purred into his ear, "Your ship isn't sinking anymore."

His penetrating gaze probed deep within her soul as he asked, "Is this why you came here today? For this?"

Her heart raced in response to his tight embrace; it was all too familiar, yet still overwhelmingly electrifying. "Yes," she murmured breathlessly, then added with an unwavering resolve, "And . . ."

His hands moved in perfect harmony across her curves as they both surrendered to the moment.

Her eyes sparkled as she murmured, "Treasure. Francis Drake's treasure."

He placed his hot hands on hers, and with a smoldering gaze in his eyes he whispered, "I've got treasure a-plenty, just for you, my love." His fingertips grazed her palms as he guided her hands.

"And after?" Zadie breathed.

His arms flexed as he pulled her close and whispered with desire, "I'll spin a tale that will make your heart race."

CHAPTER 5
CRICKET

Cricket's aged, creaking bicycle collided with the rough asphalt when a car suddenly accelerated and struck her. Tikaboo flew from the bike basket as Cricket's canary-yellow dress became streaked crimson from her fall. She'd been minutes away from meeting Bash, and now she lay motionless in the middle of the intersection, halting all traffic. Embarrassment beat down on her like a tidal wave.

"Oh my God! Are you okay?" A woman came running to her side.

"My dog!" Cricket cried, attempting to stand.

"Stay down. You were hit by a car," the woman screeched. "I'm calling 911 right now! Drivers these days! How could they miss a pretty girl on a bicycle?"

Cricket flailed around, desperately searching for her glasses, but they were nowhere in sight.

"I apologize profusely; I didn't see you when I was turning." A man's deep voice drifted above her.

"Tikaboo!" she wailed again.

A warm tongue licked away her tears, bringing some calmness within her. She nuzzled her face into Tikaboo's familiar fluffy fur and began sobbing uncontrollably. It was one thing if something happened to her — it was an entirely different thing if something had happened to her pup. "Are you okay?" Cricket's voice cracked as she enveloped Tikaboo in her arms.

"Honey, your dog is fine; she isn't hurt at all. Let's tend to your wounds now," the woman said softly, placing her hand on Cricket's shoulder. "These belong to you, I believe," she said, handing Cricket's glasses back to her.

Cricket put them on; then the woman's round face suddenly came into focus.

"Thank you," she murmured, looking around herself. Vehicles were backed up on each side of the crossing lanes, with pedestrians milling about, staring at her in confusion and shock. Someone had already placed her bike and bag beside the road for safekeeping. Shame flooded through her body like a whirlwind.

"That was my fault; here is my insurance information." The man shoved a sheet of paper in Cricket's hand. "We can wait for the authorities, or do you need medical attention?" he asked worriedly.

She forced herself up off the ground, inhaling deeply through her nose as a shocking pain seared her side. She was sure that her right leg was scraped up, and her shoulder felt like it had been struck by a hammer, but she tried to tell herself everything was normal. Her breathing was ragged from the terror of being hit, and her muscles ached from shock. All she wanted to do now was get away from this place.

Tikaboo stayed close as she moved slowly toward where her bike lay, broken and battered. "Sir," she croaked softly, gripping the handlebars with trembling fingers.

He stared at her in astonishment, his eyes wide and his

skin growing more pale by the second. "Yes?" he said with trepidation.

"I'm going to leave now," she said forcefully, despite the pain that still coursed through her body.

"Oh no, you can't do that. You need to stay here until the police arrive; it's protocol," he replied swiftly.

It didn't matter what anyone else thought of the situation—she wasn't about to wait around. "Thank you for your help; I'm leaving now." With a burst of strength, she pushed her bike into motion despite its battered state; the chain hung loose, and the front tire was bent out of shape, making for an awkward gait. On unsteady feet, she pushed forward. Tourists swarmed around her like bees as they rushed to conquer their day in the area, while she focused on reaching Bash in one piece. All that mattered was making it there and figuring out whose cursed book she had.

The winding cobblestone streets were alive with a chaotic energy today, making it difficult for her to get to the historical society. Normally, it would take twenty minutes by bike, but today it seemed as if she was fighting against the current. Even before the accident happened, maneuvering around the dense crowd of pedestrians had been tricky. The traffic lights weren't working properly; they blinked red or yellow when they should have been green. She seemed to always be just thirty seconds ahead or behind where she needed to be. As if something—or someone—was keeping her from her destination.

Cricket's mind wandered to Gran. Her heart wavered between telling her about the curse and leaving her to her happiness. The afterglow of a carefree evening with Otis shone all over her this morning. Cricket reluctantly decided that she would hold off until she knew more for certain.

"Hold on, girl, wait just a second," Cricket said to Tikaboo, who wiggled impatiently in the bike basket, just as they arrived. Cricket smoothed down her wrinkled dress. Now that she took time to look, it had several holes in it. Bloodstains pooled at the hem. She ran her fingers through her brown hair, resetting her high ponytail. Her vintage cat eyeglasses started to slide down her sweaty nose. Ignoring them, she lowered Tikaboo down to the ground. "Everything is okay. You are a good girl."

Tikaboo's tongue hung loosely from her mouth, and she whimpered with excitement. Eagerness glinted in her eyes as she plowed into the grass ahead of Cricket, waiting at the bottom of the stone steps for Cricket to hurry up and follow. Cricket smiled at the sight. She needed to try to be more like her dog: worry less, live more in the moment.

She caught a glimpse of Bash standing in the doorway at the top of the stairs. He was tall, towering over her by at least a foot. His dark brown hair framed his chiseled face with a scholarly look that brought a smile to her face. His deep-brown eyes flickered around the courtyard before he looked at Tikaboo. It brought back memories of him from years ago when she'd first met him in her college history class.

"What happened? You're bleeding!" Bash yelled as he raced down the stairs toward Cricket. "I expected you a half hour ago!"

"I had a mishap on the bike." She gestured to her scraped-up leg, and her brown leather sandals were damaged beyond repair. Now she wished she had worn her white sneakers.

"What kind of mishap?" He tugged at his collar, sweat appearing on his neck.

"Well . . . it involved a car at an intersection," Cricket replied quietly.

"My God! Cricket, you need to go to the hospital!" His leg began bouncing rapidly as he pulled out his phone.

"Put your phone away," she insisted. "I don't need a doctor. But if you have a first aid kit, I could use some hydrogen peroxide and some Band-Aids." She awkwardly lowered her bag onto the ground, pushing up her glasses only for them to tumble off again. Smooth, real smooth. They made it through the intersection to now get broken here.

"Here." Bash bent down by Cricket's feet and picked up her glasses before getting rammed by Tikaboo. "She seems okay, yes?" The pup placed her paw on his knee, and he gave her head one last ruffle before gently putting the glasses back on Cricket's nose. Though they were a little bent, they worked just fine. Cricket's face flushed red.

Bash took both of Cricket's hands into his own and pulled them against his chest as he looked into her eyes. "Come on, let's get you fixed up."

Cricket held her breath. She felt both the pull of temptation and a deep understanding of why her mother had given up her faerie powers to be with her father. She'd felt it the moment she'd seen Bash freshman year. They had been connected ever since, and yet she was unable to tell him that her entire family was fae. He wouldn't believe her. His head was liable to pop off if she told him she could time travel by touching objects; he would think she was crazy. Despite the longing, she'd vowed not to follow in her mom's footsteps—a path that had brought too much pain and suffering. Keeping Bash as a friend was for the best—it had to be this way. She knew if she let things go any further, even only once . . .

"I'm taking you to the hospital, Cricket." His face had gone a ghostly white. Clearly this reminded him of the car accident with his dad — the one that had left his father in critical condition and Bash himself struggling with guilt.

Cricket reached out and squeezed his hand softly. "This is not like the accident with your dad," she whispered soothingly. "It was just a small bike incident. I am unharmed; I can walk. And you were not driving."

Cricket moved closer. She wiggled her hands in the air, then swished her hips back and forth and turned around for him to see. They were now standing face-to-face, her gentle gaze locked on to his fear-stricken expression.

"Bash." She took hold of his hands. "I promise, if you think I should go to the urgent care after lunch, we will go together. Please, join me by the pond? I packed your favorites."

He bit his lip, his shoulders slowly releasing tension as he looked over her every inch. Then he leaned in and tucked a strand of hair behind her ear. Her heart raced at the closeness between them.

"You promise?"

"Yes." Cricket smiled reassuringly. "I promise."

"I couldn't stand it if something happened to you." His voice was heavy. "You are precious to me, you know that."

A rosy blush bloomed across her face, and she playfully exclaimed, "I promised! See? Pinky swear!" She held out her tiny finger and flashed him a heartwarming smile, while taking a step back.

"Right." He sighed deeply. "I'm going to run in and let Caroline know I'm taking my break out here," he said, his voice tinged with apprehension, "and grab the first aid kit. Just a minute."

She watched him turn on his heel and hurry back inside. She meandered into the garden and dropped down near the koi pond, with Tikaboo tight at her heels. The bright fish darted around like shooting stars — so vibrant against the still water.

Would she even make it to her next birthday? She pondered this thought as she opened her bag and pulled out one of the quilts from last night. The white-and-yellow wedding-knot pattern smiled up at her from the grass. She thought about the woman who'd made the quilt and spread it out beneath a large moss-covered tree, sending blessings to her family and wishing she knew her quilt was being appreciated and enjoyed. A wave of sadness washed over her.

She gingerly tossed a squeaky toy to Tikaboo before unloading the backpack. The faint rustle of the chips was overcome by the symphony of birds chirping above. She spread out the sandwiches, chips, and treats with care. Then she pried open the Thermos lid and poured two cups of sweet tea. Aromatic scents of nature wafted around her as she took a deep breath.

A raven swooped down into the branches of the tree, its wings flapping like wind through a silent graveyard. He tilted his head sideways and met her gaze with an unwavering eye. Her skin crawled under his cold stare.

"I'm not bothering you . . . am I?" She gazed above as two more ravens descended, all three of them fixating their eyes upon her.

Suddenly, her phone chirped loudly, and the birds responded in unison, screeching and clawing in a flurry of black feathers. She was mesmerized by their looming presence.

Babs: Hey, how are you feeling?

Cricket: Weird day, but don't worry, I'm still breathing. Working on book owner identity; will let you know if I find anything.

Babs: I'm working on "where the event took place" Might not have cell reception tonight.

Cricket: Okay, love love

Babs: Love love

"Here is the first aid kit," Bash said, giving her a comforting glance.

"I'll take that, thank you." She nimbly took the kit from his outstretched hands and started flicking through it, taking out disinfectant wipes and gigantic bandages.

"Tikaboo!" he called to summon her away from the pond. "How's our little girl doing? It's been a while since she's stayed over at my place." She snuggled tightly next to his legs.

"She's good," Cricket acknowledged. "Shadows Gran most of the time, to be honest."

He touched her leg gently with a wipe, and she winced. "Does it hurt?"

"Just a little sting, not bad," she lied.

He poured some hydrogen peroxide over the deepest scrape on her arm and spoke softly. "Magic bubbles, do your stuff." He wiggled his fingers at the wound as if to cast some magical spell.

"What was that?" she asked, suppressing a smile.

"Magic bubbles, do your stuff! Didn't your mom always say that when she fixed your scrapes?"

She shook her head but couldn't keep back the chuckle this time. "No, but I'll remember it." Her smile vanished suddenly when she glanced up to see Bash staring far away, his face drained of color.

"Bash . . . take a breath; I'm perfectly fine."

He stirred from his trance and gave her a small grin. "Yes, what do we have here? Barbecue chips? You're spoiling me." His gaze lingered past her shoulder for a few moments before finally turning to meet hers again.

"Go ahead, don't wait for me," she said with a half smile, her mind wandering to the past.

Romantic feelings between them had grown over time, yet neither of them had ever had the courage to speak of it. Instead, they'd settled into an easy fondness that made even mundane moments special.

She grabbed her bag. "I brought you something to look at."

She pulled out the stack of ruffled papers, printouts from the pictures she took of the book. Pages were no longer in any semblance of order—it would have been nice if the owner had numbered them.

"What is that mess?" Bash asked.

"I found an interesting book in our last estate sale. These are printouts, copies of—"

A vein in his forehead popped out. He was not usually so passionate, but when it came to history being taken away from museums and placed in people's homes, he got quite heated. She knew how much it bothered him that her family shop basically went against his beliefs on how history should be handled, which, according to him, was to be cataloged and kept in dusty boxes for all to check out under the watchful eyes of the curators.

She smiled as she taped a large bandage on her thigh, not letting her physical state get in the way of the conversation. "Dr. Jones," she started calmly, although with a hint of amusement in her voice. "Do we really have to have this same argument again? I know your stance on this issue, and you understand our antique store is reputable." With that, she winked at him, hinting at the fact that she found his pet peeve quite funny. "Look, Bash. I found a logbook, a diary, last night when I was doing inventory. I made copies of the pages. I was hoping you could go through it with me and help identify the time period, hopefully even figure out who the book belonged to." She glanced up to the tree branches that were now filled with black birds, their sinister eyes scrutinizing her.

She looked into Bash's eyes again, remembering all the long nights of studying together. "You always were better at figuring out the time period on items than me in school," she said playfully.

"Ah, but you always scored higher on the tests than me," he admitted with a smirk.

She loved it when they solved puzzles together, and their favorite corner of the library had always felt like a safe haven for her.

"What can I say? I paid more attention when we studied," she said, giving him a flirtatious look.

Bash ruffled through the pages. She glanced away and noticed something strange—birds started dropping to the lawn surrounding them in tandem to others forming a funnel-shaped circle above the tree.

"So, this book," he said, noticing her distraction.

"Yes, the book," she replied with a smile as she handed him a sandwich. "The book's condition was water stained and fire damaged, but not to the point that it's illegible, as you can see from the copies."

He flipped through more pages. "Material?" he mumbled through chewing his sandwich. She noticed his white shirt remained white. She would have jelly all over her already if she were eating.

The dark silhouette of the black birds perched in the trees, their beady eyes looking down upon them in an unworldly silence. They seemed to move in a synchronized manner. Their wings were motionless, and their feathers appeared matte in the sunlight. An eerie silence fell around them as the birds flew, not a single chirp or flutter of wings audible. It was almost as if they were suspended in time, their presence alone creating a tension that was palpable.

Cricket did her best to ignore the birds and focus on the pages. "Leather cover, cotton cloth for pages, so—"

"Bash." A light, familiar voice filled the air. They looked up to see Caroline, Bash's coworker.

Caroline had gone to college with Bash and Cricket. Most of their class had interned at the historical society or the Fountain of Youth. Caroline chose working here over the Fountain of Youth, even though it may not have been entirely by choice. Caroline stood on her tiptoes, teetering on her high heels, trying to keep the stilettos from sinking into the soft earth beneath the grass. Her perfect milk-white skin betrayed her aversion to the outdoors. She brushed back her shiny blond curls. "I hate to bother you on your lunch break"—she shot a quick glance Bash's way while fluttering her eyelash extensions—"but your one o'clock is here early. I just knew you wouldn't want to keep them waiting."

Tikaboo walked over to Caroline and sniffed her leg.

She jumped back, making a high-pitched screech that turned into nervous laughter. "Oh, cute puppy. So cute." She continued to laugh while rubbing her hands together. Air conditioning had turned her hands white with red blotches. "So, should I tell them you will be right in, Bash?"

He looked Cricket directly in the eyes. "Are you sure you are all right? I can drive you to urgent care. It's better to be safe than sorry."

Cricket playfully grabbed at his hand. "I am all right."

"Caroline, I'll be right in," he said, standing up and turning to Cricket. "You know I'm gonna worry about you all day, so — want to hang out here for the afternoon until I can take you home?"

"I must get back and help Gran. But I promise to take it easy," she said, placating him with a smile.

Bash's eyes softened as they lingered on her face. "If I come see ya tonight, we can go over the papers then?"

Cricket's cheeks heated as something strange bubbled inside her stomach. She didn't want their picnic to end. "That'd be great," she said quietly, looking away. She reached up and handed him his giant rice crispy square before adding, "Here, take this with you."

He smiled down at it. "Thanks. You always put the right amount of butter in them."

She rolled her eyes good-heartedly and replied, "Butter is the key. Hey, kind of random but . . . wanna go to the pirate museum tonight?"

Bash brushed at some barbecue crumbs that clung to his pants. "Yeah, sure, been a while since I've been there — you sure you're up for it?" He glanced at her bandages.

Cricket shrugged confidently. "I can handle the swashbuckling at the museum. There's something I want to check out," she said with a sneaky grin.

"Related to your papers?" he asked, glancing around at the pile of pages.

"Yep." She bit her lip nervously.

He nodded thoughtfully and walked into the building, glancing back once more before disappearing inside. "Okay — I'll text ya when I'm headed your way after work. We can grab an early dinner, then hit up the museum," he said through the crack in the doorway. "Oh — don't forget to keep an eye out for my texts!" Bash added before he disappeared completely from view.

Cricket looked up at Caroline with a warm smile, her eyes twinkling. "Hey, Caroline! It's been a while since we've seen each other. How have you been?"

Caroline smiled back. "Oh, hey, Cricket! I'm doing great, thanks for asking. When are you going to make that official?" Her eyes wandered in the direction Bash had just gone. "He talks about you nonstop. Help a girl out and put him out of his misery."

"You know we're just friends," Cricket shot back.

"Yeah, well, when you come to your senses, I will be much happier." Caroline looked her over. "Bash said you took a tumble on your bike. You okay?"

"Fine, just scratches. Hey, would you like a rice crispy treat? I just happen to have an extra one." She waved the snack toward Caroline.

"That sounds amazing, but I don't do sugar, thank you though!" Caroline laughed and brushed her fingers down her throat, drawing little circles at her collarbone. "It's a lot of work keeping this figure," she said with a wink. "But what about you? What have you been up too lately? Besides throwing epic picnics on a random workday for a guy that is just your friend." She gestured around the lawn.

"Aww, a little of this, a little of that—nothing special," Cricket said noncommittally.

Caroline brushed her hand down her baby-pink pencil skirt. "Well, that was enough outside time for me. I'll see ya later!" She waved her hand slowly with purpose.

Cricket's mouth dropped open when she saw the sparkling diamond on Caroline's left hand. "Hold on, Caroline, congratulations!" Cricket said with a genuine smile.

"Oh this?" Caroline blushed, waving her hand in the air between them. "Michael proposed last Saturday. It was so romantic! Now I'm making wedding plans, and my cousins from Chicago are coming to help with the big event."

Cricket wasn't looking for wedding bells, but that didn't stop her from being happy for her friend. "Caroline, here, take this quilt," she said as she stood up and shook out the fabric. "It has a wedding ring pattern—hopefully it'll bring you good luck while you're planning your big day! I know it will be perfect."

Caroline's face softened, and she thanked Cricket. "This is our first present," she said. "Thank you."

"You're welcome," Cricket said, reaching for the pile of papers. "Would you mind looking at these pages? They are copies from a book I found."

Cricket stepped closer and joined her on the steps outside. She handed the pages to Caroline, admiring the delicate penmanship on the copied sheets.

"Do you think they have some historical significance to St. Augustine?" Caroline asked, raising her eyebrows.

"Maybe," Cricket replied, "but I don't want to influence your initial impression."

Caroline glanced at her watch as she settled in. "Well, I could take a few minutes." She smiled, glancing at the quilt draped beside her. Cricket followed suit and sat next to her as Caroline began to flip through the pages.

"It looks like a private diary of sorts rather than a logbook," Caroline remarked as she read through one page. Logbooks would usually contain notes about weather patterns, courses set, wind directions, where they moored or anchored, etcetera; this was different.

"That may be so," Cricket agreed before pointing to a watercolor painting of a deer.

"The artwork is very detailed — perhaps it belonged to an artist?"

Cricket nodded, admiring how beautifully crafted all the drawings were. Then her gaze drifted down to an intricately drawn star chart that made her hand freeze on the page. With wide eyes, she turned to Caroline and exclaimed, "Stop there! Do you recognize this star chart?"

Caroline's brow creased as she studied it for several minutes before finally smiling widely and responding, "I think you were paying attention when we were at the Navigator's Planetarium for class! This is a representation of what the southern sky looked like back in the 1500s!"

"Well, that narrows things down."

Just then, a thunderous crescendo of bird calls filled Cricket's ears. When she looked up to investigate, the tree was alive with creatures whose forms were blacker than a night sky. Eyes that seemed to pierce her very soul, wings that beat in a chaotic frenzy, and beaks open to screech in unison created an eerie orchestra of terror.

Underneath the tree stood a daunting figure draped in darkness, who raised a single arm, beckoning her to come closer. A pall of silence descended upon Cricket as she fell into the penetrating gaze of the stranger. Cricket felt like her feet were glued to the ground. Everywhere she looked there was nothing but inky blackness, threatening to consume her very soul. Her cursed hand throbbed painfully as apprehension ran through her.

"Cricket, are you okay?" Caroline's voice quivered.

Cricket slowly turned toward Caroline, her eyes then drawn to the tree again. Nothing was there. No figure. No birds. A knot formed in her stomach.

"I'm not sure," Cricket whispered. "I don't know."

CHAPTER 6
ZADIE

Zadie lazily dried her hair, taking in the view of the breathtaking marina as Tom's boat rocked gently against the waves. The warm shower had washed away both her physical dirt and mental fatigue. She had leaned into Tom's touch like a cat yearning for affection, their bodies intertwined in a slow, sensual dance beneath the steaming jets. Now that the shower had passed, she felt lighter, clearer, and somehow more alive than before. With renewed energy and enthusiasm, it was time for Zadie to get to work—hopefully Tom had some answers.

He reappeared on the upper deck with a platter of cheeses, bread, almonds, and olives. He handed Zadie a bottle of water and motioned for her to sit down before beginning his tale.

"England was at war with Spain," Tom began, "and Queen Elizabeth had put Francis Drake in charge of traveling the high seas and besting Philip II of Spain." His eyes lit up like a Christmas tree as he said this, and Zadie could feel energy radiating off him. "St. Augustine was a Spanish settlement fit for the taking, and Drake was determined to seize it," he continued, taking a sip of his beer and popping a piece of cheese into his mouth.

He gestured over the table, revealing maps, charts, and heavily used spiral notebooks stuffed full of pictures sticking out of the sides.

"Okay, they were at war, and our city was Spanish controlled," she confirmed.

"The governor was warned that the dreaded Drake was off the coast. The town didn't have enough military men to hold the fort and protect the people and livestock. The governor ordered a retreat inland, hoping to save lives. Drake came in with his men, pleased the Spaniards had given up without a fight. But during the night, the Spanish garrison counterattacked Drake and his men, to no avail. The English outnumbered them ten to one."

"So, the English held the town. Then what happened?" Zadie leaned in, hanging on his every word.

"The next day, Drake and some of his men marched up the inlet and took the fort of San Juan. There they plundered everything they could get their hands on, but the biggest treasure was a chest of gold containing all the garrison's pay—over two thousand gold ducats. Drake took it all, burned the fort to the ground, and transported the booty back to St. Augustine. Here, love, is where the story gets interesting. It is said the moon was full that night, and an eerie mist covered the ground, as if the land itself was trying to help the Spaniards." He paused for emphasis and laid a light kiss upon her mouth, leaving her wanting more. "Rumor has it, Drake kept all of the spoils of war underground and heavily guarded. But somehow, somebody was able to take the gold all the same. Drake never found it. His anger was so great, he burned everything to the ground. The buildings were torched, the crops destroyed. Everything he could devour, he did."

"So, all of the treasure, the gold, was taken. Who do they say took it, Tom?"

"It was the Spaniards; you can bet on it. Unfortunately, luck was not on their side that fateful night, for it is said they loaded the chest of gold onto a ship and tried to sail it away for safekeeping, but it became a casualty of the sea when a storm blew in." He pulled out a waterway chart. "Back in the nineties, when I was closer to your age than mine, I gave it a go to find the lost treasure." He motioned to the waterway beyond the marina.

"What happened?" she asked, knowing he had found so many artifacts and great historical finds.

"I had a multibeam sounding system on my boat, pretty cutting edge for the time. I found the actual shipwreck. Let me show you." He riffled through several charts, settling on one heavily stained and marked. "Look here—see the restricted area directly across Anastasia Island?"

"Yes." It was several miles offshore.

"The treacherous depths of the area had turned deadly in the late 2000s, with coral spikes sharp enough to tear apart a boat from bow to stern. It's as if the sea itself is defending the wreck from being disturbed. Any sailor foolish enough to stray too close risks suffering a similar fate, their vessel sinking straight into the depths. But it wasn't always so—I used the sounding system to survey the area in this very spot." He pointed at the map. "I believe, there lay the wreck you seek, its hull sunken deep into the crack in the ocean floor. No diver now dares go near it, and to my knowledge, there are no tools powerful enough to haul up such heavy objects from such great depths. Even if it were possible to carefully navigate around the razor-sharp coral outcroppings, it is doubtful that we could manage such an undertaking."

"I get that you saw a sunken ship, but what made you think it was the wreck site of the Spaniards? It could have been any ship." Zadie leaned back on the boat's bench, out of the direct rays of the late-morning sun.

He opened his weather-beaten notebooks to reveal a page of photographs of ballast rocks and ceramic relics from the depths of the ocean. His eyes widened in remembrance at the sight before him: the figurehead of a mermaid, her body adorned with gold and jewels, encrusted into the bow of the sunken Spanish galleon—the *Dulcinea*. He flipped to the adjoining page, showcasing an artistic representation of four ships from the 1500s. There she was again, immortalized in ink—that beautiful mermaid figurehead at the forefront of the *Dulcinea*. "You're right. It's not like their flag was still attached, but the masthead was. Have a real good look at her. My research has brought me to the conclusion that the Spanish galleon *Dulcinea* was the ship at the St. Augustine fort at that time, and now sits at the bottom of the ocean miles off the coast of Anastasia Island.

"Here is a copy from the port-of-call log dating to the time of the sacking of St. Augustine. As you can see, the *Dulcinea* is on it. I looked, and this is the last place that records the whereabouts of this ship."

Zadie looked over the port-of-call list. "And the other ships that are listed here?"

"All show up at different ports. The *Dulcinea* is the only one on this list that disappeared. I'm convinced the Spanish soldiers somehow got the gold aboard, and when the storm brewed up, they sank." Tom ran his fingers through his hair. "Are you taking up the search for the missing treasure?"

"That's the plan," she said, throwing her legs over his lap.

"Well, you are welcome to take my research. But I doubt you will be able to get permits to do any work out there, since it's been deemed restricted. If the ship has fully fallen into the trench, it's a total lost cause. Even if you do find it on the ocean bed instead of in the trench, I don't think you can bring her up safely. The coral makes it impossible with the ocean current. It's a dangerous combo. But my good wishes go with you. There's nothing like a hunt. This particular treasure hunt still haunts me. It's so close, and yet so far. It would be great if you found her."

Zadie smirked, and her sea-green eyes glimmered with the possibility of adventure. Even though this task seemed impossible, she had a few tricks up her sleeve . . . or in this case, fins. Her eyes sparkled as she spoke with Tom. "The *Dulcinea* lies deep below, but I can bring her up. We just have to find where X marks the spot—shall we do it together?" She winked playfully.

He ran his fingers across the coarse hairs of his chin. "I can try green-lighting it now," he muttered, already imagining the fantasies of discovering what lay in the depths of the sea. "All I need to do is place a few calls and, with any luck, we could be planning the underwater expedition. It might be a few months before we know whether it's atop the seabed or hidden in the trench. We have plenty of time still to work out how we're going to attempt to get close safely." He grinned.

Cricket didn't have time for red tape. And Zadie couldn't stomach asking Tom to bend the rules alongside her—he had far too much integrity for that.

"Let's see what treasures await us!" He held up his beer can in salute to her water bottle.

She'd set sail at nightfall, several hours away. She clinked her drink against his and smirked mischievously. Grabbing his can and placing it back on the table, she tugged him by the arm back down toward the cabin.

CHAPTER 7
CRICKET

The woman in blue stood by the counter, holding the beautifully crafted quilt with a look of joy on her face. "Thank you for your purchase. I know your sister is going to love the quilt," Gran said.

Cricket watched on, admiring the way Gran could make even a simple exchange into something special. The woman thanked Gran with a nod and smiled, displaying a full set of white teeth.

The Closed sign dangled loosely in Cricket's grasp as she surveyed the shop. Every nook and cranny of the old antique store was filled with items, strategically placed to draw in customers with their charm and beauty. After a full day of lugging boxes from the Sub, stocking shelves, and helping customers find that special item they'd been searching for, it seemed like there were new display spaces sprouting up faster than she could fill them. There was still more work to do, but at least for now, satisfied customers left with happy faces.

During the fleeting moments of respite, she'd scoured the depths of the internet in search of knowledge about the dreaded Black Spot. She went through page after page of fictitious stories and video games, but none of it was enough to make sense of these legends. She had exhausted all her books on pirate lore, but nothing gave her the answers she sought. With only Zadie's tales to lean on, she felt like an explorer venturing out into the unknown.

Her phone chirped again, and Cricket couldn't help but smile.

"Text?" asked Gran. "You've been glued to your phone all afternoon."

Zadie was sure she knew where the treasure was, and Babs had a plan, but Cricket wasn't sure if they were really on the right track and ready to deal with Drake.

Cricket hesitated, debating whether to tell Gran what they were up to. But before she could answer, the phone chirped again; it was a message from Bash.

"Sister stuff," said Cricket quickly as she typed a response. "I just need to grab my purse and get going! This text is from Bash; we're going to the pirate museum tonight," Cricket said, trying to think of everything she wanted to take with her.

Gran smiled knowingly and said, "That sounds like fun. He's a good boy. Nice manners. You should have him around here more often."

Cricket nodded in silent agreement. Taking a deep breath, she asked, "Gran, how do you make it work with Otis? Isn't it difficult, him not knowing everything about you?"

"No one knows everything about anyone," Gran replied, stating it as fact.

"But he's human. Aren't you worried about losing yourself in him, like Mom did with Dad? The consequences are so huge. To lose the majority of your power." She sighed heavily, not sure what to do next.

Gran swiveled in her chair thoughtfully. "Hmm, I see." After a moment she explained, "I have had many human lovers over my long lifetime. I have also had many fae lovers, as is the way of our people. Your mother and aunts all were sired by different fae. How else would we be able to have all the different elemental magics in our family line? Ours has never been a purist family, and I wouldn't have it any other way. I followed my mother's example." After another pause, she continued, "The inbred fae families that stay to only one magic go mad. Worse yet, if they only breed within one magic to make a truly pure line . . ." She trailed off.

"Then?"

Finally, Gran said softly, "The magic becomes unstable, not balanced. But this is not what you were asking about. What is going on with your romantic life that has you worried?"

"I feel like I'm not allowed to be fully myself with someone else," Cricket whispered, her words nearly lost in the gentle movements of her finger tracing circles on her arms.

Gran let out an affectionate chuckle. "Nonsense, little one. You can let yourself go and be vulnerable to the right person—a fae that you trust implicitly. Or you can dabble in the human world, feeling out your human side. But remember where your power truly lies. Don't limit yourself; embrace who you are as a Culebra. Family is where your power lies, not your fae or human lineage. It's that you are a Culebra. We stay together."

Cricket was left confused and apprehensive at Gran's words. She stepped closer to Gran's desk and looked up into her eyes with trepidation. "Aunt Maj?"

Grans lips pursed into a thin line. "Aunt Maj is doing her duty. That area must be guarded and controlled. She'll be there for Zadie when it's her time to go to sea. They will be strong, together." Gran tenderly brought forward her wrinkled hand and placed it upon Cricket's heart. "Listen to your heart, child. You may feel a tug of war inside you as to your nature. Your heart is true. You are creating your own path. Follow its beat."

"I am trying Gran, honest."

Gran inspected Cricket's hidden right hand, then she took a sip of her coffee.

"You're still young," Gran said, looking back up at Cricket. "Is there anything else you want to talk about?"

Cricket's heart raced. She didn't want to bring it up till she had some answers. She began biting on the cuticle of her thumb as she nervously tried avoiding the conversation.

"Are you coming down with something? Seems a bit warm for long sleeves," she said as she eyed Cricket's batwing off-the-shoulder sweater. Cricket ran her hand across her forehead, checking if she might be running a fever.

"All of a sudden you have nothing to say?" Gran asked.

Cricket forced her feet forward, though she felt like running away from the conversation. As she rounded the corner of the counter, her shoe caught an open box of wine bottles that needed to be taken to the Sub. She stumbled but managed to regain her balance.

Gran sighed, "earth is bound by time. Each season follows the other: spring, summer, fall, winter. All have their place, and each ensues its sister in a cycle that never changes without grave consequence." She paused and seemed to be thinking for a moment. "Fire burns bright, and rages even, but only has a short period of time; then it gives way to ash." Her eyes grew distant as if she was remembering something that had happened during her youth. "Life-giving water flows directional, creating deep crevices; worn, smooth rock leaves evidence of its existence." Another silence stretched on before she spoke again. "Air and spirit, you dance with time. She invites you to have a peek into the future or go back in the past to learn to influence destiny. You are not bound by time like others are. You can move forward or backward in time, slow the passing of years or stop them completely."

Cricket didn't respond immediately. Gran often took an odd turn in conversation, giving her riddles to solve or stories to interpret as hyperboles of wisdom. Sometimes they seemed utter nonsense . . . and sometimes they felt ominous.

"I can stop time?" She remembered a rainy day when she was about five years old. Aunt Habina had been playing with her. She'd held both of her hands. They'd been spinning, laughing. She'd never felt so joyful. All the raindrops had stood still in the air. Completely still. They both had been the only ones moving. She'd thought they were just playing. She hadn't realized—

"It usually happens when you have strong emotion," Gran began. "Right now, you know how to connect with objects, things that have been filled with memories and a lot of energy, positive or negative. They help you focus and transport you back in time until you feel the power inside yourself and can move freely. It's like having training wheels. Soon, you will be able to do what your aunt Habina did. Here—"

Gran took off her thick gold chain bracelet from her right wrist and attached it to Cricket's, the light gleaming from its surface.

"Look at this bracelet," she said. "You're one link in

a long chain of Culebra women." She cupped both of her hands over Cricket's right hand, bowing her head and closing her eyes in concentration as the lights flickered around them. Softly, Gran started chanting while Cricket felt a warmth spreading through her body.

She slowly tilted her head upward. The sight of Gran's kind face was replaced by a skeletal visage, dark empty eye sockets seeping into a void that held within its depths nothingness and terror. Gran's spirit burned like wildfire, a flame which Cricket had feared since she was young. Her fire magic broiled with intensity, an unrelenting force of passion.

A field of orange marigolds sprang to life before their feet, blossoming in the warmth of Gran's power, while thick vines spread swiftly along the walls in search of nourishment. Drops of water began dripping from above, chilling Cricket's skin as goosebumps broke out across her body. A colorful mist arose from the ground, wrapping them both in shades of blue, orange, red, green. Whispers, moans, and laughter echoed around the room on a wave of cigar and rum fumes. Dizziness overcame Cricket as the colors swirled around her like an invading army devastating everything in its path. Then suddenly, unwilling laughter bubbled out from her mouth — it wasn't hers but rather the universe speaking through her. In that moment, heat coursed through her body and a wave of sorrow flooded her soul — like icy shards piercing and puncturing her insides till she felt bloated and drowned.

It was then that fire jumped out from Gran's hands like an unstoppable storm, singeing the ceiling and flowing down the walls in fierce circular patterns which pulsated with power until finally exploding in a brilliant white bubble that enclosed Gran and Cricket before blasting past the boundaries set by mere mortals and propelling itself beyond Old Town.

Cricket stretched her arms out wide, her head falling back in ecstasy. She floated above the room, above the building, above Old Town. She saw the sun rise, the moon fall, over and over. The celestial clock moved forward and forward, faster and faster as she drifted farther and farther out into the vastness of space. She was spinning, spinning. The black-cloaked figure had found her. Her hair like spiderwebs surrounded Cricket, pulling her in with no escape. A bony white hand emerged from the darkness of the tattered robe. Its razor-like nails punctured her chest and pulled out Cricket's heart. She heard Gran's voice in her head and was immediately back in her cold, sweat-drenched body. The flowers, the fire, and the ghosts were all gone from the store. Gran was staring directly into Cricket's eyes, her thumb digging into the palm of the cursed hand, clearly not pleased. For the first time in Cricket's life, she felt terror.

CHAPTER 8
BABS

The low buzzing of the beehives filled Babs with a sense of comfort as she stood beside one of the quail coops. The meticulously crafted structure, made from old barn wood and chicken wire, held six small birds inside. She ran her fingers over each bird's feathery wings, feeling the delicate tip of their feathers. Carefully, she placed the quail eggs, a jar of creamy honey, and wild mushrooms in the basket that she had just woven together from palm fronds found scattered on the forest floor. The woven basket was small enough to hold within both of her hands.

She beheld her sprawling cabin with a swell of pride. As the evening light swept across the panorama of windows, it illuminated the home that could only be described as a "fairytale haven." Babs couldn't help but feel a wave of warmth and contentment when she thought of her hard-working mother bustling around the kitchen, an immutable reminder of love and stability.

Her skull earring pulsed a steady warm heat that coiled around her neck and slithered down her body, hidden by her grey sweatshirt and torn jeans. When attempting a summoning of this kind, it was always a good idea to have an extra layer of energetic protection. Why go through all the trouble if you didn't get an answer to your question?

"Snap out of it, Babs!" Nadine hissed, her transparent body drifting closer to Babs. "You have been dawdling for far too long! Is there any point to this little excursion you're planning?"

"I-I don't know," Babs replied timidly. "I have caught glimpses of Liande, but she has never revealed her full form to me. If I had not heard the alligators' thoughts, I would never even have known of her existence or her identity . . ."

"And who is she?"

"They said that she is the guardian of the forest, and they serve her. From what I understand, Liande is a creature from ancient times."

"Who else could be the keeper of the forest but one with knowledge of forgotten times? You believe she holds the remembrance of the land?"

"Yes." Babs nodded determinedly. "If I can describe the place that Cricket needs to find, then perhaps Liande will be able to tell us where it lies."

"But these creatures from so long ago often demand —"

"We are desperate!" Babs declared. "I must take this risk."

Cricket had just texted. But even that had done little to soothe Babs's anxieties; the possibility of loss was still lurking in the shadows. Her sisters — Cricket and Zadie — her family was all she had in life, and if anything were to happen to one of them, her world would be shattered. She couldn't bear the thought of living without one of them by her side.

The night sky had arrived, and Nadine urged they set off before the moon sank too deep. Babs gazed up at its thin sliver of a silhouette, just above the horizon. A modest number of stars had begun to sparkle in the indigo sky above them, and wispy clouds were painted with a delicious hue of orange and salmon as if in homage to the setting sun that was just out of view. The stars twinkled brightly but still seemed so far away.

Babs walked in her bare feet lightly on the cool grass, damp from the evening mist. She felt small amongst the towering trees that formed a verdant canopy around them. An orchestra of tree frogs bellowed a loud melody as bats flew above, feasting on insects. Despite their quite unsettling habits, Babs found their presence strangely comforting—for even these nocturnal creatures, wary of human company, were not without companionship and a natural rhythm.

Babs's feet automatically took her down the familiar path that led to the pond, guided by an instinctive knowledge that had been built up over many years. As she drew nearer to her destination, a solitary tear trickled down her cheek. Reality shifted as she traversed one plane to another into the faerie realm, surrounded by a myriad of glowing orbs. She marveled at the beauty of the place. The energy swirled around her, strange and wondrous.

She took a deep breath and strode forward purposefully, swallowing her fear. She knew Liande would be here, somewhere.

Mud oozed between each of her toes as she dimly made out the outline of the pond. A cacophony of reptilian snapping and hissing emanated from its murky depths. Visiting during the day was one thing, but being here at night, she realized that she would make an easy target if they so chose. The hairs on the back of her neck stood up in unison.

"Nadine." Her voice was barely audible and hollow.

"I'm on it." The white figure of Nadine flew above the ground just inches away from her. Her speed was as fast a gust of wind, creating a hurricane-like force around her. Moonlight sparkled as those terrifying shadows glided toward Babs.

"Sleep, little alligator, else Nadine come to catch you."

Nadine's voice seemed to spread like cobwebs across the water. The shadows slowed considerably, almost mesmerized by her words.

"Sleep, little alligator, else Nadine come to catch you." Her voice with every repetition became stronger and more powerful. She circled the pond, silent blue flames dispelling any ounce of darkness that surrounded them, while her cloak seemed to become ever more transparent with each pass. Nadine returned to Babs's side, glowing eerily in the night air.

"Thank you, sister," Babs said.

Nadine neared, and Babs noticed her face had taken on an eerie blue hue. Icicles hung from her garments like claws grasping for life. "I am," she uttered faintly, her form flickering in and out of view, "drained. I can't stay . . . fade." A gust of wind swirled around them, and Nadine's figure dissolved into a mist that clung to the air. Her voice echoed on the wind, "Without me?" before she disappeared completely.

Babs always found Nadine's powers mystifying; it looked like fire but felt like ice. She asked about it often, but Nadine never gave an answer. Babs knew when her sister was fully recharged, she would come back to her. But for now, she was alone in the dark—a sensation that made her heart twist with fear.

Her knees trembled in the mud, her sweatshirt growing heavy with moisture. Babs slowly lifted the basket above her head and opened her eyes, surveying the still waters blanketed in blue. A faint whisper escaped from her lips into the air as she pleaded with Liande.

"Liande, I bring you offerings,
woven with my own hands.
Liande, I bring you life, scarce but valuable.
Liande, I bring you sweetness, rare and hard to find.
Liande, I bring you earth, carefully
chosen for your pleasure."

She opened her eyes and saw a disturbance in the water. The top of a green hairless head suddenly emerged, followed by its long reptilian body. Its yellow eyes glowed like flames as it stepped through the thick water toward her. Her wide lower jaw crunched on something large, and dark scales covered her from head to toe. Babs began to tremble as she beheld the primordial monster approaching. With each step forward she revealed more of her taut body, starting with her slim shoulders, then full bosom, and finally her stomach. Babs felt frozen under her gaze and lowered her head, unable to move. She stared at the creature's muscular thigh right in front of her as its thick alligator-like tail swished back and forth. Babs held her breath, not knowing what to do or how to react to the looming fear that had engulfed her.

"What force has ordained this most curious meeting?" Liande's eerie voice echoed across the water, the strange inflections suggesting an inscrutable madness. "How come you by my abode?"

Liande's eyes blazed with arcane energy as a kaleidoscope of visions danced upon the surface of the water. People and places came into focus, their secrets revealed to her. She absorbed the ancient power of the waters and pushed it into the ether. It felt like she could alter fate itself as she directed the swirling images with her will, guiding them into a new destiny that she had crafted. It was clear that Liande's will was bending fate itself.

Babs stood tall, her eyes blazing back at this powerful guardian of the forest. "I . . . I . . ." Babs began determinedly, not wanting to break her focus from Liande's yellow eyes.

"Answer," Liande said in a haughty, inquisitorial voice. Her ironlike claw rested under Babs's chin as her wizened eyes sought an answer to the conundrum she had just posed. She cackled maniacally, as if savoring her own madness.

Babs's heart raced in her chest, but she held her nerve. "Um." She swallowed hard. "I have wandered here before and sensed your power. Your name was whispered upon my heart. I seek your wisdom and counsel; it is a matter of life or death."

"It is I who have summoned you, little Culebra. It is not within your power, as of yet, to transcend the worlds without invitation." Her eyes glided over the images swirling in the pond, wild with intensity. She circled Babs rapidly, snatching at the air as she walked. "I have watched and listened; the time draws near." Liande gazed off into the trees, her yellow eyes feverish with secrets. She murmured incoherently, as if she were retelling an ancient tale to herself before turning back to face Babs again. Her tail swished wildly as she reached forward, running her clawed hand across Babs's stomach. "What dark incantations have you cast upon my creatures? Surely this power was not born of summer!"

Babs's shoulders tensed as she carefully weighed her words before speaking, her voice calm but strong: "The spell will wear off momentarily, Liande, if it pleases you."

Liande tilted her head and cackled to herself as she stepped back while inspecting the tips of her claws. Her tail twitched and swished like an agitated snake as a lethal grin spread across her face. "It pleases me," she said, her voice low and mysterious. "My favor comes at a price, one that I'm not sure you are willing to pay."

"What is your price?" Babs asked with a firmer tone, trying her best not to show any sign of fear.

"This, connected to yonder," Liande snarled, her voice dripping with madness as she exhaled into Babs's ear. She reached up and traced the silver earring in a circular motion before whispering, "Give me that which it is connected to, for I have seen it in the depths." Her eyes focused upon the still water.

Sweat dripped from Babs's forehead. "I'm sorry, Liande. I can't give it to you," Babs said, trying to ignore the quiver in her voice. She reached up and grabbed her earring, the pink light emanating from it providing a sense of protection as it surrounded her entire body. Her words echoed confidently in the small space. "Liande, I have come here for information. You are the most ancient in this forest that I know of. If anyone will know the answer, I feel it is you. I have brought you gifts and the promise of more, the terms set by you. Will you help me?"

Babs's words, carried on a cloud of pink, swirled around Liande's glistening scaled body. Her eyes dulled to a burnt orange hue, and a low hiss escaped her lips. Light exploded outward from Babs's form, fully immersing them in its protective embrace and creating a powerful barrier between them. The blue lights over the water began to go out, and dark shadows began swirling on the water again. The alligators were breaking from the spell, but none could approach without being affected by Babs's powerful aura.

"The day will come when you lament not taking my generous bargain." Liande's ominous words slithered through the dense, smoke-filled air. She recoiled her scaly arms and tapped her left foot ominously. "Let us be clear now: you are here to seek my favor, and I am merciful. Consent to one unnamed favor, and I will assist you." An eerie chuckle escaped her lips as a shrill laugh followed.

Babs understood this could easily turn into an unfortunate situation if she didn't tread carefully. To her dismay, she had no choice but to accept. "I agree."

Liande threw back her head and let out an otherworldly howl that spread across the pond like wildfire. All the lights in the area were extinguished, leaving only slithering black shadows around her, which seemed to be crawling closer and closer to where Babs stood rooted in fear. With no good plan in sight, she scanned her surroundings for any escape route that would save her — but all that greeted her were the trees swaying softly in the breeze, whispering, "Stay." She steadied her breathing and braced herself for what was sure to come.

"Ask your question," Liande said, her voice weary.

Babs let out a sigh of relief. "I'm looking for an underground cave filled with skulls and bones. The space hid gold for a short time . . . Do you know of it?"

Liande spun around, her movements frenzied and wild, as if the shadows had taken possession of her body. She strode back into the murky depths, a ghostly silhouette swallowed by the darkness.

"Hey! Hey, wait! We have a deal!" Babs called out.

Liande moved in a frenzy, razor-sharp claws scraping the surface of the pond. Droplets of water flew everywhere as her tail lashed out. Her breathing was harsh and labored, eyes scrunched tight in frustration. "My lips are sealed by orders from on high. For all that awaits you is tyranny and servitude. I have foreseen it." Her voice was hushed and dripping with dark foreboding.

"You've seen me?" Babs stammered, looking at the water.

Liande's voice faltered with a scornful tone. "I see all." Her eyes began to flicker across the lake, as her words echoed within a violent inferno. "When you find yourself on the wrong side of power—crownless—living an eternity in isolation, stripped of your glamor, haunted by the impossible tasks set out for you."

"I have no choice; I need to find this place," Babs said, determination in her voice.

Liande snarled. "You ask for guidance but cannot see what is laid out before you! I am forbidden to say more, but if you want the truth, head to Sabella—Queen of Summer—though take warning: be ready for the storm that awaits you."

Babs brushed her hair out of her face. "How do I find her?"

"Continue behind this pool and tread the lengthy road downward. I will open the way," Liande droned. "It will lead directly to the entrance of her abode, surrounded by thick mist. Call out thrice, and in this manner, she will be summoned." Liande wrung her hands viciously, and sparks flew up, forming round glowing orbs that matched her all-seeing eyes. Her breath blew them up high till they orbited in slow rhythm around Babs's head. "But still, should she fail to grace thee with her presence, a horrendous fate awaits," she added darkly. "Forget not to address her as Her Majesty." She bobbed her head on the water among all the slithering alligators. "It would be a grievous mistake to mention me; best she forgets me entirely, for the time being." With that, Liande melted into the murky depths, leaving behind only an eerie silence.

Babs wrapped her arms around herself, wondering what Liande had meant by "a horrendous fate."

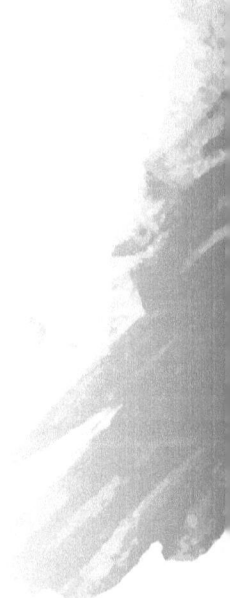

CHAPTER 9

CRICKET

They walked along cobblestone streets lit by aged lampposts, the air saturated with a heavy heat that clung to Bash's skin and trickled down Cricket's shoulder blades like sweat. Laughter rose above the murmur of the crowd as they strolled past old-fashioned storefronts and restaurants in St. Augustine's historic Old Town. A violin played somewhere in the distance, barely audible over the hubbub, and an iridescent sheen of moisture hung in the air, dampening their clothes almost instantly. Cricket rummaged through her YSL camera bag for her lipstick, capping it before rubbing her lips together to set the color. She checked her phone quickly, but there were no missed messages.

Her fingers trembled as she felt for her purse. Her heart raced with paranoia as she watched the crowd around her. Everywhere she looked, she saw the figure of the black-cloaked woman hunting her. Every fiber of her body screamed in fear and helplessness. She wanted to tell Bash what was happening to her, but how could he believe what seemed like a crazy story? She had to find out who had cursed her before it was too late—Francis Drake. She was certain he was responsible for this invisible tormenting force looming over her. If only there were answers inside the museum. Perhaps then things would begin to make sense.

"The pirate museum closes kind of early," she said, her cheeks flushing. She had changed into her favorite long-sleeved white ruffle-trim Bardot blouse and favorite jeans; both concealed the wounds from the bicycle accident and the curse snaking up her arm. But in this heat, she felt as if it might be too much—the fabric was heavy over her skin. Her hair was thrown up in a neat French twist, but a few waves of curls still framed her face.

"Leave now," Bash shouted fiercely.

Cricket jolted. His voice was urgent and his gaze laser focused. He was looking right over her shoulder. She spun around, yet there was nothing in sight. His protective instincts had been heightened, ready to face any danger that threatened her.

"What's going on?" she asked, her eyes drilling into Bash's as she saw his fear. "Tell me."

He opened his mouth to speak, and a chill filled the air. This wasn't a chill—it was like an unseen force gripping her body, trapping her in place and stealing her breath away. Panic raced through Cricket's mind, drowning all thought.

"You are mine, light wielder," rasped an ancient voice. She whirled around, searching for the source of the threat amongst the fanny-pack-clad tourists aimlessly ambling past. Her vision began to blur, darkness creeping in at its edges as she started to lose consciousness.

Bash shouted fiercely, "No! She is mine, Old One. Be gone!" He stepped between Cricket and the unknown force. Energy crackled around him as he thrust out his arm, and a mysterious power surged from his fingertips like a miniature ball of lightning. Cricket noticed something hanging from his hand. The street went back to normal, the oblivious crowd continuing their chatter as if nothing had happened.

Cricket felt Bash's strong arms envelop her in a comforting embrace. It was more than that of friendship. She could feel the heat radiating from him and a longing deep within as she gazed into his eyes. His fingers moved tenderly along her back, sending a wave of emotions that she had never felt before.

"Are you all right?" he asked. Worry emitted from his tone as he looked around for any threat. "Here, keep this on you." His voice trembled as he placed a rosary carefully in her hand. The wound on her skin wasn't lost on him.

Her heart felt as if it stopped for moment at the sight of the precious gift. The intricate metal crucifix with its weathered pearls seemed ancient and powerful—too powerful to be given away. She was having a hard time understanding what had happened. "I can't take it," Cricket murmured. "I don't understand. You saw—"

Bash ignored her words, running his fingers through her hair with an affectionate touch. "Come," he said softly. "Let's get into the museum. I think we have a lot to talk about. I'll try to explain."

Her face flushed as she quickly stood up. She had to keep reminding herself of why this was a bad idea—Bash was off-limits. But then he gazed at her with his knowing smile, and she felt like he could read her mind.

"I'm sure you have questions. I will do my best to answer them," he said in a deep, gentle voice that made her insides flip. He rolled up the edge of his crisp white shirt sleeve, revealing the new watch he had on. Cricket glanced down to see what he was wearing—it seemed they were matching in white clothes and silver accessories. Even more miraculous, he was glowing with a soft white light she had never seen around him before.

Feeling encouraged by his relaxed demeanor, Cricket tried to lighten the mood. "Yes! Let's talk inside the museum." But then reality set in; she was here for a reason—to study Drake's artifacts. There had to be some useful information on the displays. She had to find her answers tonight.

He grasped her hand firmly as they wound through the throng. His strong grip cloaked her delicate fingers; she soaked up his touch, not wanting to let go. She wondered about Gran's easy attitude towards humans—could it be because she was fully fae? Bash was something entirely different for her—an irresistible pull that had her in its grips. If she gave in to her feelings, would she lose herself completely? He was like catnip, and she feared it.

"Are you feeling better?" he murmured into her ear, his lips sending a wave of warmth racing through her body. "You look revived."

"Yes," she replied with a coy smile.

Taking the two concrete steps up to the pirate museum, their shoes made contrastingly different sounds; her nude heels clicked against the pavement while his burgundy Allen Edmonds tapped smartly with every step. Amongst a sea of flip-flops and sneakers, they looked slightly out of place. Bash stepped in front of her to open the heavy wooden door, ever the gentleman. As they entered, two black flags bearing the skull and crossbones waved gently at them from either side of the entrance.

The gift shop smelled of freshly sharpened pencils and leather-bound books—unmistakably plastic trinkets—as they weaved their way through an assortment of pithy black T-shirts and hats, walking canes and baby bibs, miniature ships and toy guns. She spotted a chest of plastic gold coins glinting in the dim lighting and wondered if her pirate would accept such "treasure."

"Ryan—" Bash yelled out.

"Hey, Bash!" Ryan said with a friendly nod. "You finally made it."

Bash smiled and patted his pocket. "Ticket for two," he said, nodding.

"No need, man. We're closing up soon anyway."

Ryan gave Cricket a long, appraising look. "So, this is her," he said with a knowing grin. Then he stuck out his hand. "Ryan. Best friend from way back."

Her cheeks reddened as she shook his hand. "Cricket," she murmured.

Ryan's gaze traveled back to Bash. "Man, I'm telling you; we need to get our bikes in gear and hit the trails again."

"Yeah, that sounds great," Bash replied, but before he could say more, Ryan shifted back to Cricket.

"Baubles and Whatnots? That's where you work? I got my dad a Christmas present from there. I think you might have helped me pick it out."

"Most likely; I live there. Literally." Cricket tucked a strand of hair behind her ear, struggling to make small talk. She wanted to know what had just happened with Bash out there on the street. How had he seen the figure? Was it messing with her? Was it threatening him?

Ryan continued, "You guys have some really cool things. I like the vibe of your store. Some days I feel like I live here too." He chuckled. "Not a bad gig, ya know. It's my uncle's museum. I help when he's short-staffed and I'm not on active duty. It pays enough for all my bike gear and then some."

Cricket smiled, half listening, and replied, "Harley?"

Ryan chuckled. "Nah, I'm a mountain biker, off road. Ya know, out in nature." He shifted his gaze to Bash. "Dude, you need to dust off your bike and get back in the game. We're planning a Georgia mountains getaway once I find time to take off. Bring Cricket with, it's all good. You got a bike, Cricket?"

Cricket's mind had drifted to the diary. She startled back to the conversation. "A bike? Umm—actually, I just damaged my cruiser."

"Replace it with a mountain bike," Ryan said with a glint in his eye. "I have a ton of them out at my ranch. I can hook you up with a good used one, totally pimped out. You know, thinking on it, I bet a fatty is more your speed. I've got a medium diamondback that should fit your height. Just promise me the two of you will come on the next big trip."

Cricket looked at Bash and shrugged. "That sounds, really interesting. Did you say you live on a ranch?"

"Ryan's family lives on the outskirts of town," Bash chimed in. "They have a horse ranch with some farmland too."

Cricket nodded, genuinely interested. She'd been so wrapped up in herself she hadn't really given Ryan the attention he deserved. She made a concerted effort to be present. "So a real outdoors guy!"

"Yeah, you could say that."

A bike excursion through the mountains. That would be fun. Meeting Bash's friend, that was unexpected. She just needed to avoid dying in the next few days.

"Ryan, I might take you up on that, thanks," she replied. "So, switching topics, are all the things in the museum authentic?"

"Oh yeah. It's for real all right." Ryan rolled his eyes as he shifted his gaze toward Bash. "Good old Bash knows all about that kind of stuff, don't you, buddy?"

"What do you mean?" Cricket inquired, her curiosity piqued.

Bash gave Ryan a warning glance before looking back toward Cricket.

Ryan grinned. "Nothing really. Just closing the place can be a bit spooky sometimes." He gave a nervous chuckle. "I'm sure it's just those ghost hunter shows getting into my head, but when I'm alone and in the dark, I start to feel like I'm not alone in there." He nodded in the direction of the first museum display.

"I'm sure it's just nerves, buddy," Bash said through gritted teeth. "Cricket, why don't you go ahead and check out the museum? I'll catch up with you shortly."

"Yes." Cricket tightened her grip on the rosary she carried, her knuckles whitening. "And, Bash, we can have that talk." She turned her attention back to Ryan. "Nice meeting you, really. She glanced down at her wounded hand hidden in her sleeve. "I do hope we get to do the Georgia trip."

"Right on!" Ryan looked genuinely pleased.

She rushed through the sprawling museum, her heart pounding with each step. She must accomplish her mission before Bash arrived. Her heels clacked against the wooden floors as she made her way to the Sir Francis Drake exhibit.

As she drew nearer, she was enveloped in a sense of awe at the artifacts lined up in neat rows inside glass cases. She stroked a worn cannonball as she made her way past replicas of Sir Francis Drake's ships that sat in dry docks. Shields, swords, and battle cannons lined the walls in chronological order from his earliest days to his last voyage. The interactive computer screens hummed quietly with stories about Drake's early expeditions and his legacy, which remained in the pages of folklore and history. A replica of Drake's famous ship, the *Golden Hinde*, stood at the center of the hall, beckoning her closer.

Unfolding the paper in her hands, she gazed upon her copy of the handwriting from the diary with desperation. If it matched Drakes handwriting that was on display, she would know she was on the right track.

A display case, covered in protective glass, held a manifest and a ship's lantern. The placard explained that both artifacts were from the *Golden Hind*, Sir Francis Drake's galleon used to circumnavigate the world. The manifest listed in beautiful penmanship signed by Sir Francis Drake:

6 tons of cloves — Spice Islands
26 tons of silver
Half ton gold
Porcelain 10 chests
Jewelry 5 chests
Coins 20 chests
Jewels 15 chests

Poring over both the manifest and sample, she felt a little thrill. The ink bled thickly at the start of words, culminating in a large flourish leaning leftward. The lowercase *Ds* were skewed to the left just like on both papers. His signature was distinct; his *F* in Francis sprawled grandly whereas the *D* in Drake was almost an afterthought. The penmanship seemed almost identical to her—did everyone write this way back then? Granted, she wasn't an expert in handwriting recognition, but with bated breath she had to admit that they could very well be a match.

Her gaze roamed over Drake's painting hanging above the manifest. He stood tall, strong, and undeniably handsome, with a sharp jawline and tousled dark hair. His eyes possessed an intensity that took her aback. It was almost as if he were staring into her soul. She studied the details more intently, taking in every single brushstroke, tracing the outline of his lips, and noting how the shadows had been expertly crafted to give depth to his chiseled features. She felt a fluttering sensation as she continued to observe him—it was like he was alive!

Cricket looked around uneasily to make sure she was alone. With a trembling breath, she gingerly touched Drake's painting, feeling the smooth strokes of oil paints beneath her fingertips. She closed her eyes and breathed in the scent of turpentine lingering in the air. Her pulse raced with anticipation as she felt an unexplained connection with this man, even though he was nothing but a two-dimensional figure painted on canvas. Taking a deep breath, she allowed the energy of the painting to seep into her, a tangible force that seemed to cause the air to ripple. Every nerve in her body felt alive. She could sense a power surging through her as if she were part of the painting itself, and suddenly she was overcome with dizziness, an inexplicable sensation, like being transported into another world.

"How long have I been here? It feels like hours!" the man groaned, shifting in the plain wooden chair. Light flooded in through three glass windows, casting a glow on half of his face

and shrouding him in deep shadows. He looked like a true man of the world.

Cricket was hiding under the shadows in the corner, trying her best to stay unnoticed — until she heard something that made her listen more closely.

"Let's pause for a bit," the painter said, wearing a muslin dress with a leather apron over it. Her hair was neatly pinned up in a bun. "I got some sack from Spain if you'd like?"

The man burst out laughing — it was startling yet strangely satisfying at the same time. "I've heard tales of our countrymen calling Spanish sherry 'sack.' But to hear it . . ." He shook his head.

The woman grinned playfully as she poured the drink into a pewter cup, handing it to him. "Have you heard what the Spanish call you?" she asked mischievously.

He laughed again, delighted by her wit. "King Philip's wobbling beard is apparently calling me 'sea wolf.' Let him call me whatever he wishes." His voice grew more serious as he added, "Our great Queen Elizabeth has bested him, and all of England is feasting with . . . sack, as you call it." He lifted his cup with reverence as a big smile spread across his face. "To our queen!" He drank heartily.

"Cricket!" Bash's voice reverberated through her like a shock, snapping her back into reality. She blinked repeatedly and tried to focus on his face, which was inching closer to hers. He looked panicked; fear mixed with worry streaked across his visage. "What is going on with you? What happened?"

She shook her head and rolled her shoulders back. "I'm sorry, just — give me a second." Between the penmanship and just seeing the man in the vision, all doubt had been erased from her mind. She grabbed her phone from her purse and quickly texted Babs and Zadie.

Cricket: Drake is our guy for sure. You were right, the Black Spot is a pirate's curse. Zadie, get that treasure. Let's beat this guy!

She hesitated, her fingers encircling the phone in her purse. Taking a deep breath, she pushed away her fear and looked up at Bash with new eyes. Her chest filled with a mix of emotions—exhilaration from the adrenaline, and trepidation at what he would think when she told him the truth.

With one last pause, she released a shaky exhale and decided it was time to be brave. No more secrets, she promised herself—not from him.

Bash shuffled his feet. "Ryan closed up already. We are completely alone. We can stay for as long as you want." He licked his lips. "I need to tell you something. It's not going to be easy to hear, and maybe a bit confusing—but I'm hoping you can be open minded enough—"

Cricket's mind was flooded with thoughts. Most of the lights had been turned off, and there was complete silence around them. "Bash, I want to hear what you have to say, truly. First—I want to show you something." Her gaze raked the floor.

"What?" He brushed a strand of hair out of her face and tucked it behind her ear.

"Where's my copy? I must've dropped it somewhere over here. Please, help me look for it!"

They scrambled around the display that held the manifest authored by Sir Francis Drake. Finally, her copy of the diary was found on the floor off to the side.

She grabbed and straightened out the paper that had been crumpled up inside her handbag. Holding it aloft, she exclaimed excitedly, "Look at this! Look!"

He glanced at the copy, then compared it to the document—he peered back and forth between them, his eyes widening in disbelief. A sweeping smile broke out across his face as comprehension finally dawned. "Cricket . . ."

"I know, right?"

They stared at each other in amazement—two scholarly geeks feeling like Indiana Jones when he'd found the Lost Ark.

"This is remarkable!" he said with an exuberant laugh. "To think you discovered a missing diary belonging to Sir Francis Drake! The museum will be so excited to add it to its collection!"

Cricket looked away, her voice almost a whisper. "Can I show you something? Please don't be scared."

Confusion crossed his face as he tried to decipher her words. She took a deep breath and raised the ruffle of her blouse, revealing the horrific wound on her hand—it was oozing black puss and radiating an ominous energy that made even the air around them seem still.

His eyebrows shot up as he scanned the gruesome injury. He gulped back a wave of nausea before he could speak. "It looks so painful; it must have been really hard when you fell off the bike." He touched her arm but she quickly pulled away.

She raised her sleeve farther and exposed a much larger wound—the dark poison crawled up her arm like tentacles. A tightness seized in her chest as she uttered in a small voice: "No, this happened before the accident. It happened when I touched the diary; Zadie said it's a curse—the Black Spot. I am under a pirate's curse."

He blinked rapidly for a few moments before finally exhaling, his eyes never leaving hers. "I'm sorry . . . Can you say that again?"

He looked around the room, then back at her. His soft gaze moved from her eyes to her lips. He stepped closer, and she could feel his breath on her face. He wrapped his arms around her like a cocoon and kissed her forehead.

"I'm here," he whispered as he rocked her from side to side in an embrace. "We'll figure this out."

She felt a wave of relief wash over her. Perhaps he did believe her after all. She pulled back slightly and peered up into his eyes. "But how?"

He let out a deep breath before answering, "I see things others can't—ghosts, spirits, whatever you want to call them. It's been that way for as long as I can remember." He paused, looking slightly embarrassed.

Cricket remembered how she had seen him surrounded by a white light when he brandished his crucifix. Maybe there was more to reality than what even she was aware of. "You can see things that others can't?"

He nodded solemnly. "Yeah. This city is full of more ghosts than living people."

She mulled this over for a moment and allowed herself to accept it as truth. She'd never seen a ghost before, but now it seemed perfectly reasonable that they might be real and roaming their streets day and night. "What did you call the one who came today?"

"Old One," he replied softly. "That's what I usually call them. Every soul that departs this world for another is ushered by someone on the other side; sometimes it's relatives or friends who have passed on before them. But I didn't sense a familial energy. Did you see or feel her presence?"

"I've felt her since the curse was uttered. I saw her under the tree, earlier today, and felt her hands on my neck out on the street, when you—"

"The crucifix. It usually sends spirits back to where they came. Not always, but most of the time. If she has been sent, and it's your time—the crucifix won't keep her away forever." Deep compassion filled Bash's face. "She called you light wielder?"

"Bash, we've been friends for a long time—"

He softly placed his finger on her lips, halting her words, keeping her from telling her full truth. His other arm wrapped around her waist, clinging tighter and drawing her closer to him.

"Cricket," he said in a tender whisper, his voice laced with emotion. He hesitated before continuing, hoping to form the right words that would adequately express his feelings. "We've been more than just friends for a long time, I know that now. If I'm going to tell you the truth—the absolute truth . . ."

The darkness of the room enveloped them. His finger slowly traveled down from her mouth, tracing the delicate edge of her jawline before resting at the nape of her neck. He gently pulled her toward him and carefully leaned down toward her, brushing their lips together with a softness like spring rain. She opened to him, allowing the kiss to linger as she savored the taste of his lips against hers. Her arms circled around him as she squeezed tight, basking in the reality of his touch.

He eventually lifted his head, still gazing deeply into her eyes. His expression was filled with love and longing as tears glistened in his eyes. "I wouldn't be able to handle it if something happened to you—if I lost you." He spoke with determination and conviction. "We will break this curse, together."

She sighed contentedly, laying her head against his chest. She could hear his heart beating fast, breaking away all barriers between them.

CHAPTER 10
BABS

Babs trudged through the mud. The smell of stale sweat filled her nostrils as she gasped for breath, her tattered and blood-smeared shirt snagging on branches and thorns. As the night deepened, the path curved downward into a velvet void of shadows and secrets. Her feet skidded over sharp rocks in a desperate attempt to keep going. The nearly full moon cast an eerie blue light across the forest, creating a scene of chaotic beauty, with screeching bats and hooting owls adding to the atmosphere of dread that engulfed her being. Sudden warmth descended upon her body as mist coiled around her legs and thighs like grasping arms, beckoning her forward. Liande's orbs of light darted in front of her, hovering silently in a lazy circle formation. Was this the entrance to the cave? An unnatural chirp sounded ahead; every instinct in her body told her to turn back immediately. She closed her eyes, took a deep breath, and forged ahead into the unknown.

She inhaled once more and, on the exhale, regained her confidence and whispered, "Your Majesty. Your Majesty. Your Majesty." With all her being she hoped this Queen of the Summer Court was close enough to hear her and would find her worthy of entering her realm unannounced and un-invited. Liande was frightening enough — to think a creature as old as Liande feared the person she was calling out to . . . An entrance to the summer court resided right behind her house, yet her mother had never mentioned it. No matter how many times she ran it through her mind, she couldn't understand why she hadn't been told. Even if no one told her, she should have been able to sense the presence of the court. She was filled with confusion and doubt. Nadine would be furious when she found out.

She needed to focus on getting answers to save Cricket. Her last text said she knew it was Drake who'd cursed her. They had to be on the right path; Babs could sense it in her bones. The answer she sought was right on the other side of her fear.

She felt a deep and reverberating growl. Babs blinked her eyes rapidly and staggered back in shock; two giant wolves blazed before her. Their eyes glowed a brilliant iridescence like a beetle's shell, their muscles coiled like springs, ready to pounce. She could hardly breathe as she stared at them, mesmerized by the power of their presence. The shimmering, iridescent power and the vibration of their energy struck ancient chords within her, stirring some long-forgotten familiar feelings that had been suppressed for years. Their noise was like the roar of a motorcycle en-gine revving up, escalating with impossible intensity until it filled the air around them. As if responding to an invisible force, a strong wind blew from behind, flinging hair wildly across her face and raising goosebumps along her skin. Babs felt herself weakening, as if something wild inside of her was being unleashed.

"Finally, the time of waiting is at an end." A voice, thick with desire and cunning, drifted through the wind. She turned to see what had spoken to her. The Queen of the Summer Court was poised before her, standing gracefully on the green grass. Her braids flew in a circular pattern around her slim face like a lion's mane. A golden crown adorned her head with a five-pointed star. The low amber moon outlined her red hair that blew ferociously around her. Thick braids framed her elongated pale face. Her features were like granite, her skin as white as marble; she seemed transcendent, knowing eyes that looked out beyond, connected and seeing all. Babs trembled before her power and felt weak and small.

A whisper cut through the air, so soft yet so powerfully commanding. "Do not be afraid. Do you not feel destiny's grasp?" Her gown billowed in the warm breeze as she opened her arms wide and settled onto a great stone. Everything around them seemed to still, like time was suspended in that moment.

Babs felt an unexplainable pull towards the queen, as if she could somehow read her mind.

"Come lay your head upon my lap," the queen beckoned.

Babs felt bewitched by the words, drawn to her alluring aura as if she were under an enchantment. She slowly walked toward the regal goddess and laid her head upon her lap with no hesitation. With a wave of the regent's slim fingers, the two giant wolves curled up and lay down, their eyes trained on their mistress.

Babs felt a warmth wash over her as the queen's gentle hand cupped her head. Time seemed to slow as scenes of Babs's life floated before her eyes, memories passing like the pages of a book. The queen seemed to read them all, searching for something hidden between the lines. Reality divided itself in two; in one moment, Babs saw Nadine for who she thought she was, while in the other, she felt Nadine's fingers wiggle inside her mind, manipulating her thoughts and memories, rigidly keeping her focus on what she desired. The queen's fingertips trailed through Babs's hair, like the brush of an angel's wings. Hot tears burned trails on Babs's cheeks, and a quiet whisper echoed in her thoughts: truth revealed.

"I can take away your pain, if you so desire."

The words echoed in Babs's mind as the queen placed her hand on her chest and pulled out all the agony, like lancing a wound she didn't know existed inside her. A gasp escaped from Babs lips. Heat like lava surged through her core, purifying her from the inside out. Her breath came in short bursts as the queen maintained her grip. Sharp nails dug into Babs's chest. She felt engulfed by flames. The delicate hand rose to the queen's mouth. Moonlight sparkled off her fangs as she blew onto her palm. Dark sleet billowed from her breath, battering the trees and shrubs. Babs fell to the ground, covered in cold perspiration. The wind grew fiercer, scattering the black hail in all directions. Cracks appeared across Babs's skin. Whereas she was broken externally, there was shining golden energy circulating inside her body—all negative obstructions were gone, and she had been reborn anew.

The queen softly laid her fingers on Babs's head, sending a wave of warmth throughout her body.

"My child, I have been waiting for you to find your way to me. The time has come for you to accept your true power and destiny. You need only free yourself from the shackles that bind you and see the truth behind them. You are being used as a puppet by the winter court, but fear not, for your fate lies with summer now. It is time for the Culebra line to take its place, to serve."

Visions of Nadine shimmered in Babs's mind.

"The Culebra bloodline is ancient and powerful. You, out of your generation, were marked for greatness. You are the vessel for your mother's earth magic." The wolves encircled her, one letting out a gentle whimper.

"You must trust in the power you possess. You will join my court and be the balance that has been prophesized. Open your ears to the call of the wolf. Your heart aches for something you cannot see; only by answering the howl can you walk the path that is rightfully yours. Reach within to find what needs to be known. I have given you the answer," she whispered.

Babs beheld a vision of Cricket alongside Drake, encased in a dreamlike slumber. A mystical sight unfolded before her, so slow and surreal she could feel each moment as it passed. The book lay featherlight in Cricket's palms, its pages illuminated amidst walls draped with bones and dust. Babs saw herself amidst the scene, taking a wolf skull, claiming it as her own. Fire exploded from the roof. The wolf came to her aid through the flames, and their bond grew within the blaze, united in purpose and strength. The queen hovered above them all, her face stoic and emotionless. Soft chants filled the air as they ascended through mud walls, past the wooden floors and stone walls, finally reaching the entrance of an ancient temple not yet seen by mortal eyes. The queen remained close, enveloping Babs in a dreamy embrace.

Tunnels of flame creaked around them, filled with fangs hissing with pain. A statue emerged that Babs had seen in dreams. Instantly she knew it was for her to find, to lead her sisters to it. Bloody footprints marked her heart, calling her forth to save her sister and take control of her destiny.

The queen's voice softly echoed around Babs: "Free yourself, claim your destiny—join me."

The words were out of Babs mouth before she knew what had possessed her. "I am yours."

The queen's laughter filled the trees as her eyes glittered with maniacal glee. She raised an eyebrow and said, "At last, you submit to me. The magic of the Culebra line is mine to wield."

Babs stared into the queen's eyes and glimpsed a feral madness. It felt intoxicating and inviting, like a forbidden fruit dangling in temptation. The feeling was so powerful that Babs wanted to give herself over to it completely. All her questions vanished from her mind as she let go of all inhibitions.

"The seer will guide you. Trust him."

CHAPTER 11

CRICKET

The hot bath salts surrounded Cricket's skin with a bubbling foam, making the aches and pains unnoticeable. Her long light hair was freshly washed, nails were scrubbed, and toes worked into a soft pinkness. The clawfoot porcelain bathtub was her favorite part of her vintage bathroom. She could really think while she was soaking in the tub.

Here she was, so worried that she was going to freak Bash out, but as it turned out, he had a secret of his own—he could see into the spirit realm. Maybe if they made it through this mess unscathed, Bash could teach her what he knew? Wouldn't that be fun?

She sighed deeply as she lay back against the edge of the tub and let the memory play on repeat in her head. For a day that started with a car scraping her up, things were not turning out that bad. It was amazing what a first kiss could do to lighten your mood, and the possibility of a romance if she beat this wretched curse. But could she be romantically involved without losing herself? Without losing her powers, like her mom had? Just like Gran said, she could have fun.

There was no reason to not live life because of fear. Better to let the heart guide than the fearful mind.

She had meant to tell Bash that she was fae, but revealing that she was cursed was enough for one night. She would find the right time to tell him, after they beat the curse.

She was coming off her high from the confirmation that they were indeed dealing with Drake. Now, there was so much work to do. She squeezed lavender vanilla soap on her sponge and began scrubbing at her leg.

Zadie had texted that she was out looking for the treasure tonight. She promised to call on Aunt Maj for backup if she needed it. That was a good sign. Usually, Zadie was all fins up without a plan. If she was thinking of Maj, she had thought things out.

When Babs texted Cricket back, her good news was that she knew for a fact where to return the treasure. The bad news was that the only way to do it was to use the tunnels under town in the Subterranean. She needed time to figure out how to unbind the tunnel. Even with all the times she had fortified it, she never imagined she would want to unravel the spells.

First step, Burt. Cricket knocked on the bathroom wall three times and waited. She could hear something scrabbling inside the wall, behind the plaster and wood. He always took his sweet old time responding to her and often scrambled back into the walls before she'd even finished knocking. She was sure he'd pestered her aunt Habina when she'd lived here, probably even Gran when she'd been young. Who knows, maybe further back than that? She always found it creepy when listening to things in the walls — mice, bats, the occasional opossum? The scratching noise came again, and she heard a quiet *cluck* in response.

"Burt."

Aha! She heard his distinctive noise. Burt was quite the master of the house, their Duende. They called him Burt because . . .

"Burt." There it was again.

For as long as she'd known him, he had belched constantly, and it sounded like . . .

"Burt."

He drank the mouthwash, seriously. He had a thing about cleanliness.

Through the crack in the door that led to her bedroom crawled a spider about as big as her hand. On its back rode Burt. A floppy green pointed hat balanced atop his pale green head; his elongated ears stuck straight out on each side of his melon head like bat wings. Spindly legs wrapped around the belly of his spider, reminding her of Jack Skellington, only her Burt wasn't as jovial or ambitious.

The comical duo promenaded across the uneven wooden floor and climbed the ledge of the clawfoot tub with confidence—there was no telling how long they had practiced this routine. The skin on Burt's hands grew white and wrinkled as he gripped the tiny arachnid closer to him until they disappeared behind the lip of the tub. She imagined them nestled together behind one of the feet, waiting for a chance to stumble upon someone who might be in need of an ambush.

His head came into sight again. "Good evening, my Little C," his featherlight voice said slowly as he cocked his head to one side, his eyes wide like an innocent child's. He had always called her Little C. She wasn't sure why. He was so diminutive in stature, she must have looked large to him. But she didn't mind the nickname. Irony was cool.

She slowly bent down to his level. "Good evening, Burt. How is your day? I bought this new toothpaste I thought you might like. It's cinnamon."

Duendes were meticulous; they believed everyone should be clean and tidy before bed. She had experienced the consequences of not following suit—a few scratches from her Duende's attempts to help her out without waking her up. Ears were his area of obsession—she made sure to never forget washing behind hers.

He tilted his head toward the crystals of the ceiling light and gave a wide grin back at her. "Burt likes the toothpaste," he declared.

"That's great! Is there anything else you'd like me to get for the bathroom?" Conversation was key in the world of Duende culture, niceties were expected before any request were made.

He began stroking one of the spider's long hairy legs as it lay across his lap. "You need a new toothbrush," he squeaked. Despite her own being only a few weeks old, she knew better than to argue with him.

"Yes, I'll get one next time I go out shopping."

That appeased him.

"Burt, do you want to play Find with me?" she asked with a sparkle in her eye.

"Ohhh, I'd love to! Find is my favorite game, especially when it's something missing." He beamed and rubbed his hands together eagerly.

"This one is hard though," she warned. "It's not in the store or in our rooms. It's—below. Have you ever gone down there before?"

"Not in home?" Burt frowned in concentration. He was usually content to never roam.

"We'll wander away under the house tomorrow and see if you can find our way back home," she challenged him with a hint of mischief in her voice.

"Ohhhh, yes!" His eyes lit up as he laughed and jiggled in excitement.

"I'm glad you're excited about it." She smiled, watching as he shook the spider near the edge of the tub. "We will play tomorrow; Babs and Zadie will join us."

"Splendid!" Burt exclaimed, already imagining their journey of finding things that were lost or misplaced and figuring out where they belonged.

"Okay, Little C," he repeated in his squeaky voice as he turned his spider around. It spun its spindly legs around and released a thin glass thread, which whipped through the air like a fiery strand of gossamer silk. With this lifeline between them, the two dropped down to the ground and landed softly.

Cricket moved the bubbles around and turned a trickle of hot water on to heat up the tub. She looked down at her body. Long livid marks marred her entire right side from the car incident. Her cursed hand was purple with black streaks that threaded along its length and up her arm. It was as if her body was rotting from the inside out. Everything ached. She needed deep sleep.

She pulled the rubber plug out of the tub and watched the water form a funnel, flowing down, circling the drain. When the tub was completely empty, she stepped onto the rug, put on a robe, and wrapped a bath towel around her hair.

Cricket had a daunting task ahead of her. Inside Aunt Habina's diary, she'd found a binding spell that could have been the original spell, or at least akin to what was used to seal off the tunnels downstairs. It seemed they had constructed it so that only one way was blocked originally. But Gran and Mom had woven together their life energy to cast an even more powerful spell, one that blocked both directions. Cricket had only worked with it in that state.

She focused intently on constructing a reversal of the spell, envisioning it in her mind like an intricate knot that needed to be untied. It was no simple task; this enchantment was strong and complicated, created by powerful fae who all had a connection to the magical realm. Cricket felt herself rising to the challenge as she began manipulating the energy around her with assurance.

Cricket, exhausted after hours of spell work, fell into bed. The cool sheets were a welcome relief against her hot skin. She placed Habina's diary on the bedside table and admired her freshly scrawled notes. From the open window, she could hear the contented coo of a pigeon above the laughter of pedestrians walking by on the streets below. The streaks of black on her hand reminded her of the preciousness of an average day. As she closed her eyes for a moment, thoughts of future bike rides and treasured first kisses danced in her mind.

CHAPTER 12

ZADIE

Yara, the sun has been down for hours. It's time to start our treasure hunt," Zadie said, looking over the nav charts one more time. At this point, she had it memorized. The salty ocean air felt like silk across her skin as she leaned over the starboard railing, letting its spray cool her face. The dark waters were unusually still, and her ship, *Yara*, glided forward with hardly a sound with the masthead in control. Her thick golden hair cascaded over her delicate shoulders, moving with the gentle ebb and flow of the sea.

"I'll say it again: this is not a good idea. I don't want my hull ripped apart by jagged coral." Zadie heard *Yara*'s voice in her mind.

Yara had always been the practical one between them. It was risky, and Zadie hated to put *Yara* even close to danger. She was her best friend; to be honest, she understood her better than even Zadie's family, being that *Yara* had at one time been a mermaid. She had been enslaved by a cruel captain when he had captured her while sailing and strapped her to the bow of his ship. It was fate that brought Zadie to this old vessel, still holding *Yara* in its embrace, merged into one. After all these years, *Yara* had become the ship.

From the moment she'd sensed *Yara*'s spirit and knew her sad tale, Zadie knew she would stay with *Yara* no matter what the sea threw their way. "For a ship, you are very squeamish. I'm not going to let you get hurt. Let's not fight. I don't have the energy to spare."

Zadie's mind drifted to her very sexy morning with Tom. It had felt like a vacation from her quest for *Dulcinea*; he was the comfort that she had needed. She knew Tom would have some answers about where to look for *Dulcinea*, and although the heat that stirred inside of her was not because of the warm breeze, she couldn't help but smile at the memory.

Zadie ran her fingers lightly over *Yara*'s wheel. "Cricket confirmed that it's Drake's treasure we are after, and Tom's information is always solid. It's out there for the taking. We have got this. You and me."

So far there hadn't been anything the two of them couldn't do once they were in sync. Zadie just needed her buy-in.

"Is Tom solid?" Yara mocked. "But seriously, I may be more than a ship, and you may be Mer . . ." The boards below Zadie's feet made a deep creaking noise. *Yara* was obviously agitated. *"This is a lot for just the two of us. Why didn't you ask your sisters along?"*

Zadie looked down at her thigh, a smile gracing her features. "It's three; we have Kraken." She sighed. "You know my sisters are useless on the water. Just as useless as I am on land. I can't do a deep dive and be worried about them falling overboard. Babs freaks out the minute land is out of sight. Fear on a boat drowns everyone," Zadie said.

"You are in a testy mood and spouting nonsense. You still have the capability to go on sea and earth. It's a blessing, not a curse. What I wouldn't give to have my true form again. To walk, to truly swim," Yara mused.

A wave of her sadness washed over Zadie. Yara's longing to be on land, to stand on two legs, was hard to think about. Zadie imagined her in the height of her beauty. Her long golden locks, her piercing azure eyes. She could lure any seaman she chose. Zadie's cheeks felt hot with shame.

"I'm sorry. I'm agitated. I shouldn't take it out on you. I need to find the treasure before the Black Spot overcomes Cricket." She paced back and forth along the bow, her legs restless. "Once we have the treasure, we have to get it back to the place where she was cursed. Babs is working on that. Ugh—I poked at her last night. I think she's still mad at me, and probably Cricket. It's never fun when she's out of sorts." Zadie ran her hand along the back of her neck, massaging the tight muscles. "We are up against a ridiculous timetable."

"I understand curses, as you well know. But we should ask for help. Call for Maj; she will come if you need her," Yara suggested.

She had had the same idea. Aunt Maj was backup who could offer real help. Zadie's pride wasn't going to get in the way of saving her sister. This was a no-brainer. "You are right. I will call on the Mer, once I lay eyes on *Dulcinea.*" There was no point calling them till they had found the ship.

"Dulcinea? Are you serious?" Yara shivered. The boards creaked all over; the mast heaved to one side, then counterbalanced to the other, rocking the whole boat feverishly. *"I know her!"*

Confusion clouded Zadie's mind. "You couldn't have known her; she went down in the—"

"*Fifteen hundreds; yes, I know. I will last forever. My immortality fused with the ship. Don't we look good for our age?*" She laughed.

Zadie had never thought about how old the ship was. That was old!

"*Younglings.*" Yara was bemused. "*Zadie, listen to me. Dulcinea is my sister. If you know where she is, we need to find her and bring her up. If we place her on a new boat, she could still yet live. What if she has been conscious all these centuries, lying on the bottom of the sea, waiting for someone to rescue her?*"

"You mean the masthead?" Zadie asked, not understanding what *Yara* meant.

"*Yes, more Mers than you can count were captured by greedy captains. They saw us as prizes, profit, a way to protect their ships, their cargo, their lives. When they realized that boats would accept Mers and merge with them, we were prized, coveted. Our capture was boasted about. Any of the pirates you can name, I would guess to a man, captured a Mer and rode her over the sea,*" she said.

Over the years Zadie and *Yara* had been together, *Yara* spoke often about other Mer ships. Zadie knew there were more still out there like her. *Yara* always got so excited when they passed near one. It wasn't often, but it happened. Most sailors, if they had ever heard of Mer ships, believe it a legend, nothing more. That kept them safe; the Mers usually didn't reveal themselves to the captain. Zadie hadn't thought of what happened to them if they went down. She'd assumed they were no more.

"*Who knows the sea better than a Mer?*" Yara asked.

"No one," Zadie admitted, rolling her shoulders back, content with trusting *Yara*'s knowledge. "Which is why we will be successful in retrieving your sister, *Dulcinea*, and her treasure. We will save our sisters, together."

Yara's wood set off a low glow as she and Zadie aligned wills. How serendipitous life could be at times. Beautiful, really, how an event can lead you to another; one just needed to take time to notice, like searching for the perfect seashell at low tide.

Zadie loosened the line and pulled the main tight to hug the wind. The engine purred as they glided softly through the dark, star-filled night. Airplanes flew high above their heads; little lights of white, green, and red speckled the sky above. The humid evening breeze blew Zadie's long hair wildly about her like tiny whips; goosebumps rose on her arms as she closed her eyes, feet set, wide hands lightly touching the wheel, sailing with the ocean. She let out the jib, the wind filling it like a pocket stuffed full of sweets. Zadie could smell Cricket's magic in it, attracting only fair wind to pull them along. She cut the engine. They could hear the sea, its breath, its movement. They were one with her, gliding along the surface.

A white cloak of clouds surrounded *Yara*, nestling her in a tepid, wet blanket as she increased speed. High, white waves crashed over her bow, soaking all in salt water. Clammy cold reached deep into Zadie's bones, stripping her of any heat she had left. Her feet quickly became blocks of ice, her fingers numb, thick, and nearly useless. *Yara* rose and fell, rose and fell; crashing waves beat at them rhythmically for what felt like hours. Zadie's thoughts drifted.

The secret of the sea is knowing she is always in control. The only way to survive is to let go and let her happen to you. Pay attention and listen. She tells you what she wants. If you want to survive, submit.

Zadie felt a shift in the water. "*Yara*, drop anchor. You can't get any closer. In these waves, you will crash into the coral. I will swim over and down."

"Are you sure? I could get a little – " A wave crashed over the bow; the boat shifted deeply to the right, then left.

"Here, anchor here. I'm strong enough to swim it." She hoped her anchor chain and rope were long and strong enough to hold. It would be disastrous if they dragged anchors into the coral.

Zadie felt *Yara* drop both anchors. The sea continued to buck. Zadie jumped off the starboard side and did her best to ignore the shock of cold. The waves threw the top half of her body left and the bottom half right.

If she remained close to the top, her body would be shredded like a frail strand of seaweed.

She forced her head down and kicked as hard as she could, clearing the top. She placed her palms on her thighs and closed her eyes. Heat soared through her abdomen; like liquid, lava filled her legs as they fused into one. Her powerful tail pushed against the current as she swam deeper.

She turned her ring and touched her stomach. *Kraken, I release you*, she thought.

Kraken slithered out of her side and sped down ahead of her. Down and down, they went. He twirled and twisted. Happy to be back in the water, where he belonged.

A heavy burst of current smacked Zadie into a wall of coral. The right side of her face numbed immediately, and her right arm burned as if it was being shocked. She was weightless and powerless, drifting with the current toward the tubular kelp beds farther down. But even then, she couldn't evade the towering fronds of coral that punctuated the seafloor like tall trees. They beat her again and again, until every inch of her body felt impaled on their jagged peaks. She couldn't see Kraken but felt he was near and all right.

The current's surge whipped strongly as they continued the descent. Her eyes adjusted to the lack of light, all reds and oranges gone, only blues and greens remaining. Cool and cold. The coral was jagged, growing in wild columns inhabited by all manner of sea creatures. Kelp danced back and forth with the ocean, puffs of sand kicking up at their roots. Zadie scanned for signs of a shipwreck, but nothing was obvious.

Kraken came into her vision, coming close to her side. They dove down lower, staying just above the edge of the trench at the bottom of the sea. It was about as long and wide as a football field. Its darkness hid its contents and its depth.

She hovered above where she thought the ship had lain in Tom's pictures. There was no ship to be seen. Her gut seized. It was clear she had to go into the trench and find out if the ship had fallen in. The only logical explanation was that it had. Or, if it was not there, someone else had already found the ship and taken it up. But if that had happened, everyone would have heard about it. *Right?*

She hesitated. She wanted to see the ship before calling Aunt Maj; but going into the trench by herself was just stupid. The uneasy feeling in her stomach remained. Her head ached from descending so quickly. Her body was on fire from the coral. She listened to her gut.

She threw her head back and sang the Mer song. Notes vibrated through the water like waves of gold and silver. In the water, you are never alone. You are connected to everything and everyone; every movement and sound is felt and shared by all. Perfect unity. Of course, this meant anything that felt like having a Mer snack had just gotten an announcement of where to find her. But her worry fell away as her skin tingled at the vibration of her kin's Mer song sung back to her. Their voices intermingled and grew more powerful as they grew nearer to her.

Zadie swam to keep warm, but not so fast as to lose her strength. It would be a long night. Kraken enjoyed the play time, oblivious to the bitter cold. After what felt like forever, the murky dark water parted to reveal Aunt Maj, the Admiral General of the Merpeople, who was flanked by several mermen: all clad in bronze-colored armor. Each gripping keens. These small slender objects, no larger than a baton, propelled them through the water at wicked-fast speeds. They used them for long distances or to speed away from predators. With the keens, Mers could outswim anything in the sea.

"Zadie." Aunt Maj's deep voice greeted Zadie's ears as Maj removed her helmet and attached it to her belt. Tiny shells were woven through her many blond braids. Her vivacious blue eyes shone with cheerfulness. Looking at her, Zadie knew exactly what she would look like in time. Maj embraced Zadie. Zadie winced as the pain of her injuries sent sparks through her system. She closed her eyes and swallowed it. No time to deal with pain now. She loved being in Maj's arms. They felt like home.

When Zadie'd been little, she loved cuddling on Maj's lap, her shimmering hair a curtain closing them in to their own private world, and they would sing. Zadie would mimic all the sounds Maj made till they fell into laughter.

Swimming back a stroke, Zadie bowed her head in gratitude to each merman in turn, then a generous bow to Aunt Maj, as was due her rank. They may have been family, but when in front of Maj's men, protocol had to be followed.

"Admiral General," Zadie said, looking straight ahead. She felt Kraken swimming by her waist.

"Niece." Maj's amusement flickered through her eyes. "Would you mind telling us what brings us to these depths in the middle of the night?"

"Would you like the long version of the story or short?" Zadie asked.

The two mermen took off their helmets and put all their gear away on their belt, just as Maj had.

"It's the middle of the night, and the waters are rough; let's go with short," the general said.

"I think there is a ship down there, and I need what's with it, a chest of gold, and the Mer masthead. *Yara* is anchored away from the coral but in choppy water, so we have quite a task to get the treasure and masthead up to *Yara*. Uh, I mean, *we* if you want to help me."

Murmurs broke out at the mention of a Mer masthead.

"Who do you think is down there?" Maj asked.

"*Dulcinea*. *Yara* thinks if we bring her up, we can put her on a ship and bring her back to life," Zadie said.

Maj shook her head. "I don't think *Yara* is right. As she knows, once the Mer is bonded to the ship, it's not reversible. When a ship goes down, the masthead dies with the ship. We would have heard her if she had survived. We would have come for her."

Zadie winced. There was no way she could come up with the treasure and not *Dulcinea*. "I promised *Yara* I would try," Zadie pleaded.

Maj looked at her men. "Okay, *Dulcinea* is gone to us. But maybe it will help *Yara* to see her. What about the chest?" she asked, one eyebrow raised.

"Long story—really need it, and the sooner the better," Zadie said quickly.

Maj looked at the trench, then back at Zadie. "We will help you; there is no way you could bring anything up without us." She reached into a bucket bag attached to her waist and pulled out an extra keen and a gold wristband with a flower motif on the top and handed it to Zadie. She in turn strapped it on her wrist and pushed the center button. It illuminated the whole area. Each of the Mers pushed theirs as well, and they dove into the trench.

Their light, as bright as the sun, chased all the sea creatures away. They swam in unison, the lights making their path easy to navigate. The ship lay on its side in two separate pieces. Relief flooded over Zadie. It was here. The two mermen swam past her to inspect the farther half. Zadie dove down to do the same in the part that was nearest them, the aft end of what was left of the ship. Time's quiet fingerprints lay all over the ship. Jagged broken wood decorated by human skeletons, claimed by rough coral and barnacles, dominated the scene. Broken pottery shards littered the interior. Zadie followed Kraken to a corner where an oil lamp remained perfectly intact. It looked strange in its current surroundings. She felt Kraken's joy as he let her know that he'd beaten her to the ship. Always competitive.

Zadie saw a coral-encrusted chest and felt her heartbeat speed up.

She'd found it! Everything was going to work out. Things would be okay. Cricket would be okay. Her hands had a slight tremor as she used her diving knife to help pry open the trunk. Kraken felt the edges with his tentacles. Zadie felt a touch on her shoulder. Maj swam in from behind her.

Maj pulled a slim cylindrical tool off her belt, then sang a high vibration, causing the tool to shoot a dark blue laser beam at the seal of the trunk. Bubbles billowed out of the lip of the chest, reminding Zadie of the cheesy plastic treasure chest in fish tanks.

"Grab that side." Maj pointed to one side of the chest.

Zadie swam to the edge of it. Maj took her place on the other side. Together they forcefully pulled the top off the chest. Dust and debris floated all around them. Zadie held her breath, trying to keep it from getting into her lungs, as she sifted through the contents of the chest. Barnacled pottery, some silverware — no gold.

What if they had the right ship but the wrong story? Doubt in herself and shame of failure in front of Maj froze her in place.

"Chin up, little fish," Maj teased. "There are many more hiding places for us to seek. You don't think ships are limited to one chest, now do you?"

Zadie took a deep breath. Her body was weary, but Maj's words encouraged her. She'd asked them for help, not to do it for her. She needed to dig deep into herself and find the energy to see this task through.

They swam around for what felt like eternity, checking out both parts of the ship. Zadie dove down below, and there found the masthead *Dulcinea* pinned under the ship. Her beautiful form looked like it had not been affected by the water or time, but Zadie did not feel her, and her heart broke for it. Zadie sang out to the others. Their song resonated on her skin as they came quickly.

Maj handed Zadie a gold device shaped like a pinecone. They each pointed the tips of their instruments at the time-worn ship. They sang a low vibration, activating the devices to glow green. Beams of focused green light shot out of the ends, lifting the ship off *Dulcinea* and resettling it on its side, so they could pull the masthead off the decaying ship. Sand floated off the ocean floor, momentarily blinding them all.

Zadie called out to *Yara*, telling her that *Dulcinea* was coming. *Yara* cried out her own song, letting the search party know her exact location.

The mermen pried the masthead easily away. With somber faces, they pointed their cones at *Dulcinea*, lifting her up to take her to *Yara*.

Maj swam to Zadie. "We haven't found the chest."

Desperation flooded Zadie. "Please, can we look a little longer?"

They were all exhausted. The water was colder at this depth than any of them were used to. Their fingers were numb from lack of circulation.

Maj nodded her head in resolve. "With the ship resettling, be careful. It will not be secure."

Zadie nodded in agreement, hope rekindling in her heart.

They both dove down to where the front of the ship had resettled. Loose planks were floating in the water. Something silver caught Zadie's eye. She swam to it. It had been a drinking cup. This was new; she hadn't seen it before. She looked around. A new hole had been ripped into the bottom of the ship when they'd moved it to free *Dulcinea*. She swam through the small hole. There in the space, she saw two cannons and a chest. Again, her heartbeat sped up.

This really is it. It has to be.

Maj was right behind her. She smiled when she saw what Zadie was looking at.

Again, Zadie used her diving knife and pried at the top of the chest, which opened. Visibility was next to zero. She turned down her light beam; floating debris swirled around them.

Zadie heard Kraken and felt his joy. He crawled into the chest. When the water settled, she saw he was writhing in coins of gold. He was beyond happy with himself that he'd found it first.

"Your cephalopod seems happy," Maj noted.

Zadie felt so relieved. They'd really found it. Almost there.

They pulled their pinecones out and pointed them at the chest. Singing their low vibration, the devices turned green again. They focused the sound to lift the chest and swam out backward. Kraken curled around Zadie's arm, merging with her.

Zadie cried out to *Yara*, and she answered. Zadie and Maj followed her sound, guiding the chest in front of them. The water became fierce as they neared the surface. Zadie's muscles began to fatigue and cramp, but she kept pace with Maj.

When they reached *Yara*, Zadie felt her sadness but could not hear her voice. She'd walled her off. Zadie could understand her need for privacy. Zadie could see the mermen had placed *Dulcinea* next to *Yara* at the front of the ship. She and the boat had wrapped themselves around *Dulcinea*, integrating her into them, but *Dulcinea* remained lifeless wood.

The mermen helped guide the chest out of the water and onto the boat. *Yara* was still cloaked in mist. Other seamen passing by would only see an eerie green light in the morning dawn.

Maj embraced Zadie. Zadie could have fallen asleep in her arms; she was so tired. Zadie took off the bracelet and handed it to Maj, along with the pinecone.

Maj slipped them into her bag. "You know you belong with me and our people. Your place is out here in the sea. I need all the help I can get. Guarding the triangle, it's nearly more than we can handle. We need the help of every Mer."

Guilt flooded through Zadie. "I know. I just can't leave my sisters. Not yet." She felt so torn.

She felt, in her core, a pull to the sea. She did have an obligation to embrace her duty, to join the ranks and serve under her aunt, but her sisters on land still needed her. Self-ishly, she wanted to be with Tom. She wanted to enjoy her human life for as long as she could, before it ended, and she became Mer only.

"I know your inner struggle, for it was mine as well. Don't wait too long, like I did." Maj looked away. Then added softly, "Habina is dead because of me."

She dove, and the Mers dove right behind her. Even with all Zadie loved and wanted on land, it took all she had not to follow.

CHAPTER 13
CRICKET

T hank you so much for your purchase," Cricket said to her latest customer. "This pattern is beautiful," she cooed, holding up one of the teacups that the woman had picked out for the recipient back home. The brunette woman's eyes sparkled behind a pair of antique sunnies in a classic Jackie O style. She was dressed in a flowered sundress and espadrilles, and her hair was piled atop her head like an architectural model. She turned, offering Cricket a better view of her dainty up-turned nose.

"Oh, thanks. It's just perfect. I'm getting it for my daughter's birthday. She is away at college; I thought it would be nice if we could video chat and have tea together in matching cups."

"What a lovely thought. I am sure she will appreciate it." Cricket finished carefully wrapping the last porcelain cup-and-saucer set in pink tissue paper and put the set in a white paper bag that had their large Baubles and Whatnots black script printed across the front. She closed her eyes and sent a blessing to this woman's precious daughter.

Cricket coughed, her eyes watering. The chills had come again, and she shook so hard that she stumbled into the wall of vintage books behind the counter. She had been pushing through work, but it was taking its toll on her body and spirit. Her concentration kept slipping, and she was unable to form a single coherent thought or decision before moving onto the next one. She felt like she may fall over at any moment.

"Are you all right, hon?" The woman backed up in alarm.

The coughs kept coming. She grabbed a tissue from behind the counter. "Fine . . . Thank you . . . allergies," she managed between the fits. Allergies were easier to explain than death by pirate curse. The cough startled her. She had never coughed before. Her fae blood protected her from most illness.

The bells tinkled in a cheerful melody as the woman walked out the door. The warmth of the day created a soft haze that filled the streets and gave everything a lovely glow. Cricket watched as the woman's brunette hair blended into the crowd, her figure becoming just another in the bustling street full of people.

Simultaneously her phone vibrated on the counter, bringing her awareness back.

> Zadie: Got the treasure, come get it and me.

> Babs: I know where we need to take it. Cricket I'm on my way to get you.

> Cricket: Thanks guys

It was all coming together. They were really making progress in the fight against this curse. She knew she could count on her sisters' help. She could hold on. She had to.

Just then the doorbells jingled. In walked James, the FedEx guy. James's chest stretched his navy polo in all the right places. Clearly, he lifted weights on top of his regular lifting during his nine-to-five. Tikaboo ran out from under the counter. James promptly pulled a dog treat out of a pouch on his belt, like he did every day. Tikaboo ran around the corner, practically levitating, slid into his legs, and climbed halfway up his leg, mouth wide in a smile. "Who's my favorite girl? Who's my favorite baby?" James cooed, bending low to the ground to accept some puppy kisses. Nothing was as sweet as a big guy baby-talking a little dog. Tikaboo made a snuffle noise in thanks and went back behind the counter to eat the treat in privacy.

Cricket took a moment to finish her text.

Cricket: See you soon

"You are her absolute favorite, you know." Cricket suppressed a cough while looking up at James. "What do you have for me today?"

He brushed his sun-kissed hair away from his wrinkled brow. "Looking good there, Cricket. 1950s vibe today? It looks great."

"Thanks; yeah, it's vintage." She felt horrible. At least dressing properly, she could fake it till she made it. She swished her high ponytail back behind her shoulder, blew her bangs out of her eyes, and ran her fingers over her strand of white pearls. Her thin white long-sleeve shirt skimmed over her long black-and-white polka-dot wrap skirt that covered all her odd scrapes from the bike accident.

"Of course it is. You are always in old clothes." James flashed her a wide smile.

"Perk of the job. I get to find unique items in the estate sales." She did enjoy that her fashion was authentic and classic. She didn't keep up with the newest trends but did tremendously treasure the old ones. She didn't care what color was *in* this season. She knew what she liked and what brought her joy. She didn't take fashion all that seriously. It was more like playing dress-up to her.

"That's cool; I guess that would be fun. I'm usually in this uniform." He glanced down at his tight navy-blue shorts and adjusted the boxes and tablet in his hands. In her opinion, he wore the uniform well. "Did you know that a flock of ravens have completely taken over the sidewalk in front of your shop?" His lips lowered into a concentrated frown.

The smile dropped from her face. "How odd." A wrinkle formed on her brow. She changed the subject. "How many packages today?"

He looked down at his tablet. "Only five packages. Is Gran slowing her roll?"

Cricket rubbed sanitizer on her hands, then walked around the counter toward him. "Um, never." She rolled her eyes as she signed his sheet.

He handed her two small boxes.

"I'll be right back with the remaining three. They require the dolly. I'll try not to let any of the birds in."

Creepy. She looked around, but she didn't see anything unusual in the shop. She closed her eyes and breathed in deeply. She didn't feel anything either. If Death was here, she was playing hide-and-go-seek. Maybe it was best not to know.

She returned her attention to her phone and called Gran.

Cricket hoped she was on her way already. It rang and went to voice mail. "Gran, hey, when you get this, can you call and let me know when you think you will be in today? I need to run an errand with Zadie and Babs. Thanks, love you." She hung up.

"Burt."

Uh-oh. She looked around the room but didn't see him. She was running so much later than she'd thought she would be.

The bells jingled relentlessly as the front door opened. In stepped a tall, spindly man and his petite companion. She barely came up to his armpits, dressed in a sundress and hat that shadowed her sun-kissed face. The sound of their flip-flops clacking against the stone floor echoed in the small shop. They gave off the vibe that a beach trip was on the horizon.

Cricket forced a cheerful voice as she welcomed the customer. "Hi there, welcome to Baubles and Whatnots. Is there anything I can help you find?" Her head pounded dully, and her skin felt like it was on fire from the relentless itching. This morning she'd woken up covered in a dark scarlet rash that refused to be soothed by antihistamine cream. It was an itch worse than anything she had ever experienced before, and with each twitch of her fingers came a sudden jolt of pain that drove her crazy.

"Oh, no, we are just looking," the young man said, waving a long thin hand her way.

"Take your time, and if you have any questions, just let me know," she said, closing her eyes and focusing on her breath.

"Thanks," the woman rang out cheerfully.

"Burt" echoed through the room.

The couple looked at her, puzzled.

"Excuse me," she said, covering her mouth. They turned back to their browsing. She hurried over to the music system, her shiny red heels clicking lightly across the floor. She turned up the volume. Smooth jazz filled the room. "Burt, play Find." She looked over to find Burt standing on the cash register. He had a huge grin on his cute tiny face. She rushed over to him.

"Burt, thank you for remembering," she whispered. "We are going to play Find, but I need a little bit of time to—"

The doorbell rang again. James the FedEx guy was walking backward with the three boxes stacked neatly on a dolly. She grabbed Burt and shoved him in the pocket of her voluminous skirt. A tiny, startled squeak accompanied the movement.

"Where do you want them?" James called out.

"Here would be lovely." She pointed at a cleared spot by the door leading to the Sub.

He expertly slid the tower of boxes onto the exact spot, spun his dolly around, and smiled. "See you next time, Cricket."

"Have a good one," she called out as he headed out the door. She needed to grab an aspirin.

The couple seemed to enjoy browsing. They were cute together. They talked in low tones, and when they laughed, it was like their joy entwined and was sent out to the world. Good vibes. She wondered if she would get a chance to leisurely saunter through Old Town with Bash when this was over. That would be so lovely, just walking about, getting an ice cream, listening to the music. Not feeling sick, not fearing death. She rolled her eyes at her own mental drama.

She rustled through the second drawer beneath the cash register and found two Tootsie Rolls and a bottle of aspirin. "Burt," she whispered. "I need to finish up some things. Will you stay in my pocket for a while? I have candy for you." She slid the two pieces of chocolate inside the pocket.

"Burt."

She took that as a yes.

The bells rang again. In walked Babs without her usual swagger, wearing army-green sweatpants, a black V-neck tee, and her combat boots. She didn't have her normal makeup on, only lip gloss that contrasted against her pale, sunken completion. Her eyes remained hidden behind her sunglasses.

"Can I make you coffee?" Cricket asked tentatively.

Babs walked around the desk and plopped heavily into Gran's chair, throwing her head back and saying nothing.

"Let me rephrase that. I'm making you a latte. We can have a coffee break together; I could use a moment."

Gran had spoiled her by getting an espresso machine. She loved starting her day with one. And on crazy days, like today, it was nice to have a second in the afternoon just to keep her going.

The smell of coffee floated through the store. Cricket handed the large white mug to Babs, who cupped it with both hands, brought it up to her face, and inhaled deeply. She took a sip.

"Thank you!" the woman called out to Cricket as her companion opened the front door for them to leave.

"Thank you for stopping by. Enjoy the rest of your day," Cricket replied. The bells on the door jingled as it closed.

Cricket brushed her bangs out of her eyes, grabbed her matte red lipstick from the counter, and reapplied. She felt a bit warm but was sure it was from running around;

she hoped that was the reason anyway. She checked the thermostat and turned it a few degrees lower. Time to make herself an iced latte. She glanced at Babs, taking in her slumping figure.

"You feeling okay?"

"Just tired, that's all. Didn't sleep much last night." She swiveled the chair lazily back and forth with the heels of her shoes. "Do you think I should hide it under layers of lipstick like you? You don't fool me. I know you don't feel well," she said flatly.

"I've felt better, but it's not horrible. Like Elizabeth Taylor says: 'Put your lipstick on and pull yourself together.' That easy." There was no reason for Babs to be anxious about her symptoms; there wasn't anything she could do about it; plus Cricket hated complaining. "So, you know where we need to take the treasure?" she asked, redirecting the conversation.

"Yep," Babs said, not facing her.

She hated when Babs was in a mood. "Well?"

Babs took a sip of her latte. "We have to return it to the catacombs under the Cathedral Basilica. Lucky for us, we have a way in." Babs pointed to the ground below them.

Cricket thought about the room she had been in. The bone-lined walls, the crucifixes. Catacombs made sense. "And you found this out how?"

"A spooky night in our woods talking to the Queen of the Summer Court. You know, your usual weeknight when you've reached the bottom of Netflix," she sniped.

Cricket shivered. She absolutely preferred spirit travel to actual physical contact with another unknown fae. Much safer. Well, maybe not. She was the one cursed, and it had happened while spirit traveling. "Who?"

"The Queen of the Summer Court," Babs repeated.

"Huh? In *our* woods?" Cricket's jaw went slack. "There aren't any faeries anywhere around here except us."

"Believe what you want," Babs quipped.

"You met with the Queen of the Summer Court? How does one even do that?" It was more than Cricket could comprehend.

"Long story. I'd rather not go into it right now. Enough on our plate and all that."

Cricket shifted her weight from one heel to the other, the hair on the back of her neck rose as a horrible thought overtook her mind. "Babs." She felt the blood drain from her face. "You didn't make any deals—" She felt like she was going to throw up. "You didn't make any deals for *me*, did you?"

Babs swiveled in her chair lazily. "It's complicated, but nothing for you to worry about. It's my business."

"Since when did we start keeping things from—" Cricket felt deep regret for their fight about Nadine the previous night. She should have trodden more lightly.

"I'm not keeping anything from you. Stop being so sensitive. Now is just not the right time to get into it. I did my part. I know where to return the treasure." Babs closed her eyes and took a large sip of her drink. "There's no reason to make this harder than it already is. Keep it together."

"Right." Maybe she was being sensitive. She didn't feel well. Maybe she should just drop it. "Sorry. Of course, we'll talk about it when you think the time is right."

Babs let out a long sigh. "Thank you. So, getting back on topic, I texted you last night. Did you find a way to undo the spell that seals the tunnels in the Sub?"

"Yeah, about that. The men in the vision, they were coming in and out of stairs, like a hatch. Maybe we don't have to use the Sub to get to it," she suggested.

"That old entrance is paved over; the catacombs are vaster than you can imagine. They are sealed off from the town entirely." She flourished her hand, indicating the streets outside. "The only way to get to it, that I know of, is through our Sub. We are going to have to unseal our area. We don't have time to find a different entrance," she reasoned.

"Are you absolutely sure that is the only way?" Things were bad enough. She hadn't brought Gran in on this. That was one thing. But to directly go against Gran's rule? They had never dared do that before.

"Yep, I'm sure, and no, I don't think we should do it. And yes, I know we have to." Babs's voice was devoid of emotion.

Cricket worried that Babs was still mad about the *Nadine conversation* the other night. Anger was coming off her in waves. At least Cricket thought it was anger.

She set her cup down on the counter. "Look, Babs, about the other night . . ."

"Cricket, not today—I just can't." She spun the chair around, leaving only a view of her back.

Cricket decided to ignore the bait. Fighting with Babs never led to anywhere good. Her head was pounding, and her skin itched. She couldn't add to it ticking Babs off, yet again. "Okay, well, if the tunnels are the only way—I did work on untangling the spell. I think we can do it all together, the three of us." She took a sip of her coffee. "Also, bonus, I figured out how to keep us from getting lost. Well, we might get lost, but this guarantees we can get back."

"Oh yeah, how's that?"

Cricket gently pulled Burt out of her pocket. "Look."

Babs turned around; a small smile tugged at her lips. Cricket sighed in relief.

Point for Cricket.

"Hey, Burt. Are we going to play Find?" Babs reached out to him. He walked onto her hand, holding half a Tootsie Roll. His face gleamed sticky from the candy. "Smart—reverse game of Find," she said.

"I was worried we would get stuck down there, but with Burt, we are sure to *find* our way back home."

Tikaboo stepped out of her bed and sat on Babs's foot. She was never one to be outshone.

The bells on the door rang. Cricket turned to see Bash, cheeks crimson and breathing heavy. His white shirt collar betrayed a wet stain ringing his neck. His slightly curly hair lay flat, drenched from his excursion. Cricket glanced at Babs, who grinned, tilted her shades down, and winked at her.

She cupped Burt in her hand. "Cricket, I'll be back. I'm just going to run upstairs for a minute to play dress-up with your makeup. Hey, Bash." She glided past him and up the stairs. "Tikaboo!" she called out, and the dog ran right up behind her.

Burt really did turn Babs' mood around. Cricket would have to remember that.

"Cricket." Bash's long strides brought him to the counter. "Outside," he said, his eyes scanning the room as he gulped air into his burning lungs.

"Yes, outside?"

"I'm glad you texted." His voice was near manic.

"Yesterday?"

"No, today. You texted *See you soon* and didn't reply to me when I texted back," he huffed. "I assumed something happened with the curse. Clearly something is going on. The birds are right outside." His words came out all in a rush.

Her phone revealed her mistake. She'd accidentally texted Bash instead of Babs and had missed five texts from him asking if she was okay. "I'm sorry. I didn't hear my phone. That text was meant for Babs. I didn't mean to worry you," she explained, heat flooding her cheeks.

Her phone vibrated. They both peered at it.

"I've been worried about you all night. I scoured the internet trying to find anything on Drake or pirate lore of the Black Spot," Bash stammered.

Her phone continued to vibrate. "I'm sorry, just a second. I must take this. It's Gran." She pointed at the mini fridge with water bottles. He headed over to get one, then veered to the window to stare outside.

She was overwhelmed. Why were the birds outside? Her first encounter seeing Death was right here inside the shop with Gran. But that was in a vision. Cricket focused to the right of their shop's doorway; three candles were lit on their ancestral altar. Maybe the ancestors had formed a physical barrier of protection.

"Thank you," she whispered. She answered the phone. "Gran?"

"Cricket." Gran's voice was scarcely audible. Roaring sounds filled the background. "Not coming back today . . . Daytona . . . Races . . ."

"Gran, I can't really hear you."

Banging noises shot through the phone, and Otis's baritone voice bleated loudly. "Cricket! We are at the races! We are in Daytona! We won't be back today." And the phone went dead.

"So, Gran's at the races," Bash said.

"You heard that?"

"I think SpaceX heard that. You are manning the shop then? How can you be manning the shop when your life is in danger?"

"I hadn't planned on it; I didn't expect Gran to be out of town. I need to run an errand with Babs, hence the text you received that was meant for her," she explained.

"Do tell," Bash said, rubbing the back of his neck.

Here's to letting him in all the way. She took a deep breath and exhaled. "Zadie found the chest of gold I am bound to return to Drake. It's on her ship down at the marina, and we need to transport it here. Babs and I are running over in her truck to grab it."

As if on cue, Babs's footsteps could be heard descending the stairs.

"Are you serious? She found Drake's lost treasure?" His face went pale, then broke out with a smile. "You are overflowing with chests, aren't you? Chests with diaries, chest of gold from the sea. This is what you need to break the curse?"

"You told Bash about this?" Babs growled.

"Yep, he was with me last night; we had a talk," Cricket explained. She walked over to Bash and slipped her hand into his. He looked down at her and kissed the top of her head.

"When is Gran getting here?" Babs replied.

Cricket pursed her lips. "Gran isn't coming in today."

Babs rolled her eyes. "Cricket, put the Closed sign up. Bash, you sit in back."

CHAPTER 14

BABS

H e's so cute! Why did we have to leave
him at the store?" Nadine excitedly
cooed while Babs turned the truck
onto the main road that led to Zadie's marina.
The traffic was slow as snails today. Babs lightly
tapped her fingers on the steering wheel, willing herself to be patient. The pedestrians slowly meandered in large herds through the crosswalks.

Nadine had been gone since helping with the
crocodiles in the woods with Liande. Babs's experience
with the summer queen had been so intense, when Nadine
popped up again, queasiness filled her stomach. Fortunately, Nadine's focus had been on Burt all morning. As
unsure as Babs was feeling, right now was not the time
to examine how she felt about it all. She needed to stay
focused on the task at hand. Put one foot in front of the
other. Her own issues could wait. Cricket was what mattered right now.

Babs's eyes locked with Nadine's in the rearview mirror.
She was sitting in the small back seat with Bash, Cricket riding shotgun.

At least Nadine seemed to be in a good mood and not testy.

"We will get back to the store soon," Babs said in a low voice.

Bash glanced at Babs quickly and looked away.

"Yeah, this won't take us long," Cricket replied. "The marina isn't that far away, and traffic isn't that bad in the morning. Bash, do you have the whole day off?"

"Yes, Caroline covered my shift for me. I'm in. Whatever you need," he said and laid his hand lightly on Cricket's shoulder.

Babs slammed on the brakes and the horn simultaneously. Two bikers were crossing with the traffic. A guy in a car was texting on his phone, about to run the red light into a turn directly into the bikers. Everyone slammed on their brakes in response to her horn's loud sound. The texting man's car stopped inches from the biker closest to him. His eyes were wide, face drained of blood. She could see him mouthing, *Sorry*.

"That was close," Cricket said through a cough.

Babs eased on the gas and moved the truck out of the cross section. "You okay?" she asked, as Cricket kept coughing. Babs reached in her center console and pulled out a weather-warmed water bottle. Cricket took a swig. It was startling to hear her cough.

"Thanks, yeah. I have a headache. But I took some aspirin, so it should go away."

The truck stood still as they waited at yet another light. "I'm really worried about you. Maybe you should stay in the truck and try to sleep while we unload the chest from *Yara*," Babs said.

"No, I want to come. I'll take it easy. I promise," Cricket replied. She was drenched in sweat.

"Do you need anything? We could stop at a drugstore," Babs offered.

"Nope, all good," Cricket replied while resting her forehead on the window. Babs watched as little clouds of condensation formed on the windowpane where Cricket's warm breath met the cool surface of the glass.

"She really looks sick," Nadine commented. "Look at those deep circles under her eyes; her skin has gone yellow."

Babs peered at Cricket's hand, but it was covered by her long white cotton shirt. Her face was glistening in a sheen of sweat, her body crumpled into itself like a wadded-up piece of paper. Babs wanted to talk to her, but not in front of Bash. There were some things only family should know. The list of private topics in the Culebra line was considerable.

"Bash, you look tired," Babs said, locking eyes with Nadine in the rearview mirror. Cheshire grins crept across both women's faces.

"No, I'm rested enough," he protested, locking eyes with Babs in the mirror.

Nadine floated closer to him and brushed at his hair. She put her lips to his ears and whispered, "Sleep, precious one, else Nadine come to catch you."

He shuddered and glanced in Nadine's direction. He started to mutter something. Crazy, it looked like he could see her. She continued to brush his hair, sending shivers throughout his body. She laid her head on his shoulder. He jumped back. Babs gauged his reaction. *He must be sensitive*, she concluded. Some people were — the psychics and mediums, saints and mystics.

"Sleep, precious one, else Nadine come to catch you," Nadine droned on.

"No, you don't," Bash growled. He had moved out of

the rearview mirror's vision. All she could see was part of his neck; he was breaking out in a sweat.

Cricket turned around. "You all right back there?" Her brow furrowed in concern.

Babs heard shuffling as she finally glided the truck through the last traffic light for this trip.

"Yeah," he responded, "just clearing space back here. Babs," he called out.

"Uh-huh." She turned the truck into the marina.

"I'm not sleepy at all. You got that? I am here to help, and I can help. Let's work together." His tone was resolved, hard and abrasive like a diamond.

Babs turned her head for a quick glance in the back seat. Nadine was gone. In all her life, no one had ever seen Nadine, let alone interacted with or apparently sent her away. Babs was freaked. Her gut reaction was to get this asshole out of her car. She needed time to work it out.

"We'll see. We will talk about this later," Babs said to him. "Cricket, show me your hand," she said.

"What?" Cricket asked, panic tinging her voice as she tugged her sleeve down lower.

"Your hand, let me see," Babs insisted.

Cricket glanced in the back seat at Bash, then reluctantly pulled up her sleeves, revealing what looked to be purple-and-black bruising all over both of her arms. She raised her tee to show her stomach covered in a deep purple-red rash.

"Oh, man," Bash breathed as his face grew ashen.

"How long has it been like that?" Babs asked.

"It just steadily got worse throughout the night." Cricket looked down at the water bottle. "It hurts and itches—but I'm still breathing."

Babs pulled into the parking space reserved for visitors and killed the engine. Thank goodness Zadie had given her a sticker. Parking could be monstrous in Old Town. She was too curious about Bash to wait. Babs had never seen anyone react like Bash did to Nadine. She was taken aback by his obvious determination to help and wondered what exactly qualified him to stand alongside them. He seemed to be struggling with something powerful but wouldn't say a word. Babs felt the urge to interrogate him, but she knew that she would have to pick her words carefully. The last thing she needed was for Cricket to get hurt because of some guy's inflated sense of ability. The right way would be to take some time to think, but she felt a volcano in the pit of her stomach, churning. She needed to deal with this before she exploded. They all had to be at their best before going into what they were about to face. "Cricket, go ahead and let Zadie know we are here. I need to talk to Bash for a second. We will be right behind you."

Cricket furrowed her brow and gazed into Bash's eyes questioningly. Even that small act seemed to drain her.

"I'm right behind you," he said, smiling at her.

Cricket got out of the truck and shut the door. Silence enveloped the cab. Babs took a deep breath and exhaled slowly, trying her best to approach this calmly and methodically. "Let's take this one step at a time, okay?"

"She isn't a ghost," Bash said, ignoring her lead. He crossed his arms across the front seat, leaning in and closing the space between them.

"What?" Babs asked as she twisted around to face him fully. She crossed her arms across her chest, forming a barrier between them.

"Nadine—that's what she called herself, right?" He brushed his bangs out of his eyes, "She isn't a ghost. She isn't human either, or at least fully human. That doesn't make sense, does it?" He ran his hand through his hair. "I don't know what her origin is—I wasn't around her long enough—but I can tell you, when I see these types of entities, it's never good. They are not on the love-and-light side of the spectrum. They are dangerous. She felt cold—Yes, cold is the word that comes to mind. Does that mean something to you?"

The seer will guide you, trust him.

He was confirming what the summer queen revealed.

"You saw her?" she asked, hoping to slow this conversation down. She needed time to assess the situation and think about how best to handle it. "What did she look like to you?"

Bash's eyebrows shot up. "Well, to be honest, she looked exactly like you. But she didn't feel like you. She feels dangerous—really dangerous."

Could it be true? Was Nadine not her sister? Had she lied to Babs her whole life? Was everything she believed a lie? It was just so hard to accept. As messed up as their relationship was, Babs needed her. "How could you know that, Bash?" she protested as stinging tears clung to her eyes.

He lowered his head. "You also need to know that she is firmly in control of you. Her power is surrounding you, oppressing you. She has a thick colorless fog all around your mind. Can you feel it, even now? You need to get rid of her. If you need help—"

"Okay, I get that you see and hear more than the average human. What does that make you?" Babs asked, trying to sidestep the subject just a bit, just to give herself time to digest it all.

"Human?" He seemed to weigh her words. "I'm just a guy who doesn't appreciate someone trying to have their bestie, non-corporeal mean girl knock him out," he said, his eyebrows lifting in unison, his lips forming the tiniest grin.

Babs looked into his fierce eyes. They showed more depth than she had originally noticed. She was starting to see why Cricket was drawn to him. He was geeky, passionate, and unexpectedly fiery. Just the type her sister would fall for. "Look, Bash, I'm sorry. I wanted to talk to Cricket and didn't want you to hear. How was I to know you were cool with — unexpected things?"

The Culebra family never told anyone outside the family anything — personal. Letting him in was a total deviation from the norm. It at least warranted a conversation, a heads-up from Cricket. She wondered how much he knew. Was it just about the curse, or had she told him — everything?

As if reading her mind, he replied, "I am here with full understanding that Cricket has been cursed, and we can only lift it by getting the treasure back to the spot where the curse occurred. Look, Babs, I'm not happy just sitting in the back seat. I'm going to help. Death is literally after her. I've seen it. I'm going to be a part of stopping it. And when you're ready, I can help you with your issue too, if you want it," he declared.

"Honestly, this talk has been more helpful than you know. My *issue's* name *is* Nadine — at least that is how I know her." She paused and took a few calming breaths. "It's really complicated," she said as the tears finally released, creating streams down her cheeks.

"No, Babs, it's not. You have an entity that's oppressing you. You must decide if you want to continue to live this way, or if you want to declare your freedom and live life on your own terms. It's as simple as that."

Babs sighed. "Can I trust you to keep it between us? At least for now? Cricket has enough on her mind."

Bash extended his hand. "Truce?"

Babs reached forward and grabbed it with a firm shake. "Truce."

CHAPTER 15
ZADIE

The smell of vinegar wafted about Zadie while she finished stuffing the signed documents into the plain oversize envelope. She planned on handing it off to Tom the next time she saw him, but for now it could go in the drawer at the navigation center.

She paced back and forth along the bow of the boat, helplessness overcoming her. It was a good thing Babs and Cricket were on their way. *Dulcinea*'s death was spreading into the ship, and she feared for *Yara* herself. Rot was creeping down the side of the boat. She had no way to fix it on her own. Water was seeping through the compromised section into the cabin below. Her hope was that Babs could use her earth magic to work within the wood of the ship to at least stop the spread, if not reverse it.

"Hey, we are here." She could hear Cricket's quiet voice coming from the dock. Her tone was more subdued than usual.

"Come aboard," Zadie yelled back while walking toward the aft of the ship to meet her. Cricket was already on the ship, sitting on the chest, conveniently set on the starboard aft nearest to the dock.

"We brought reinforcements," Cricket murmured before a fit of coughing seized her. She was cradling herself as if she were in pain. Her skin glistened and was covered in red splotches, like a rash or a bad fever. Zadie turned to see Bash and Babs board the ship.

Interesting. She was surprised to see Bash with her sisters. There wasn't time to think on it. She had more pressing matters.

"Great, more hands make light work," Zadie replied. "Happy to see you, Bash."

"Hopefully I can be of help," Bash said, wobbling a bit as he came aboard.

No sea legs on that one. The sight brought a smile to her face.

"Let's do the thing," said Babs as she took large strides toward Zadie. "We are in a hurry to get back. Whoa! You stink!" Babs stumbled back away from Zadie, her face wrinkling up in disgust.

Good grief, how immature. She gardens with actual manure, and she can't stand the smell of vinegar? Sisters!

"Fire coral. Had to treat it with vinegar. I'm good, thanks for asking, sis." Zadie frowned.

At once, the sound of the anchors being raised could be heard, and the boat began gliding out of the dock slip and toward the sea. Everyone stumbled except Zadie. All eyes landed on her.

"Are we going somewhere?" Bash asked, his eyes betraying bewilderment.

"Here, Bash, have a seat." Zadie patted the only slightly dirty cushion at the aft table. She took a mental note to add *replace outside cushions* to the never-ending list of things to do to care for *Yara*. She reached into the mini fridge and handed Bash a bottle of water. "Enjoy the ride. Cricket, here, sit right by Bash. You look like you could use a minute of rest anyway." Zadie handed her her own water bottle, while looking over her sister's long-sleeve shirt and long flowing skirt. The red heels were the true telltale sign. Cricket was covering up how bad she felt with her clothing choice. That was a good sign, Zadie decided. That meant she still had some fight in her, no matter how ashen her face appeared. "Babs, want to help me navigate from the bow? Let's just give these two a little boat ride, shall we?"

Babs's face took on a greenish hue. She moved as close to the center of the boat as possible, holding on to the cabin door as if it alone was her salvation.

Zadie reached for her hand; it was warm and moist. "Babs, look at me."

All the muscles in Babs's face had tensed.

Zadie put her lips to Babs's ear and murmured a siren song in an ancient language. Its vibrations flowed up and down Babs's spine, calming her nervous system. Babs's breath normalized, matching Zadie's. Zadie continued to sing. Babs's shoulders dropped down; she began to sway slightly. Her eyes slowly blinked.

"There you go, sis. All better, right? I'm right here. You are not alone. The water can never hurt you with me here to protect you." She backed up, giving Babs a reassuring smile as she wiped at the corner of Babs's eyes.

"Thanks for that," Babs whispered.

"We are kind of in a hurry." Bash's voice carried on the wind.

The automatic roller furling began to buzz. The main sheet rose high above their heads, gulping all the air and setting them a-sail.

"You two just stay right there and enjoy the ride," Zadie yelled back while grabbing Babs's arm and pulling her toward the bow.

"Why is your boat kidnapping us?" Babs asked, her voice serene—airy, as if she was floating on clouds.

"We have a problem," Zadie replied.

Babs shook her head, pulling her thoughts together. "Yes, we do. We must get the treasure chest back to the catacombs before Cricket croaks. Did you get a look at her? She isn't doing so hot. We need to go now. There isn't time to play pirate," she lectured. Even with Zadie's calming spell, her eyes were beginning to go wild, and Zadie noticed for the first time that Babs's hair was unusually unkempt. The stress was clearly getting to her. Zadie couldn't blame her; she was unraveling too, but whereas Babs tended to explode, Zadie would find ways to channel the energy—positively.

"Did you get it all out?" Zadie paused for emphasis while tapping her fingers on the railing. "Ready to listen?" She stood patiently, waiting for Babs to calm down. Years of sisterhood had taught her to slow down and wait for Babs on her emotional timeline. Rushing her didn't do anyone any favors.

"Fine. What?" she spat out while holding on to the bow pulpit with both hands' knuckles white, looking over the horizon.

"'Fine. What?'" Zadie mimicked in a baby voice.

Okay, maybe she exploded some too.

"Look down over the edge, and you will understand the immediacy of the situation."

Babs closed her eyes and took a deep breath. "I can't. You know I can't."

Zadie's voice dropped an octave and slowed, "Look over the edge."

Babs's body went rigid. She stiffly leaned over and looked at *Yara*. Her arms were wrapped around another masthead. Rotten wood spread down the side of the boat, clearly emanating from the second masthead.

Babs straightened, took a few steps back, panting heavily—and glared at Zadie. "Don't do that shit to me! Don't ever do that to me! Using the Mer voice on your own sister—No one manipulates me!" Rage came off Babs in waves, knocking Zadie off her center. Her knees buckled, and she stumbled, barely catching herself.

"I'm sorry, you needed to see. We don't have limitless time to deal with this."

Babs took several breaths to calm herself down. "Short version and to the point, explain what is going on with your ship."

"Okay, here's the ask: Can you use your earth magic to heal the wood and bring *Dulcinea* back to life?"

Babs looked up at the sails for a long time, her lips pursing, and finally let out a long sigh. "I assume *Dulcinea* is the figurehead *Yara* is holding? She is—or was—like *Yara*?"

"Yes," Zadie reassured, her head nodding furiously.

Babs shut her eyes and put her finger up to her lips. She opened her eyes, leaned tentatively over the bow, fighting her fear. Her gaze slowly moved toward *Yara*. "I think I can infuse my earth magic into the wood to force out the death, then draw enough water magic from you and *Yara* to permeate into *Dulcinea*. I don't know if we can bring her back, but we should be able to save *Yara*. Earth magic should have no problem reversing the rot. If we're lucky, the water magic, fueled by you and *Yara*'s life essence, could spark *Dulcinea*'s life back into existence—like magical CPR. Then simply being held by the living sea should heal her the rest of the way."

Zadie understood how their fae magics could work together. Babs was always so good at puzzling things out. *"Yara?"* Zadie asked, making sure they were all on the same page.

"Yes, yes!" Zadie felt her say.

Babs stared Zadie down. "Are you sure you are well enough? This is really going to drain you. It's going to take everything you have."

What wouldn't Zadie give for *Yara*? She would do anything to keep her safe and to give her a chance at having her sister back. "I am fighting fire coral scrapes. No big deal. Nothing like what Cricket is dealing with." She downplayed her issues. *Yara* was being negatively affected. That had to be fixed, immediately.

They sailed out of the marina completely. The waves were low and soft. *Yara* glided over the sea as if it were glass. There was an eerie quiet. The morning sun shone bright, without a cloud in the light blue sky.

"Okay, reach out and put your hand on *Yara*." Babs wrapped her arm around Zadie. She placed her free hand on *Dulcinea*.

They leaned together precariously over the railing. Zadie closed her eyes. She could hear her sister's voice in low mumbles swirling around them like a cold mist. Heat left Zadie's body through her hand and into *Yara*. She felt wet and bogged down, bloated. Forgotten. Salt water began running like a stream out of her mouth directly back into the ocean. Seaweed beat against her skin. Her legs gave out; she lay heavy against the railing. Darkness overwhelmed her senses. Loneliness overtook her. She shifted her awareness from the fountain that was her mouth, expelling all the silt and saltwater to the heat from the hand on her back, willing it, pulling it into her. Her mind reached for Babs's voice, ignoring the seaweed tangled in her own throat. Zadie let Babs's heat fill her. She greedily gobbled it till she was as toasty as if she were sitting by a fireplace.

After what felt like an eternity, Babs and Zadie fell to the ground. They lay there, letting the boat rock them. Zadie sensed *Yara* speak — no, it was *Dulcinea*. They were talking to each other. Zadie lay there, listening. It had worked. She couldn't move. She felt Babs shake her. Babs was in a complete panic. But Zadie couldn't make her eyes open, her lips refused to move. She was so heavy, like a soaked log. Then pure fire hit her head. She sat up, blinking. Cricket and Babs were staring down at her. She kept blinking — no, just Babs was there; she was just seeing double.

"We did it," Zadie said in a whisper; her throat hurt so badly the words were barely a croak.

"Yes, we did." Babs glanced across Zadie.

Bash's voice thundered above all. "Turn the ship around; we need to get back now! Cricket just collapsed."

CHAPTER 16
CRICKET

The torches were lit. Their light reflected off the walls of dark stone in the ceiling and walls, casting a warm glow everywhere that was not interrupted by the flickering shadows of flames. Where the shadows fell across her body Cricket could see, but she couldn't feel the heat. A strange white mist had descended over her vision. She was lying on the sofa in the Sub, covered in a heavy crochet blanket. Someone had lit the fireplace and activated the guardians; their gaze was directed inward at the glowing crystal skull resting on the diary in the middle of the mantel.

Babs and Bash were fussing with the chest of gold, placing it on a dolly. Zadie lay across the floor with a sad expression on her face. Tikaboo licked at her cheek. A devastating wave of remorse swept through Cricket. This was all her fault. Her sisters were at risk because she had taken a reckless gamble. Babs would never have been so thoughtless; Zadie would never put her family in such danger. She'd let Bash into this mess, too. Weariness overwhelmed her, and she felt empty inside, as if nothing mattered anymore. Maybe it was time to just give up, to close her eyes and let the world forget about her — allowing everyone else to be safe.

Yes, that's right — just let go. The foreign voice echoed through her mind. It seemed the logical thing to do — *just let go.* Her breathing slowed, then stopped.

Cricket's lifeless body remained as still as a statue. She hovered near the ceiling, looking down on the room.

Follow me.

Cricket couldn't decern where the voice was coming from. She looked about the room, her interest waning.

Bash's voice echoed around her like the howl of a banshee, an irritating sound to her ears in the face of oblivion. But suddenly, her sight went dark, she felt warmth envelop her skin, and a gust of wind blew around her motionless form. Heat penetrated her stiffening core, and light blinded her closed eyes. Though she heard Bash speaking, the words were incomprehensible in her weakened state. Cricket struggled to move or even speak, but her limbs would not obey. Suddenly, a beam of bright light appeared before her, starting small but quickly growing in intensity and volume until it was overwhelming. A deafening roar filled her eardrums, and she instinctively took a deep breath. As she blinked open her eyes, she saw Bash holding on to her tightly, Babs and Zadie at his side, eyes filled with horror.

"Don't you even think of leaving us. You are strong enough to make it through this. We'll make it through together." Bash tenderly kissed her lips in reassurance. His love embraced her, giving her the strength to carry on despite the pain that wracked her body. She wanted to scream out of anguish and defeat, but instead she gritted her teeth and tried to maintain some semblance of dignity and courage.

Babs put her finger to her mouth, staring seriously into Cricket's eyes. "Zadie, come with me. I have an idea."

Zadie winked at her, then her sisters moved out of her vision.

"You've been through worse, you know," Bash uttered. He had moved to sit on the couch with her, careful to be gentle with her tender skin. He swayed her slowly back and forth, like the limbs of a willow tree in a gentle breeze.

She inhaled his cologne, concentrating on his steady heartbeat. Her shoulders relaxed, and her breath deepened. "What was worse?" she asked, pretty sure she had never felt this low. Her mind was wallowing in a pit of self-loathing, a party for one.

"Sitting through the first *Hobbit* movie in the theater." He chuckled.

She grinned, appreciating his nerdy side.

"When the goblin king started singing, you spat your soda—" He loosened his embrace. Tikaboo jumped to her side, laying her head in Cricket's lap.

"That movie was really horrible. What were they thinking?" she asked, grateful for a fun memory to focus on.

"I have no idea." He took her hand in his and caressed it ever so tenderly. "But I know what I'm feeling right now."

"What's that?" She nestled her head into his chest, the soothing rhythm of his voice lulling her thoughts.

"All I can think about is how relieved I am that we talked. I'm grateful to be here with you, just like this," he said before softly pressing a kiss to her forehead.

A peaceful tranquility washed over her. The future no longer mattered. For that moment she felt nothing but contentment in the present. "You know, I want to give you the same comfort," she whispered, gazing deeply into his eyes.

He brushed her cheek gently, and she let out a relieved sigh.

Zadie's voice boomed through the room. "I knew it! I totally called it. Babs, pay up."

Babs rolled her eyes and mockingly replied, "Okay, fine. Here you go." She threw a bag of sugar-free chocolates at Zadie. Tikaboo leaped off the couch, eagerly eyeing the treats.

"Hey! Get your own," Zadie said with a smirk.

"Ah, you two," Babs said with a sly grin, rolling her eyes. "We both knew it was just a matter of time." Babs smiled up at Zadie, then turned her attention to Bash. "Come on over; this is my favorite chair down here. Right by the cozy fireplace. We have a sister thing to do."

Bash and Babs seemed to be getting along well. It was usually hard to win her over. Cricket couldn't help but wonder what had been exchanged between the two of them earlier that day in the truck.

"Okay," Bash said, sliding his hand down the length of Cricket's arm and gently squeezing her hand before getting off the couch. He crossed over to the chair and plopped down, then bounced a few times. "Yep, nice chair, Babs, nice and close to the fireplace."

Cricket tugged at her sleeve. "Ah, Bash, keep an open mind." A flood of worry washed over her.

Both her sisters' heads turned to look at her.

"I thought he was filled in?" Babs asked.

"Mmm." Cricket bit her bottom lip as she crossed over to the chair and stood by Bash's side. "So, yeah, I told you about the curse."

"Yes," he replied quizzically. "Spirits can curse from the beyond. It's the first time I have ever encountered it, but it's been documented countless times."

"Right, um, my sisters and I, ah—my family, we—" She grabbed his hand with both of hers.

"Oh, this should be good. Babs, you got any popcorn?" Zadie quipped.

"Knock it off. It's not like you have ever had the guts to do this," Babs chided.

"Or will ever choose to." Zadie rolled her eyes.

"It might be hard to understand, but given you aren't exactly a stranger to the *wider* world around us, the spirit world," Cricket continued as she became aware of her clammy palms sweating.

"Cricket," Bash interrupted, catching her eye, "you can tell me anything."

She took a deep breath in and slowly blew it out. "I'm fae. Well, half fae. My, our, father is human, but our mother is fae."

Bash blinked rapidly. "Okay, I'm not sure what that means. But okay."

"Well, you'll figure it out soon enough." Babs laughed. "Let's get this going."

Cricket looked from one sister to another. They both seemed fine with the fact that she had just revealed their family secret to a human. She leaned in and kissed Bash softly on the lips, savoring the moment. "Thanks for being open minded."

"I would rather live in a big miraculous world, full of wonder, than shuffle through a mundane existence," he replied.

Babs rolled her eyes. "You two can have the extended big talk later. We have work to do now. Cricket, Zadie, to the fireplace. Zadie, remember to focus on the intention."

Cricket removed her red heels and carried them loosely in her hand as she padded over to Babs, as did Zadie after finishing her chocolate. The sisters in unison kneeled in front of the fireplace and raised their hands, each throwing in a few strands of their hair.

Blue-green fire jumped high. Its warm kiss spread across Cricket's face; she was grateful for the feeling. The eyes of the sentinel dogs bore down upon them. Cricket lifted her open hands as she closed her eyes and began to chant along with her sisters.

"Ancient protectors of the Culebra line, we summon you now.

Grant us strength to keep our inner balance and ward against outside forces.

Guide us through this quest for self-mastery and assistance to others.

Strengthen our power to remain true and keep our intentions pure.

Shield us from danger so that we can shield others in turn.

Raise the veil so we may call upon the magick of the faerie realm.

Unite us together, let three now become one unified soul sharing our strength."

Gold-and-silver sparks of faerie magic shimmered around and through the trio, binding them together in a bond stronger than blood.

Cricket could feel Zadie's and Babs's power and the strength of the sentinels radiating into her weakened body. Energy pulsed through her veins, revitalizing her body with healing magical energy that soothed her wounds and eased her pain. She opened her eyes to see both Zadie and Babs staring at her intently, their faces illuminated by the glimmering golden faerie lights that shimmered around them.

"Thank you." She felt emotionally stronger as well as physically. She absentmindedly twisted at her ring.

"Did it help?" Zadie panted.

"Yeah, I'm sure that it did," Cricket replied.

Babs interjected, her voice low and resolute. "I'm going to brew a strengthening potion. Its effects usually last for several hours. Being at our best will be essential if we're to navigate the tunnels undetected. I want us all to be super-charged just in case."

"What will it do, exactly?" asked Bash, his eyes wide with awe.

Babs brimmed the kettle with water and placed it over the fire, then began to go through her pouch of herbs. She sprinkled them into the bubbling liquid, chanting ancient incantations under her breath as she did so. "It will magnify your strengths," she said finally, looking up at him. "You can partake if you wish."

"Have you all taken it before?" Bash asked.

"I haven't," Cricket admitted.

"Nope," Zadie replied.

Babs let out a breathy whisper as she carefully arranged the freshly picked herbs into cups. From her hands, golden sparks scattered and danced around each cup, infusing them with elemental strength. Babs poured the steaming water from her kettle over them, completing the spell. Her senses were heightened, and she could hear the rustling of the trees in the wind from miles away, feel the rushing energy of animals nearby, and became one with their natural environment.

"Trippy," Zadie said while grabbing her mug.

Cricket grabbed a steaming mug as well.

"Cricket, I'm not sure you should take it. You are air, and the veil being thin with you already—"

"Babs, I need any advantage I can get." She took several sips.

The velvety potion filled her mouth and coursed down her throat. An ethereal sensation flooded her body, as if she'd been filled with the clouds themselves. Thoughts and ideas danced across her mind's eye, lucid and clear. The world around her fell away, and soon the only thing left was clarity. The ring on her finger became like a tether to reality, keeping her aware of the moment despite the ethereal spell of the tea.

Cricket's voice floated around her sisters. "Aunt Habina inscribed the ancient rite into her diary. Gran, Mom, and Maj must have weaved their energies in perfect harmony to bind the tunnel with a force of great arcane power." Cricket watched as an invisible pulse radiated from the entrance, ethereal tendrils breaking around them like a rippling rainbow. It was like looking upon a living dream.

Zadie's voice echoed through the hallowed chamber, a siren song calling forth the spirits. With a gentle push of her hand, she guided the dolly with its heavy burden across the stone floors until it reached the entrance to the forbidden tunnel, sealed by generations past. Zadie's siren song gave Cricket the impression that Zadie knew the three of them would be enough to break the barrier and reveal what lay beyond.

Babs mumbled something under her breath.

"What's that, Babs?" Cricket whispered, feeling the air around her buzz with magical energy. It was as if an ancient power had been released inside of her, and each exhale carried with it a wondrous incantation. She felt suspended in time, lost in a trance between this world and the next. An invisible connection to the sky above tugged at her core, urging her to take flight.

"Gran, Mom, and Maj were the only ones who made it out the last time this tunnel was open," Babs whispered in fear. "The faint echoes from within that tunnel are more than enough to strike terror into my heart. I can't help but feel a shiver when I think of what happened in there. So traumatic that they all stayed silent about it. So horrible Maj left."

"The loss of Aunt Habina," Cricket mused. "We are not them. All three of us are making it out, and Zadie isn't going anywhere. Right, Zadie?" Cricket asked. Whatever broke Mom, Maj, and Habina apart, they were determined not to carry that ancestral baggage forward. Nothing would separate her and her sisters. Nothing. Not ever.

She imagined all three of them much older, laughing together over coffee, Zadie still in her human form.

"Well—" Zadie stammered, a blush filling her cheeks.

"That's right, Zadie isn't going anywhere," Babs answered.

Cricket gingerly untied the Culebra cigar bundle, releasing a cloud of smoky mystery in its wake. She handed a single cigar to each sister, speaking these words: "We use this ancient rite, the symbol of our family's faerie magic. The Culebra cigars are stronger bound together and more powerful than ever before."

Her lighter flickered to life as they simultaneously lit their cigars. A flurry of sparks burst around them with every deep draw. As one, they blew on the wall. Suddenly, iridescent blue strings appeared, fine as spiderwebs, darkly creeping across the entranceway.

"Join your hands. We must intertwine them and move counterclockwise." Cricket's cursed hand entwined with her sisters as they slowly stepped backward, unravelling the enchantment. They blew plumes of smoke toward the ceiling. It drifted to the wall like tendrils of fog. They could feel the web of the spell start to unravel. The blue electric light began to dim. The three continued their sacred ritual. The blue light dwindled as they drew and breathed. Cricket led the chant:

> "Dissolve these ties that bind.
> Undo what has been done."

Babs and Zadie joined in, harmonizing their voices into a single song that sliced through the spell, causing the wall to become translucent. Cricket could hear distant echoes around them — the intonations of past generations. Whispers on water droplets running down the walls of the cave, murmurs reflecting off the legs of beetles — all combined and imprinted over the three of them. Their voices melded together until it was one single voice resonating through time, their voice imprinting over the past. Time itself seemed to dissolve before Cricket's eyes as she witnessed the other side of the tunnel come into view.

The stone floor was jagged and uneven, not like the smooth granite from the entrance. Lit torches adorned the walls, giving the area an air of ancient power that seemed to be both forgotten and remembered at the same time. Cricket could sense intense energy radiating off the walls, as if two different intentions clashed with each other. A chill ran through her body as the hairs on the back of her neck stood up.

A hole in the enchantment had formed, large enough for them to wiggle their way through. The piercing look on Zadie's face and the tense set of Babs's shoulders were familiar, as if they'd done this a thousand times before. But Cricket felt like she'd lost her footing. Her stomach was a tangle of nerves, filled with dark imaginings that belonged only in nightmares. Her emotions were so volatile. She slipped on her red heels, wishing she had picked flats for the day.

"Just a minute," Babs said. She went to the corner and looked in her backpack. She gently lifted something tiny out from the darkness of the bag. There was Burt, sticky from sweets. His eyes blinking rapidly from the light. Cricket had completely forgotten.

"Burt, we are going to walk far away, then play Find. Are you ready?" Babs handed him off to Cricket. She focused on the light weight of his body in her hand. He nodded quickly, like he always did when he got excited about something.

Babs slung on her backpack, taking care to load it properly. Her fingers tapped the straps. The weight of the pack seemed to fill her with resolve and determination.

"What's that for?" Zadie asked. "We aren't going for a hike."

"I'm ready for anything," she said, glancing at Bash.

Bash's cup was empty, lying ominously at his feet, his eyes glazed over and wild. A guttural moan escaped from his lips, his eyes glistening like dark pools of secrets. "She is coming," he muttered through a slacked jaw. "She is here."

Suddenly, hundreds of black birds swooped in from the chimney, with a thunderous roar of wings like an incessant drumbeat. The acrid smell of singed feathers filled the air.

"Go," Bash bellowed above the clamor. With one fluid motion, he reached for a sword on the wall and brandished it before him. His form was engulfed in white-and-gold light, power radiating from him in spectacular pulses, shaking the very foundation beneath their feet. He readied himself for battle—his eyes ablaze with determination and ferocity — as the cacophony of caws and fluttering wings grew ever louder.

Cricket's jaw dropped in awe as the figure of Bash emerged into her vision. She could scarcely comprehend how he had amassed such unmeasurable strength. Her heart raced at the sight of him, and it took all her control not to gasp.

That was some tea indeed.

She felt a pull at her arm. Turning, she saw Zadie had already climbed through the opening of the barrier and was in the tunnel. She glimpsed Babs's form farther out than even Zadie. A blast of cool air hit her, and she shivered in her feverish state. The dark smell of moisture surrounded her as she passed through the entrance. The dampness of the tunnel soaked into her bones, cooling the heat that had built up in her body. She heard the drip, drip, drip of water echoing from all directions; its ominous intonement a slow torture to her ears.

"Come on!" Zadie pleaded. "Should we seal it off?"

Cricket's gut said they needed to. If those birds came in the tunnel, it would surely disturb whatever was down here. At least alert them to their presence. But she couldn't seal Bash in there by himself. Her head was numb; her stomach twisted.

"When we get back," Cricket answered, taking a few more steps into the tunnel.

"Let's just hurry and get back quickly," Babs said from several yards ahead.

"Something could get out; we wouldn't even know. Gran sealed it for a reason," Zadie protested.

"Then let's stop arguing and get this done." Cricket turned and started walking with urgency. The world shifted around her, revealing the hidden realm that coexisted below the mortal plane. Flickers of light danced in her vision, illuminating the path before her like a mystical guide. She knew the spell they had cast to enter was powerful. It had to be detectable by anyone nearby. Even a human would have at least experienced an uneasiness.

Babs's tea had opened her mind to a place she had never dreamed of before. It was exhilarating yet terrifying to be walking in both worlds simultaneously for a sustained time. She was acutely aware of the dangers lurking in this unseen dimension. They walked in silence for what seemed forever.

"You're stumbling like a drunk, and you're not keeping up. You were too greedy with the tea," Babs said. "Give me a second. I'm not sure which way to go." The tunnel was split in two before them. Babs closed her eyes and opened her palms toward the sky, then took three deep breaths.

Cricket was pretty blissed out. Babs's grouchiness didn't even matter. For a flicker of a moment, Cricket saw Babs dressed in red robes and wearing a crown, surrounded by wolves. Her face set in stone, power coming off her in waves.

Babs bowed her head and brought her folded hands to her forehead. *"Queen of Summer, you showed me the way. You know what I seek, and I have your blessing. Guide our feet and fortify our hearts. Protect us from what lies ahead."*

Cricket heard the birds in the distance behind them and Bash's commanding voice but couldn't understand his words.

Babs rolled her shoulders back and said, "Now we can go. I know the way." She looked over her shoulder and paused. "He will be okay, and so will we," Babs whispered as she led them down the tunnel to the left.

"Watch out!" Zadie wailed from behind as they turned the corner.

The tunnel was full of tall, fanged creatures that looked like grotesque statues. Their skin was grey and leprous with a light covering of frost. Their breath steamed from their jaws as they hissed and moaned, yet it seemed these creatures were frozen in the act of screaming by a spell. They stood silently watching, unable to move.

"I have seen these creatures in my mind!" Cricket murmured.

"We have to weave our way through," Babs said.

Their skin crawled as they slowly walked past the frightening creatures. Zadie and Cricket pushed the dolly inch by careful inch. Cricket's heart screamed to go back and help Bash, but her feet shuffled forward. The sooner the chest was returned, the sooner the curse would be lifted. The wheels of the dolly continuously found holes in the floor to lodge in. Torch light cast long shadows around them, giving the impression that the creatures were moving.

They turned down so many different tunnels, she soon lost her sense of direction. It all looked the same to her. There was no way she could get back to their entrance on her own. Other than the occasional doorway, the tunnels had the mirage of going on and on. A repetitive squeaking noise emanated from the dolly wheels as they went along, punctuated by Burt's muttering and Zadie's labored breath mingled with hers.

They weaved their way past all the tunnels filled with cursed creatures, which was a tiring and nauseating job. They rounded a bend and found themselves walking over a field of rotting corpses. An avalanche of bodies stretched out to the walls. The flesh was long gone, eaten away by vermin. Armor draped over moss-covered bones as the earth claimed what belonged to her. The passageway reeked of death, but it was not an odor that could warn them off.

Zadie's voice pierced the air. "Habina! Aunt Habina must be in here. Forgotten, left like this! No wonder Gran can't talk about it. This is horrible."

"Just try to be careful where you step," Cricket said. Her stomach lurched as she felt bone beneath her feet.

After several miles of stumbling through snakelike tunnels that twisted and turned and grew narrower and thicker with bodies the farther they went, a vast cavern opened before them, clear of any signs of war.

Petroglyphs covered the walls in vivid red, yellow, and black. The style reminded her of Sumerian or Egyptian hieroglyphics, but it was uniquely its own, wilder and loose. It seemed to document a great war.

Winged women shot bows and arrows at the people below as they marched forward across a plain. Piles of dead bodies set aflame sent plumes of smoke into the air just above their camp in the distance. The piles grew larger with each successive drawing until finally it looked like a mountain beneath a star-filled night sky filled with constellations. Mounds were drawn beneath these constellations and connected by light lines running down from each point. Intuitively Cricket felt these mounds had been built for some purpose once lost to time. Her mind raced to puzzle out what it might be. The constellations she knew were a map, but one she didn't know how to read. She placed her hand on one of the drawings. Energy surged out and swirled around her. She jumped back, bumping into Zadie. *A portal?* she wondered.

Zadie's breath was coming in ragged, deep inhalations and quick exhalations. Cricket was doing her best to ignore the fact that her legs felt like rubber from the long walk and that her arm muscles ached from righting the dolly. Babs was the only one who seemed physically unaffected. She trudged along without ever breaking stride or concentration.

The wall opposite them stretched upward, reaching for the heavens with the sheer height of it. A waterfall plummeted down like a relentless assault of an army in battle, forming a crystal-clear lake below. The aquamarine color of the water was a startling contrast to the mud-red walls of the cavern. The roar of the falls filled Cricket's ears and made her feel small and insignificant.

In front of the waterfall, a statue that reached halfway to the ceiling, seated on what appeared to be a throne, dominated the space. Torchlight gleamed off her gold surface, casting an ethereal glow around her. Her hair was in braids, each strand as intricate and detailed as if it had been woven by gods themselves. She had horns on her head and a crown with a five-pointed star, both of which seemed to shimmer like polished diamonds in the flickering light. Her eyes and mouth were closed, as though in silent contemplation or deep meditation.

Her arms outstretched, resting on two giant wolves that flanked her like loyal guardians who would do anything to protect their master. The wolves themselves appeared as large as a house, but their eyes glinted with an intelligence that betrayed something more than mere animal instinct.

Cricket surmised they had stumbled into a temple dedicated to this goddess-like figure. She had the overwhelming irrational urge to bow before the statue, prostrate herself at its feet and offer humble praise. A feeling of familiarity swept over her—belonging or was it remembering? It felt like she had come home after years away.

As she stood there in awe, taking in every detail with

wide-eyed wonderment, Cricket realized that this place held secrets beyond imagining, stories that begged to be told.

She followed the seated woman's gaze to look at the lake. Dark shadows glided beneath the surface in a slow, rhythmic dance. The place was eerie and calming all at once, like walking into your favorite dream.

"We need to get behind the waterfall. That is where the secret entrance to the catacombs is," Babs said, breaking Cricket's trance. "Once we place the chest in there, we can head back and seal our entrance. I will run ahead and work on getting the way opened." She paused and looked at the statue with the wolves. Then she sprinted behind the water-fall, her backpack jostling up and down.

Cricket closed her eyes, willing her body to be well enough to do this, willing her spirit to stay in the now. She turned and locked eyes with Zadie. They picked up their pace, but time felt like it was moving slowly. Babs was already out of sight. Cricket tried to ignore the tightness in her chest. She focused on thoughts of Bash but couldn't conjure him in her vision. Burt continued to make noises on her shoulder.

The mist from the roaring waterfall caressed her face and hair like a ghostly touch. As they climbed closer to the cascading water, Zadie pushed on the dolly with all her might to maneuver it over the jagged incline. Suddenly, a rogue rock tripped them—the dolly, Zadie, and Cricket—and she landed painfully on the wet, rocky shoreline. Cricket's infected hand clumsily sank into the edge of the lake. An echoing rumble shook the cavern with its intensity, and her hand lit up as if electrified by tiny pinpricks. As she tried yanking it free, something strange brushed against it—a warmth that sent waves of dread through her body. The more she pulled, the deeper her hand sank.

"Get up, get up!" Zadie's high-pitched yell raked Cricket's ears. She had already righted the dolly. "You can't just lay there."

The lake erupted with a thunderous roar, and from the depths of the still water flew a magnificent swarm of gigantic fae men, at least seven feet tall. Clad in silver armor and brandishing weapons of death, their luminescent ragged ice wings created an ethereal aura as they blazed through the sky like arrows. Frigid wind swirled and screamed around her, racing by her ears with each gust. Cricket's heart raced faster than ever before as she stared helplessly at them flying above. Their icy-blue eyes scanned the area with inhuman precision, seeking out anyone who dared to engage them.

Crawling out of the lake on all sides were more fae men, dressed in the same armor, brandishing swords that glowed blue. These fae were large, and they radiated an uncomfortable menace with every move they made. Blue electric static scurried across the ground with every step they took, causing frost to cover the rocky ground.

Understanding dawned on Cricket that the living beings around her belonged to the same species as those who had perished in the tunnels. The armor was the exact same.

Burt cried out. Cricket's hand was free of the water. She picked him up from the ground and put him back on her shoulder.

The black birds from their Sub swiftly entered the cavern the same way she and her sisters had come in. The birds formed a giant black cloud, swirling and darting viciously above the lake, circling the floating fae.

Cricket looked back and her heart dropped into her stomach. There stood Bash with gashes all over his body. Blood had seeped through his white button-up shirt. In his hand was one of the swords that had been hanging on the wall by Babs's chair. It was covered in blood and feathers. Behind him she could see the dark hooded figure trying to get past him. She reached for the rosary at her chest, which Bash had given her, without thinking. His eyes darted around the room in great concentration, taking in the foreign sight. Recognition crossed his face as he saw her. He ran at a full sprint, ignoring all but her form, Tikaboo at his heels.

A dark, thick rumble permeated through the room. She turned to see the statue rising out of its chair. Rocks from the walls and ceiling began raining down.

"Zadie, get the chest to Babs," Cricket yelled over all the noise. "Use the waterfall to lock yourselves in. Find a different way to get out. Don't come back this way. I'm going to get Bash and Tikaboo out of here and seal our entrance." There was no way they could leave the entrance open with these things down here. Those birds had just given them an obvious signal that there was a way in.

"I can't leave you!" she cried as her eyes scanned the room.

Cricket grabbed both of her arms. "Yes, you can, and you have to. Go!" she yelled, leaning in to kiss her salty cheek.

Zadie struggled, pushing the dolly behind the waterfall. A few minutes later, the water spread itself around, locking tightly against the walls. Cricket lightly ran her hand along the water, feeling it was as solid as stone. She had no idea what could be on the other side of the waterfall, but her sisters had to be safer on that side than this one.

Cricket's body twisted around, her voice trembling in fear. "Bash, I'm coming," she croaked, but her legs felt like lead weights. They wouldn't move no matter what she tried. The curse was overtaking her mind and body.

Bash gritted his teeth and steeled his resolve as he barreled forward, despite the caws and screeches from the merciless flock of birds that relentlessly bombarded him. He kept his gaze determinedly ahead, willing himself to reach her side and protect her no matter what may come.

The statue stood in the animate lake, her gold exterior now a vibrant red. She waved her magical staff in the vast water, stirring up a raging whirlpool. An ancient hum coursed through the room, reverberating off every surface and causing rocks to come tumbling down.

Shadow forms of female fae phased through the walls, becoming solid and life-like. They were dressed in loose white linen pants, hair pulled back in elaborate braids. Thick leather belts hugged their waists, carrying multiple blades. Red cloaks clasped with large red stone brooches swirled out behind them as their silent leather-boot-clad feet brought them near the water's edge. Blades were out at the ready, bows trained on the invaders. Curiosity and wonder crossed their faces as they beheld the black birds and their dark mistress.

In front of some women stood huge feral wolves, their eyes blazing like coals in the darkness. Among them, one woman stood out: her long brown hair cascaded down to her shoulders, and she raised her hands as if summoning something from deep within. The female fae warriors joined their hands together and chanted in a ghostly harmony, sending an eerie light pulsing through the cavern. As the warriors sang, their beauty shifted to ferocity, and it became hard to distinguish where reality ended and fantasy began.

From the bubbling depths of the lake, a captivating figure emerged. His broad chest was encased in shimmering golden armor, framed perfectly by his long silver locks, which were bound neatly beneath a crown of what appeared to be icicles. Soft blue eyes that glowed like pools of sapphires stared majestically into the torchlight as his loyal troops looked on in admiration. His royal presence was like a breath of fresh air, and he flew gracefully with wings of woven branches and bright red holly berries, landing gracefully onto the bank of the lake.

The gold statue in the middle of the lake moved in an eerie, mechanical way. A deep reverberating clang like a war drum emanated from it. She raised its staff above its head and let out a loud, piercing cry. The sight was startling and made Cricket feel lightheaded. She reached for Burt on her shoulder and placed him in her pocket.

The fae drew their swords and howled ferociously, saliva dripping from their razor-sharp fangs. Cricket felt a sudden fear as she realized the gravity of the situation: these were not just winged warriors; they were vicious predators ready to spill blood at a moment's notice. She had never witnessed this kind of savagery before.

Bash, his face a mask of strength and courage, thrust himself forward as the ultimate barrier between Cricket and all the chaos that lay beyond. He bellowed out a defiant "You can't have her!" in one final stand. Cricket quivered slightly as she followed his gaze to the black-cloaked figure that had finally come for her. He stretched out his hands, and suddenly they were surrounded by a penetrating white light that was quickly consumed by powerful black wings and beaks. The looming figure of darkness silently descended upon them, its feathered minions barraging them both with their gnarled talons.

CHAPTER 17
BABS

Y ou'd never believe what's going on
back there," Zadie said, releasing
the dolly that carried the treasure.
She wiped away her sweat before hurrying to the
back of the falls. Its cascading droplets drenched
her in seconds. "I sealed us off from that giant
mess. I'll hold the water so you have enough time to
return the treasure."

Babs aimed her foot at the jagged rocks beneath her,
sending a flurry of dust into the air. The stones scattered
and settled around her feet. "Where's Cricket? You didn't
leave her—"

"You're not paying attention!" Zadie exhaled, her voice
muffled by the sound of rushing water. "Everything is in
chaos back there. Bash appeared out of nowhere, and now
everything's gone haywire. We don't have time to discuss
it. Grab the treasure and get it back to the catacombs immediately. Cricket needs that curse lifted without delay, and I
need you to hurry. Connecting to fast-moving water takes
up a lot of energy—it's like having to say please a thousand

times per second. It's not hard, just exhausting, and I'm already exhausted."

Babs observed Zadie reach out her palms and softly caress the water's surface. Her lips moved, and her eyes were shut tight. Suddenly, she jerked back as if a jolt of electricity had shot through her body.

"What's going on?" Babs questioned as she moved the dolly with the treasure inside.

Zadie's eyebrows shot up, her eyes wide as she replied, "The water is confused. It thinks it's in ancient Britannia."

"That's odd. Have you ever encountered disoriented water before?" Babs reminisced, recalling times walking through the woods where she swore time had been reversed. Of course, land mostly stayed in one place, while water was always traveling.

"No way. I've come across water that was unaware of its age, but never water that had no idea where it was. This ought to be an intriguing conversation." Zadie grinned.

Babs smiled and said, "I'll leave you to it then."

Zadie's lips moved as she shouted something, but Babs couldn't hear a thing due to the deafening roar of the waterfall. The powerful cascade blanketed the edges of the cavern, and its spray soaked Zadie completely.

Zadie frowned in Babs's direction and mouthed the word, *Hurry.*

Babs quickly pushed the chest forward toward the catacombs, careful not to let it tip over. The walls around her transformed into a skeleton army in full body armor, all standing at attention. Thousands of eyeless skulls formed crosses and stars as she stumbled through the darkness. The sound of the waterfall gradually faded as Babs made her way to the center of the underground cemetery.

"Can the people in the pews above even guess what lies beneath them?" Nadine asked, hovering behind Babs as she made her way down the constricted passageway.

An unwelcomed foreboding spread through Babs as she realized Queen Sabella's vision was coming true. "Wherever you trod upon this earth, aren't you treading over countless deceased?" enquired Babs.

"I believe that's so," Nadine responded, startling Babs by speaking right into her ear.

Socrates had famously claimed that an unexamined life was not worth living. Babs pondered how many of her choices had been made to escape the feeling of loneliness, and with Nadine she had never felt alone—but at what cost? An intense melancholy crashed down on her as she realized what she needed to do, but wondered if she could overcome her fears.

"Are you afraid of the bones, Babs? You don't need to be. They can't do anything to you." Nadine stepped in front of her and started caressing one particular skull. Babs observed her feline-like curiosity.

"I wonder what kind of life this one had," Nadine pondered.

"I hope it was a good one. Look ahead, the end of the tunnel is coming up soon."

"Do you recognize where we should put the treasure?"

"Not yet; the space has changed. I'm a bit disoriented."

Babs's voice echoed off the solid earthen walls. She set the dolly down and began searching. Everywhere she looked, there were bones scattered across the floor. The air felt heavy and oppressive. She noticed on the floor a space where an old staircase had once been, and directly above that was the doorway that Drake's men had used for entry and exit; however, it looked to have been sealed long ago. In the vision given to her by the queen, Babs had seen how entry to this room had come through one single long passageway. Now, as she gazed around today, it seemed like several tunnels came down and made a cross shape, with Babs standing in the middle of a round room at its center, connecting all four pathways together.

Nadine pointed up at the ceiling, which was grimy and blackened with soot. Through the dark grime were shades of blue. Babs paused for a moment, trying to focus only on the feeling of this place. A low hum rose in her ears, and she squatted down, letting her hands wander through the grains of dust on the floor. She wiped some of the earth onto her face and neck, wanting it to know her. This dusty ground held secrets and knowledge that went deep, layer after layer.

She murmured to herself, "Yes, this is where my vision has brought me. This is where I'm supposed to be in body and spirit." She saw a vision of Drake screaming at his men, who were cowering in confusion. It played over and over in her mind. She couldn't help but think that she'd be angry too if someone had stolen her treasure. Perhaps all Drake wanted was to please his queen or gain a bit of fame and glory. It was hard to guess what motivated people.

The tunnel where Babs had entered must have been here during Drake and his men's time, but it had been cleverly hidden from them. The priests had likely assisted those who absconded with the treasure in a desperate attempt to save the city; they surely were the ones responsible for the secret chamber beneath the church. Unfortunately, their help hadn't been enough—the treasure had lain at the bottom of the ocean, taking with it many people's dreams and desires.

"We ought to put the treasure here. This is where Drake stood in my vision. Although, I don't feel his presence."

"There's conflicting layers of energy in this place. Kind of confusing, if you ask me. Like a tornado of vivid colors." Nadine prodded, "Should you say something?"

Babs wished Zadie was with her. Their plan ended at *get the treasure back to the correct spot*. What came next?

"Hey, Drake, here is your treasure. It was a pain in the ass to get here, so you're welcome." She paused and listened. Nothing. "Just for the record, my sister didn't steal it. So, if you could kindly lift your curse off her, that would be great."

"Maybe throw in a compliment," Nadine urged; her figure glided to the other side of the room.

Babs rolled her eyes and paced back and forth. "History has been kind to you. You are still remembered. Your name fills books," she praised. "There's even a yearly parade."

The flames of the torches wavered in the darkness. An electric buzz filled the air. The ground below started to shift and churn until, finally, the chest sank into the earth without making a sound, leaving no trace of where it had been.

"Do you think that means it worked?" Nadine asked, floating to Babs's side.

Babs shut her eyes and concentrated on Cricket; she kneeled and made a pattern of circular lines in the soil with her outstretched hand. She kissed her forehead to the ground, traveling through the dirt into the tunnel, skimming by the waterfall until arriving at the gigantic cavern. She felt Cricket's soul intertwined with the earth. All of Babs's strength was devoted to reading Cricket's energy. She looked for any sign of danger, but all she could feel was peace. Babs rose up. Contentment filled her being. "She is safe. Cricket is safe."

"Well, that was . . . strange," Nadine mused.

"I'm not complaining, at least it's over. I don't have the ability to travel through time, and from how Cricket described Drake, I'm glad I didn't have to do one-on-one negotiations. I'm fine with some things staying out of my awareness."

A part of Babs wished to stay where she was and savor the accomplishment she'd achieved for her sister, but another part of her knew why she was there. Taking a deep breath, Babs steeled herself to confront her fear and stood up. She remembered what the queen had shown her in her vision and turned left toward a tunnel she'd been through before in spirit. As she marched down the hallway, determined in her purpose, Babs reached out with her left hand and lightly brushed against the delicate bones that lined the walls.

Step by step, she made her way closer to her fate. The world flickered in and out, and her sense of self changed by increments. She was no longer in the same realm. The energy around her prickled between hot and cold, primordial and sensual. A warm mist hung over everything. The ground changed from hard rock to soft grass. The energy of summer swelled around her as she staggered forward.

"Queen of Summer, I am here. I'm ready," she whispered. "I will trust you."

The passageway lit up with red fire, lighting her way. Babs embraced the power of summer that filled the space. She was surrounded by the skulls of the wolf—the guardians of the summer court—and could feel their energy dancing around her. At the center of it all lay a wolf skull wearing a bronze helmet: exactly what she was searching for. She stood still, hesitating as she reached out to touch it. All these years she had believed in Nadine and defied everyone else's opinions; now reality hit hard, and it hurt no matter how much she wished it didn't.

Nadine's eyes grew wide with alarm. "Babs, what are you doing?" She spoke quickly, almost in a panic. "Let's go back to Zadie. She must be tired by now."

Babs put her bag down and held the wolf's skull firmly in her hands. She invoked its spirit as she replied calmly: "I'm done taking orders from you, Nadine."

"What selfishness compels you to take that skull? We already returned the treasure, and now it's time to go." Nadine's voice shook with indignation. She cut off Babs's escape route by hovering over her menacingly. Her eyes filled with confusion, then seethed with white-hot rage. "We leave NOW!" The air around her hands crackled as they lit up like flaming torches.

Nadine's tantrums used to paralyze Babs with fear, but she no longer feared her. Her vision had given her clarity. Nadine seemed so small and powerless instead of dangerous. It was almost comical how Nadine tried to wield control over Babs's life. But it all made sense now; Babs had enabled and excused Nadine's inappropriate behavior for so long out of a misguided need for companionship. Babs scoffed, unwavering in her stance against Nadine's manipulative power play. "The days of me bowing to your every whim are over."

"Is this because Bash could see me? Because he could send me away? He's just a stupid human! He doesn't know anything about us."

Babs held the wolf skull in her hands, and a primal force swept through her body. She felt as though all of nature had intertwined within her being. The skull trembled and ignited with flames, which formed a luminous portal, summoning the spirit of the wolf to enter this plane. Bones began to form, crafting a grotesque figure of muscle and sinew. Fur slowly sprouted from its skin, and it was completely reanimated. The newly formed wolf stood beside Babs, its fierce eyes locked onto Nadine. Nadine cringed at the creature's snarls, as if she felt its rage flowing through her form.

Nadine trembled fearfully as she stammered, "How dare you use the power of summer? You're not trained — it's impossible!"

The wolf's dark fur bristled, and a deep growl rolled through its throat. Its eyes blazed with hatred as they fixated on Nadine.

Babs trembled as the scorpion-like sting of betrayal, lies, and deceit pierced her heart. She seethed with rage, "You pretended to be my sister! You tricked me into believing my family was against me!"

Nadine stared at the wolf; her entire body tensed like a bowstring. "I am your sister!" Her eyes went wild. "You can't trust the summer court," she spat through gritted teeth. "The queen only does what is best for her! You don't mean anything to her, but you mean everything to me!" Nadine pleaded, letting her hands fall limp as her fire extinguished. "I don't expect you to understand. I did what I had to, to be able to be near you." Her desperate plea rang in Babs's ears. "It was the only way!"

"You are not my sister!" Babs roared, her voice raw and broken, tears streaming down her face with relentless ferocity.

Her real sister had never been there; this Nadine was an imposter. She'd accepted the hard, heart-wrenching fact that when they were born, only one twin had survived. Her real sister had died then and there.

Nadine's tear-filled eyes pleaded desperately as Babs erupted in a rage. "You're nothing but a liar! I won't stand for it anymore!" Her fists clenched tightly, burning with the fury that was boiling inside of her.

"I have always protected you and been there for you," Nadine begged, her voice quaking with emotion. "Don't trust the queen! Don't give yourself to her!" But her words were no use — Babs had already made up her mind.

"Be rid of you!" Babs screamed as the wolf lunged at Nadine. The beast summoned legendary magic to rip apart Nadine's spectral body hurling her to the ground. Nadine was helpless in the grip of the wolf's mystical powers as it violently shook and tore her soul apart. As chunks of her spirit were thrown out of the wolf's mouth, they disintegrated until nothing was left but a haunting memory.

Babs collapsed beside the wolf, her tears cascading into its fur. The old pain left her, and she felt restored.

Babs's lips uttered his name, "Gwylm."

CHAPTER 18
CRICKET

The wings of the ravens beat in long, slow strokes as they swirled up above Cricket and Bash and flew toward their mistress. Her cloak rose up around her like a storm cloud.

Bash's chest heaved as he tried to pull air into his lungs. His shirt was shredded and soaked with blood that streaked down his arms and torso. Cricket's skin had taken on a grey-green hue, her eyes vacant. Her breath came in short gasps.

The grim figure of death shuddered. A haunting wail escaped her pale lips as it echoed off the rushing torrents of the waterfall and through the glassy lake below her. Everything in the cavernous chamber seemed to freeze. Hundreds of fae eyes were transfixed on the writhing shadows that embraced the dark, shrouded intruder. Her head tilted as she listened to the faint whispers of an unknown presence, sallow face contorting in misery as if she were hearing a call from beyond. With a single fluid movement of her arm, her form dispersed into nothingness, leaving only an eerie silence behind for a few heartbeats.

The ravens croaked in distress, calling out a sorrowful song. Bash gathered Cricket in his arms. Her eyes began to flutter, her wounds began to mend, and her skin shone with an otherworldly radiance as she emerged from the brink of death, the curse that had cast a dark shadow over her body visibly fading away.

Cricket's head rolled to the side. She felt all eyes turn to her and Bash. Deep growls emanated from the wolves by the warriors lined along the cavern walls. The sound sent tremors through her body. When she observed the fae flying above the lake with crossbows and swords in hand, a foreboding feeling began to manifest inside that things were about to take a turn for the worse.

Bash quickly studied the scene in the room, noticing the guards standing watch around the lake. "Where did your sisters go?" he asked cautiously.

She murmured a response without looking at him, her eyes set on the closed-off waterfall. "They went ahead of me. They must have returned the treasure to where it belonged," she said quietly.

Bash's mouth began to form a reply, but he was cut short.

"Ambrosias, you were not summoned. What is the meaning of this unannounced intrusion?" The cavern was deafened with the reverberation of a voice, which carried a clear sense of anger.

The hair on Cricket's arms stood up. A tiny, pale woman with brilliant green eyes and long red hair gracefully sauntered out from behind the giant empty golden throne, flanked by dozens of winged fae women. She radiated an eerie glow, power pulsing off her in waves that rippled through the air like heat lightning. Her skin was so white it almost gave Cricket vertigo to look at her for too long without blinking. Her power and strength pulled all eyes to her. Her menacing smile revealed long, glittering fangs. All had gone still awaiting what would come next. Cricket was frozen in place by hallowed awe.

"No, Mother—Queen. I was called. No need for hostility," Ambrosias boomed with a baritone timbre that resonated throughout the room.

Cricket's gaze remained transfixed as Ambrosias gracefully approached his mother. His enormous wings appeared to be made of hardened vines, stirring up tiny ripples on the surface of the lake as they moved with great agility. The intricate patterns of vines, thorns, and bright red berries sent lumbering reflections dancing across the water, creating a dark medley of chaotic shadows that grew and receded, causing a hypnotic effect.

His broad, muscular frame rippled with every step, evoking a sense of power that was both captivating and calming. His pale silver locks waved gently down his back. His crown of lustrous blue ice shimmered under the firelight like stars in the night sky. Beneath his serene mask lay a smoldering passion that seemed to beckon to Cricket.

The queen's entire body shuddered in revulsion, her lip curling at the sound of Ambrosias's voice. "Then why do your men carry weapons? Have them stand down," she demanded callously.

Ambrosias's features softened, though his eyes still held a sharpness. His mother had a way of hurting him. He waved his arm casually, and his men unclenched their weapons.

He whipped around, his gaze a powerful force that pinned Cricket in place. His eyes glowed like starlight, and her heart raced as he flew toward her, sending shimmering ripples through the lake with every flap of his majestic earthy wings. The room melted away until only the two of them existed, locked in an unspoken connection. He glided closer, each movement fluid and perfect, as if some magical force kept him suspended inches above the ground.

"I heard your call," he purred, "and I have come to answer. I have waited for a long time."

A current of energy ran through Cricket as she stammered, "No, I . . . didn't."

He placed his fingertips on the tops of her shoulders and dragged them down her arm. When their hands met, something stirred deep within her soul.

"The connection between us is magnetic, imbued with destiny from the beginning of time. We were always meant to be entwined this way." He moved their hands over her heart and stepped closer. She watched as the vines of his wings writhed as he spoke, animated by his words.

Bash charged toward him but was immediately restrained by two of Ambrosias's soldiers, their grip on him tight and unyielding.

"Let all those present bear witness that the eldest, wielder of light, from the Culebra line has summoned me. I accept this fae as my own," boomed his powerful voice that filled the room. "Mine alone."

Cricket's stomach sank as understanding dawned on her. "Oh—wait—no," she stumbled out, feeling the heat rise in her cheeks. "I didn't call for you, I just fell! My hand slipped into the water; we were just returning. You see, I—"

Ambrosias's powerful gaze seemed to suck the oxygen from the air.

She slowly lifted her head, meeting his gaze. His eyes held hers, and a deep rumble shook the ground beneath them as he raised his hands forward. His chant echoed through the air like a divine proclamation that reverberated with magical power. Their arms began to glow an ethereal blue, and intricate symbols of ancient power flowed in perfect harmony around them. A soft warm energy surrounded them, and it felt like they were floating in a cloud of magic. As the power inscribed itself into their skin, it began to pulse with light, and she felt an indescribable force binding them together.

"It is done," Ambrosias intoned, his voice as deep and dark as the night. His eyes burned with passion as his thumb traced the winding mark on her arm. Matching his own design, it snaked its way around her skin like vines of energy. Cricket felt a pull inside her chest like an invisible rope that tethered her to him, binding them together with magic, and something else. She searched his face and felt as if she knew him, had always known him, from long before this world, when they were two souls entwined in another realm of existence.

He spun to face the queen, his face becoming a stone mask as he spoke. "Mother, you gave me to the winter court when I was nothing more than an infant. I have done my best to bring honor and respect to that court in your name. I have tirelessly strived for peace between our worlds—a laborious and thankless task." He paused for a moment, measuring his words. "The winter king grows weary of waiting for what is rightfully his." His tone was as sharp as a blade now, threatening and determined.

"It is *Your Highness* to you, Ambrosias." The queen fumed and glared at the prince. "The land has taken it, as the winter king well knows. It's hidden from my sight. The one that could wield the power to bring it back is too weak to do so—having given up her power for the love of a mortal." She turned her glare on Cricket. "I suggest you ensure the summoner does not follow the same path as the one before her."

Cricket was utterly lost. She hadn't meant to summon Ambrosias. How did these fae know her? Her family? The weight of it all beat down upon her until she felt like Alice in Wonderland trying to sort things out while everyone around her spoke gibberish. Wasn't it enough that they had just broken the curse? She hadn't even one moment to breathe between surviving that and landing right in the middle of — whatever this was.

"My chosen has nothing to do with this, as you well know," Ambrosias said through gritted teeth.

"We'll see about that." A vicious grin crossed the queen's face. "The hostage will have to continue to appease your king for now." Her voice was sharp and her eyes aflame with deranged fury.

"No more will you disrespect winter!" he growled, eyes blazing with fury. He reared his sword above his head, and in that instant, the room erupted into chaos. The flying fae unleashed a hail of arrows. The winged fae of summer took flight to meet their giant foe, fangs bared, wolves unleashed. The air crackled with energy as all the warriors prepared for battle.

Burt tugged on Cricket's ear, bringing her back to her immediate surroundings.

"I've got you, Burt. We must leave this place."

With the chaos ensuing, Bash freed himself from the one guard that still held on to him. He grabbed Cricket, and they started moving along the wall toward home, careful to not get too close to anyone. The women who stood along the walls began to chant again; a high-pitched wail that sounded like glass breaking on marble. The sound stabbed at Cricket's eardrums, and she clapped her hands over her ears. She couldn't think straight—her head felt fuzzy and thick, her vision dimming. Something wasn't right. Her world became out of focus, as if a fog had settled over it. She leaned against Bash, and he wrapped one arm around her protectively.

"You don't know where home is, Little C?" Burt asked, his grip tightening on her tiny ear.

She surveyed the room with a growing unease. "No, these tunnels are too labyrinthine," she muttered in dismay, her vision swimming in the hazy mist. She couldn't even make out the entrance from which they had come; its location remained shrouded in obscurity.

Burt stuck his finger out. "That way," his tiny voice squeaked directly into Cricket's ear. She motioned to Bash the way to move.

Tikaboo wildly darted around them, her tail twitching with anticipation. Suddenly, one of the female fighters stumbled back into Cricket's path, blocking their way to the tunnel entrance that led home. She showed no remorse as she wielded her sword at her opponent, thrusting it ruthlessly into his flesh before violently kicking him back into the lake.

Cricket rolled her shoulders back. What was once a clear mission of returning treasure to break a curse was now an evening cloaked in mass chaos. She and Bash were trapped in this nightmare. And she worried for her sisters. Were they faring any better?

The water had turned red from the blood spilling from the fighters' weapons, and streaks of crimson washed over the ground. Apparently fae could die. She studied the fae fighter right in front of her and realized that she had purposely blocked their path. Cricket's eyes widened with recognition as she understood who was standing before her.

Two gigantic, winged warriors descended from the sky, their colossal wings churning up polluting clouds of dust. The dark-eyed giant lunged forward, pushing Cricket to the ground as Bash raised his sword, poised to strike the descending foe. In a flash, another warrior flew toward them with a spear aimed at Bash. But just as quickly, Cricket's savior appeared — the warrior woman shot in between them and locked her hands onto the assailant's throat before he could reach Bash. As if possessed by some frenzied force, the two clashed against each other, their eyes wild with rage. Yet still she managed to hold them back from attacking Cricket. As Cricket watched the woman battle it out with both enemies, something stirred in her memory — that same warm familiar feeling she had felt during air practice years ago . . .

The giant glanced back to the warrior woman, confused. He fell backward as she rolled to one side, slashing viciously at his side. The heel of her foot connected with his, sending splinters of ankle bone into the water behind her.

The solid smack of a stone, thrown with such strength that it whizzed through the air like a deadly arrow, struck Cricket on the right cheek — so hard that her head spun from the force. She fell back several feet and landed next to Tika-boo, who licked her face and whined softly.

Bash scooped Cricket up from the ground and pulled her to his chest, concern crossing his face. "I think we are batting out of our league." His lips formed a frown.

Burt crawled out of her pocket where he had been hiding.

Cricket scanned the room; wolves were everywhere, fighting alongside the red-cloaked warrior fae. The circle of chanters remained unbroken, their voices making it near impossible to think. The giant statue stirred the water with a sword raised high. Steam rose like fog as it met her blade. The ravens had scattered about the room, unorganized. Cricket put one arm around Bash's chest; she could smell his blood and see where he'd been hurt. His left side was covered in gashes.

"I don't know why or how you two are here, but obviously you are not safe. Let's get you out," the familiar fae said, lifting Cricket's chin to examine the gash left by the stone. Strong comforting musk emanated from the woman as she turned Cricket's head back and forth.

Cricket looked closely into the eyes of the woman. Tiny braids snaked through her dark ponytail, and bits of dirt had become tangled in them. Condensation from the steam beaded on smooth skin near a scar that bisected one almond-shaped eye; a blemish on perfection. Her expression was guarded from emotion. Her fangs were longer than her crimson lips.

Cricket stammered, "Habina?"

"Yes, Cricket—it's me. We can talk later, *summoner, wielder of light.*" She spared a half grin. "Stay behind me, both of you." She shot a quick glance at Bash, who nodded in agreement. She pulled a dagger out of her belt. "The copper will keep anyone from the winter court from trancing you. We can't let Ambrosias steal you away to winter—Just try to stay away from anyone flying around, especially the ones that are bigger; they are older. Your mind is vulnerable to them, copper or not."

They weaved their way through the battle.

"What is this place?" Bash asked.

"This lake is a portal. It is water between worlds. You shouldn't have touched it." She glared at Cricket. "You let them in. Whether you meant to or not, you did summon

Ambrosias — if what he said was true." They dodged around a group viciously fighting. "We can figure that out later. Right now, they are trying to push them back in and lock the waters down. When we were summoned, we thought they were breaking the treaty, but apparently, they were invited." Her eyes bored into Cricket's while she handed her the blade. Their hands touched. She had missed Habina so much.

Cricket tucked Burt back in her pocket. "Stay by me, Ti-kaboo. No heroics," she barked, trying to keep her mind on the issue at hand.

"I think Babs's tea has worn off. How about you?" Bash asked. He rolled his shoulders back.

Cricket felt light, and although everything was colored by the thick haze, she still saw colorful bubbles of light surrounding most of the beings in the room. Bash was surrounded in a white glow. "Mine hasn't worn off yet."

They wove their way through the murky, hot steam that rose from the ground like a grimy mist. They kept as close to the wall as they could. Cricket's heels splashed in puddles of blood strewn across the rugged ground. The sharp aroma of adrenaline and death was thick in the air.

Something sliced deep into Cricket's back; she felt a searing pain, like fire, radiating from the wound. An ear-piercing bellow escaped her lips as she stumbled backward. She spun around and saw an unfathomable giant looming over her, his eyes fixated on hers with a sinister sneer stretching across his face. His ironclad grip paralyzed her body and lifted her off the ground as his razor-sharp icicle wings kicked up dust all around her. The winds created by his wings whirled into a frenzied dust storm, blurring Cricket's vision. Without hesitation, she clutched the copper knife firmly in both hands and stabbed wildly

behind her. Although she wasn't sure where she was strik-
ing him, wetness covered her back with each thrust even
as she was carried into the air. Although she felt sick to
her stomach, Cricket gritted her teeth and willed herself to
keep going; survival instincts surged through her now that
she had broken the curse.

A moment later, he released his viselike grip, and she
expeditiously plummeted to the ground. Every inch of her
body throbbed in pain, but she was victorious—she had
saved herself from capture.

"Grab her and go!" Habina ordered while pointing at
Bash.

An eternity seemed to pass in only a few seconds. Cricket
saw the sword of the winged warrior, suspended in midair
and aimed directly at her aunt Habina.

Her heart thudded in her chest as she thought about
being reunited with Habina after all this time, only to lose
her now. She felt a force inside her core, empowering her,
causing time to slow down around them—except for herself
and Habina.

She was silent, but her lips formed the words to Habina:
"Look behind you!"

In an act of sheer strength and agility, Cricket leaped
forward and catapulted into the air, flying by will alone.
Everyone else was motionless, apart from her and Habina,
who seemed to have stepped outside of time. She sent the
warrior flying backward into the lake with a loud splash.

Exerting all her power, she pushed his head down until
he was completely submerged. She made her way back to
shore and picked up Tikaboo in a protective embrace.

Meanwhile, Habina had dispatched three other huge
soldiers into the lake with remarkable swiftness, weaving
between them like a gazelle dodging predators. Finally

facing Cricket, they shared an approving nod as the spell ended and they reentered time. The cacophony of sound came rushing into Cricket's ears.

Cricket couldn't tell whether it was due to being close to her aunt or something else entirely, but she felt her head clear and strength flow through her body. She hastily patted her pocket, checking that Burt was still tucked away safely.

"Run to the tunnel. I will catch up with you," Habina yelled as she continued to cut down her enemies.

Cricket clasped Bash's hand, and together they raced alongside the lake, pushing any enemies in their way that were close enough to fall. She jumped up, snatching rocks out of the air meant to hit the chanting women and their ferocious wolves.

Bash leaped toward Cricket's direction with force, sweeping her into his arms and spinning them to the ground. Tikaboo flew away from Cricket's grasp, and Bash clamped his arms around her tightly, as she felt a warm liquid drenching her torso. With urgency she pushed him away to see an arrow lodged in his lower back. Terror struck Cricket's face as icy tendrils surged from the arrow, enveloping Bash's body in a deep coldness. His cheeks started to pale, and he seemed disoriented. The arrow glowed an icy blue, and droplets of an unknown liquid seemed to be coating his skin. Suddenly, Bash's eyelids drooped heavily, and he looked around in confusion, not seeming to recognize his surroundings.

"We have to find Babs and Zadie," Bash mumbled, but the energy it cost him was evident on his ashen face.

"I already told you that they aren't here—" Cricket became aware of her panicked voice before she could think further. She stared at the arrow piercing Bash's skin. It was slowly taking over his body. It was freezing him!

Habina let out a grimace of recognition. "Winter arrows." Her voice quivered as realization sank in. "It needs to be pulled out. It's just a flesh wound, but if we leave it, he will freeze to death."

"Help me lay him down." Cricket clasped his hands tightly, tears streaming down her face as Bash's skin remained icy to the touch. "Please don't leave me," she whispered softly into his ear, Tikaboo licking affectionately at his pale cheek.

Cricket braced herself, and with one swift motion, she yanked at the frigid arrow perched in Bash's side. He moaned as it remained stuck inside him. She pulled through the resistance until finally, with a sickening sound, it shot out of the wound it had created.

Cricket applied pressure to the injury, a wave of nausea washing over her. She grasped the copper blade, her hands shaking as she cut her sleeves off to use them as temporary bandages.

Habina helped heave Bash up into a seated position as Cricket expertly wound the fabric around his wound. The warmth that had been absent from his body was gradually returning as the enchantment of the arrow faded away. The sight of his pink skin was a relief as she inspected the dressing; there was minimal blood loss.

"We have a clear way to the tunnels," Habina yelled over the noise. She dropped down by Bash's side and secured his arm around her neck. Then she helped Cricket lift his other arm around her shoulders, and together they supported his limp body as they carried him toward an oval of light in the dark tunnel.

Tikaboo's fast feet ensured beating them all to the tunnel.

"Burt Find," Burt said, tilting his small head to the side with a mischievous grin.

"Yes, Burt, Find home."

CHAPTER 19
ZADIE

Zadie huddled on the hard cavern floor, the cold seeping through her scales. Goosebumps rose as rocks dug into the flesh of her shivering elbows. While on land, she was more sensitive to temperature changes.

Ignoring the chatter of her own teeth, she caressed the waterfall with her fingertips. In her mind, she begged for concealment from the chaos just beyond, where she had left Cricket. Worry for her sister sat in the pit of her stomach.

The thoughts of the water moved rapidly. She was trying to catch them all, like tiny fish flitting away. They changed from one form to another with a dynamic and enthusiastic energy. The water's tone was elevated and ethereal. From this body of water, one could learn a lot about acceptance; its vibrations remained high, giving it the capacity to adapt quickly. However, this body of water was unlike any other that Zadie had encountered. Like all water, it seemed to have an infinite memory and knowledge—but it appeared to be confused. It insisted it was in medieval Britain and surrounded by a grove of ancient, twisted trees tended by a secret society of druids.

Zadie was astounded to find that the water seemed to know her mother. Before her eyes, it created images of her mother's reflection past and present. She watched as the pictures went further back in time, until she saw her mother at the same age she is now. Excitedly, she couldn't wait to tell her mom about this strange occurrence.

She reclined, stretching her arms out above her head to dip them in the water. There was a large rock wedged between her shoulder blades, making it uncomfortable to lie down. Her knees may have been relieved from being off the ground, but it felt like the wounds on her back from the coral were burning. She just couldn't find a position that wasn't uncomfortable.

Zadie's gaze rested on the rough cavernous ceiling above her. Light filtered through the water and threw moving reflections that danced throughout the space. Dark blue pigment dominated the ceiling, with bright yellow star constellations painted at each of the tunnel openings. She was lying in an oval alcove that connected three separate tunnels. The way she and Babs had come in from showed the Draco constellation flanked by two winged figures. An ornate dragon flew above them; his scales were a shimmering white, his eyes sky blue.

Zadie's smile slowly faded as she looked above the tunnel that Babs had disappeared into. She noticed a pattern of Canis Major, with Sirius, the Dog Star, painted in bright red, exaggerated in size, set as a jewel in the crown of a beautiful horned woman who stood with a wolf at her side. Zadie couldn't quite make out the third tunnel's constellation. It appeared burnt and chiseled, deliberately deleted from history.

Navigation by the stars was one of her strongest suits. The blanket of the heavens was comforting to her. If she could see the sky, she knew where she was. But she didn't have a clue what these ancient pictures meant.

Zadie couldn't help worrying about the distance Babs might have needed to travel. Would she be okay returning the treasure alone, and what unseen dangers lurked in her path? The day so far had been anything but ordinary. Here she was sitting idly in the middle while one sister faced danger and the other dealt with a pirate's curse. Holding a barrier, while important, didn't feel very heroic.

Her imagination was trying to work out what was going on in the cavern below. Cricket must be beyond freaked out to be down there. Hopefully she was able to weave her way back to the tunnel entrance and get to the Sub unnoticed.

She wished she could release Kraken to relieve the boredom and help keep her mind off how uncomfortable she felt. But Kraken rarely listened, and most likely he would dive off the waterfall. She wouldn't have a chance at finding him then. He could be so infuriating. He enjoyed being chased around more than anything. Kraken was beyond amazing; he could get through the tiniest spots, blend into anything. She couldn't imagine being without him.

OMG, Babs, hurry up! I'm going crazy sitting here by myself!

Yara must have been enjoying her conversations with *Dulcinea*. Zadie wished she could be present to listen to the tales they would tell, having been apart from each other for centuries. Frequently, she pondered what it would be like when the moment arrived for her to depart and embrace life beneath the waves as a mermaid. Despite the great distance between them, would she be able to sense if either Cricket or Babs were in danger? Right now, it felt like they were all safe and sound.

"Who is *Yara*?"

Zadie craned her neck to the right as a tiny water sprite stepped out of the spray. The water trickled off her body, sliding down her smooth skin. Her webbed hands and feet moved her slowly toward Zadie as her large slitted eyes looked on with curiosity.

"My friend," Zadie answered. "Do you know what is going on down in the great cavern?"

"How would I know? I'm here with you."

The way her eyes open and close rapidly is akin to the movement of a frog's eyes, Zadie thought.

"You were listening to my thoughts?"

"Of course." The sprite took several hops and landed right by Zadie's head. "That's why I came. Your arms and back are hurting, huh?"

"Yes," Zadie replied, her voice wavering slightly.

The sprite gazed at her inquisitively. "What are you waiting for? Come on, give me a lick."

Zadie cocked her head in confusion. "Lick you?"

"I'm sure you know—my skin is a natural analgesic. It's truly remarkable." The sprite leaned in.

"Are you joking?" Zadie laughed.

"Not at all," the sprite said earnestly, gesturing for Zadie to continue. "Go ahead. I want your pain to stop—it's bothering us all. We don't put up with unpleasantness around here. So, lick or let go."

"Well, letting go of the waterfall isn't really an option." Zadie sighed.

Zadie's eyes cringed shut as her tongue brushed against the slimy surface of the sprite. An acrid taste flooded her mouth, causing a wave of nausea to wash over her. With a loud retch she shuddered, desperately trying to avoid the bile inching its way up her throat.

Yet, to her surprise, a tingling sensation slowly began to crawl its way through her, and within minutes she was able to feel the stress of lying on the ground ease. The tightness in her back melted into release, and warming energy coursed throughout the entirety of her body, leaving little more than contentment and relaxation behind.

"You're welcome," croaked the sprite as she hopped back into the waterfall.

Zadie felt the burning sensation emanating from her back continue to dissipate as her arm cramps melted away and were replaced by a sense of ease.

"Hey, you." Babs's black converse appeared in Zadie's view.

"Finally! Mission accomplished? Is Cricket safe?"

"Yes, actually it was anticlimactic." Babs frowned. "What's wrong with your face? You look kind of — green. In fact, all of you is kind of green, even your hair!"

"Oh no." Zadie frowned. "I think it's a side effect from the sprite, but hopefully it doesn't last long."

"Sprite?" Babs asked. Catching Zadie's grimace she continued, "Never mind — fill me in later. You ready to get out of here?"

"I thought you would never ask." Zadie shimmied, "I have an idea, but I'm not sure it's your thing."

Babs cracked a smile and nodded.

"I wish to ask the waterfall to take us up," Zadie blurted out.

"We don't know where 'up' is though," Babs commented.

"I know that whatever is up there, home is walkable, because we walked this far down here," Zadie reasoned.

"All right. So, what's next?" Babs inquired.

"Quite the change of heart," Zadie said with a raised brow. "What happened to the good old 'we can't do this' speech?"

Babs simply shrugged and winked. "Let's just say I feel relieved of a heavy burden."

Zadie's face contorted with concern. "Are you sure you're, okay? Did you hit your head?"

Babs laughed and pointed behind her. "Let me introduce you to my new friend." Out came a large wolf, its muzzle wet and paws caked with red mud. "This is Gwylm."

Zadie let out a gasp. "Where did it come from?"

"I'll fill you in later," Babs said. "Does your plan work for all three of us?"

Zadie groaned sarcastically, rolling her eyes. "You want to cling onto a giant wolf and see if the water can move us fast enough so that we hit the surface without both of you drowning?"

Babs grinned and held out her arms. "I guess that's the plan! Are we game?" Babs turned to the wolf. It sat unflinching.

Zadie smiled at Babs. "Right, I guess we take that as a yes from the giant furball? Sis, I need your help to sit up."

Babs came to Zadie's side and lifted her up off the ground.

"I will jump hard into the water when the water is ready; just cling onto my waist and try to keep away from my mer-tail. You okay with this? Are you cool, Wolfy?"

"Gwylm," Babs corrected. "Yes, he's in."

The sisters shared a look of understanding before Zadie asked in a gentle voice, "You nervous?"

"No, I trust you." She shrugged. "I love you, sis." She gave Zadie a tight squeeze.

Babs wasn't one to share her feelings, and her fear of the water was usually overwhelming.

"Back at you." Not wanting to be a codfish, Zadie replied, "There isn't anyone I would rather be going up this waterfall with than you." She kissed Babs on the cheek, then closed her eyes and waved her arm gracefully through the rushing drops. She felt its embrace and knew when it offered an invitation to push off from the ledge. At that moment, Zadie opened her eyes and yelled to Babs and the wolf, "Now!"

The trio leaped off the rocky ledge. With each powerful beat of Zadie's tail, they moved closer to the surface despite fighting against the current. A faint green glimmer washed over Zadie's mermaid form, and as the intensity of the light grew, so did her vibrational song. The waterfall responded by reversing its course. Zadie swam with determination, as if she was on a mission; she felt every ounce of fear Babs and Wolfy experienced and was determined to deliver them safely to the surface. In answer to their worry, dozens of colors—reds, greens, blues, yellows, and purples—swirled around them. The water sprites danced in a circle, sharing Zadie's music and creating a pocket of air for their two land guests.

After what seemed like an eternity of swimming, Zadie's song reached a crescendo, and they were thrust into a small calm lake. They had made it! Zadie thanked the sprites for helping them reach their destination.

The three swam to the shore. Babs clambered out of the lake first, coughing desperately and trying to catch her breath. Zadie followed behind in a fast transformation into her human form.

"Everyone okay?" Babs gasped between coughs while pointing frantically. "Those bubbles — the sprites — "

"Pretty cool, huh?" Zadie said as she looked around, squinting in attempt to find any hints of where they had ended up. "Can't make out much, though. Trees are too thick for me to see the sky."

Babs lay down on her back, closing her eyes with a sigh of relief. Gwylm flopped onto his stomach and nuzzled into the dirt, delighted to be on dry land again. After taking a few moments to just breathe, Babs abruptly shot up, scanning each direction intently. She slowly pointed farther ahead with a determined expression on her face. "It's that way," she said confidently.

"What's that way?"

"Our farm is that way. Just a few miles from here. The walk shouldn't take us that long. From there, if we take my motorcycle, we can get to Baubles and Whatnots in no time. We can even hook up the sidecar for Gwylm."

"I'm not getting on that deathtrap!" Zadie protested.

"Hey, I've worked on that old Indian motorcycle for years; it was a piece of junk when I found it. Now it looks brand-new; it even sounds great!" Babs insisted.

Zadie shuddered. Babs was a Daytona girl at heart. She only knew one speed: pedal to the metal. This speed addiction of hers was way less nerve-shattering when riding in her big honking truck. But two wheels — terrifying.

"Just think of it like a wave runner. I am as good at a motorcycle as you are at a wave runner. Trust me."

"I do trust you; it's just uncomfortable for me," Zadie said.

Babs started tugging at her ear. "You don't say. I just clung to you as we went up a waterfall. I think you can handle a motorcycle ride to Old Town. Come on, let's go—my skull earring is burning. Something is going on in the Sub."

CHAPTER 20
CRICKET

Cricket cradled Burt in her free hand. His pointy green hat fell, crumpling to the left and covering one of his wide childlike eyes. His long pointy ear swiveled as he listened to the chaos behind them. She marveled at his calm disinterest. Perhaps living in the walls at home gave him a sense of invisibility. Of course, his small stature protected him as well.

Habina's voice broke the awkward silence that had settled between her and Cricket. "Ready to play Find?"

"Okay, Little H," Burt replied warmly with a wink.

Cricket glanced across Bash's ashen face and stole a glimpse of Habina's almond eyes softening at the sight of Burt. Her lips were in a tight grimace, betraying how much Bash's weight was costing her. They steadily, slowly, took deliberate steps.

"That move we pulled off back there was pretty amazing," Habina said cautiously. "We sure made a difference in the fight. You are more experienced than I expected—having the ability to link with me and maintain the spell without physical contact." She stopped speaking for a moment, as if trying to figure out how to phrase something, then looked at Bash. "And include him too."

Cricket stumbled over her words, her mind racing. "Actually, this was my first time traveling without using an object focus," she murmured.

"You have forgotten how we used to play together," she said softly. "So, you're used to holding objects and taking trips through time? For the shop, right?"

"Yes," Cricket answered firmly.

"Well, what made it so incredible was the speed at which we were both able to move — faster than time itself — but still without having to touch each other."

Cricket nodded. Bash groaned in pain. They stopped moving for a moment to give him a rest.

"I'm sorry, we'll go a bit slower," Habina said as she eyed his bandage. It was not blood soaked; that was a good sign. "The bleeding has already stopped. Just one foot in front of the other."

"We can rest soon," Cricket murmured in Bash's ear.

Through gritted teeth, Bash said, "I'm sorry I'm slowing us down."

"Nonsense, you took an arrow for me. The least I can do is help shuffle you back to safety."

Bash gave a weak smile, turning his attention to his feet. "Quite a first experience with — your world. I don't understand how all of that can be going on and no one know about it."

"You're telling me!" Cricket exclaimed. "I didn't know it was going on, and I am fae! It was literally right there, and I was clueless."

Habina guided them to the left of the tunnel to avoid wading through a large pile of bones. As they came to a fork, Burt pointed to the left, and they followed his lead. "Let me see, you should have finished school by now and be helping your gran with the shop, right?" Habina asked.

Cricket shifted her arm around Bash before answering. "Yeah. I check and ground the energy of the objects that need it before we sell them. Just like you used to do." She felt her ankle twinge as her heel caught a divot in the tunnel floor.

"Babs is helping at the farm with your mom?" Habina asked, keeping her eye out for more obstacles.

"Yeah. Babs mostly runs the place. Mom travels a lot. She's actually gone now."

"Um-hm." Habina's eyes followed the fast-waving tail of Tikaboo, just turning out of their sight.

"Maj and Zadie breaking hearts all over town?"

Cricket paused for a moment before responding tersely. "Aunt Maj is no longer with us. She left after thinking you were dead, Aunt Habina." Her thoughts started to clear, and anger welled up inside her — Why did her family have to keep so many secrets? Why couldn't they just be open about things? And yet, wasn't she continuing the pattern? She should have talked to Gran about the curse.

They stopped walking.

"What do you mean Maj is gone? She shouldn't leave for at least another — "

Cricket snarled, "All I know is something horrible happened, you *died*, Maj ran away, and Gran and Mom refused to speak a word about it! They blocked our tunnel and told us not to ask any questions. Gran runs the store and teaches me how to take care of your old job. Babs helps Mom with the farm, and Zadie, well, she does her own thing since Maj left." Cricket's chest heaved as she shouted angrily, "Why is everyone so convinced that you're dead instead of knowing what you really are? A vampire?"

They took several steps, following Burt's tiny finger pointing to which tunnel they should take next.

Habina chuckled. "No, no vampire here! I've just become more powerful in the fae way."

Cricket's face crinkled in confusion. "Gran doesn't have fangs or anything like that."

"No," Habina said with a grin. "Gran still lives in the mortal world. When she comes back to the faerielands, her physical form will slowly shift."

"What do you mean?" Cricket probed, eyes wide, her anger subsiding.

"It has something to do with how we absorb energy from the ley lines around us. That kind of charge can enhance our abilities and change our physical forms too," Habina explained. "Does that make sense?"

"Kind of, I guess. Do the fangs do anything, or are they just decorative?"

"They give life. The last time Gran, Maj, and your mom saw me, I was close to death. Apparently, they thought I was dead, or they would have never left me. We ran into trouble when using the tunnels. There was a lot going on back then. We were greatly outnumbered. Fortunately, a healer from the summer court found me. She opened her vein with her fangs and fed me her sacred life-giving blood." Habina paused to take a breath before continuing, her words now full of emotion. "After several days I recovered my strength, and since then I have been repaying the life debt by serving the queen."

They focused on keeping Bash as comfortable as possible. Cricket kept an eye on Tikaboo as Burt continued to point.

Cricket dragged her aching limbs forward, lost in thought. Her fury at Habina's absence had gradually subsided, replaced with a feeling of sorrow and empathy for all she had endured.

After some time had passed, Cricket couldn't keep herself from asking, "Did I cause all the fighting back there?"

"Oh, there doesn't need to be any reason for the summer and winter courts to fight. But your clumsiness did give Ambrosias an excuse to come to summer and cause a stink. He uses any excuse to cross the worlds. But that he claimed you — publicly — this is a political move I don't yet understand."

Cricket's eyes widened as she replayed the scene in her mind. "He called me *light wielder*. How did he know who I was? Or what family I am a part of?"

Habina shook her head and smiled. "It's the knowing. We are all connected. You have it too, just hidden."

"Let me guess," Cricket interrupted, her voice filled with newfound understanding, "because I live outside the faerie realm."

Habina nodded in the affirmative.

The image of Ambrosias entered her mind, setting an electrifying sensation through her. She felt that same pull at her stomach, a longing she instinctively wanted to deny. She shifted her feet awkwardly and lowered her voice, blushing slightly as she asked, "So, *the knowing* — does it give you an aphrodisiac feeling? Like, does it have a strange magical effect?"

Habina's eyebrows shot up. "No, at least that hasn't been my experience." She looked sideways at Cricket. "I'm sure you felt the normal connection." Habina smiled. "Are you beginning to understand how much you give up by living in the mortal realm?"

Cricket looked at Bash. "I like my life just fine, thank you."

Finally, they turned to see at the end of the tunnel the opening to their sub. Several ravens clung to the walls, watching them.

Tikaboo pelted down the tunnel, her loud barks ricocheting off the walls. She chased after the birds as they flew through the entrance until she couldn't spot them anymore.

Burt yelled, "Find — I win."

Relief washed over Cricket. She mulled over all that Habina had said, reaching to see things from her point of view. But one thing she just couldn't grasp. "Why didn't you let Gran know you were alive?" Cricket asked, her voice wavering.

Habina spoke with confidence, her voice gentle but resolute. "I knew the best course of action was to leave my old life and move on to my new one."

Cricket felt a volcano of emotions erupt within her. "Oh, really? Maj was so torn up about losing you that she left. Gran and Mom can't talk about it. We all choke on the grief!" Tears threatened to spill from her eyes.

Habina stopped walking, gently cupping Cricket's face in her hands. "Cricket, look at me," she said softly. She lifted her head and stared into Habina's gentle gaze. "I never stopped loving you. The path I chose was one your mom would never want you to take. I showed her my respect and you my love by staying away." She paused, wiping a tear from Cricket's cheek with her thumb before continuing. "I am sorry if that wasn't enough."

Cricket's chin quivered; the emotion was too much. Her mind switched gears. "Do you think just the two of us can do the spell to seal off the tunnel?" They neared the entrance to their Sub.

The effects of Babs's tea had completely worn off. Between the tea and adrenaline, she'd been able to carry Bash with Habina for the past few hours, but she felt her strength giving out.

"The three of us are more than enough." Gran stood alone, encircled by dozens of blackbirds' lifeless carcasses.

"You were in Daytona!" Cricket exclaimed. She felt a mixture of dread and relief. Dread because she was embarrassed about all the problems she caused. All the decisions she had chosen wrongly had cost not only herself, but the ones she loved. She hoped to have had it all cleaned up before Gran found out. But she felt relief because she knew Gran could fix it. It was going to be okay.

"I sensed the seal go down and came home to find the shop closed, you gone, the tunnel open, and this mess." She waved her arms about the room. "You can explain yourself after we fix this. How bad is the boy's injury?" Gran asked, staring at Bash's limp body handing between Cricket and Habina.

"The bleeding has slowed considerably. I'll make him comfortable while you ready the spell," Habina said, avoiding Gran's gaze.

Gran's face went pale, her eyes wide. She quickly pivoted to Cricket. "Do you have the Culebra cigars?"

"Yes." Cricket handed her second bundle over with the lighter and placed Burt on the ground. He quietly scuttled away. Habina and Cricket sat Bash awkwardly in the chair, Tikaboo at their heels.

"Cricket, where are your sisters?" Gran asked.

"They fixed a complication we had with a cursed object. They'll be back soon. They're not coming through this way."

Gran settled in front of the large fireplace; lifting her hands above her head, she intoned,

"Protectors of the Culebra line, one of your oldest is here.
We seek your help and protection.
Give us strength for the task before us.
Heal the one who has fallen.
May our energy stay pure and strong,
That we will continue to be a stronghold."

The protection spell heated the room.

The stone dogs leaped from the fireplace, forming a circle of protection around the women. Tikaboo joined their ranks. Two stone dogs went to Bash and began licking his wound. Cricket could see the wound melt out of existence. The knot in her stomach loosened. He was going to be okay.

"Let us begin," Gran intoned.

Cricket noticed she had yet to make eye contact with or touch Habina, even as she placed the cigar in her aunt's mouth and lit the end when Habina took a deep draw. Cricket worried the magic would be affected by the tension. It was hard enough to summon when you were calm. This kind of strain could be explosive. Then again, maybe they could funnel that energy into the barrier.

It was her turn next to draw on her cigar. She was ready to follow Gran's lead.

"Your arms," Gran commanded.

Cricket caught Habina's eye; she had been staring at the raised markings on Cricket's forearm. "Will you be stuck on this side, Aunt Habina?"

"No, we will make it to keep out not keep in," Gran answered.

She nodded, closed her eyes, and inhaled on her cigar. A dark, gurgling noise, raspy and unsettled, came out as she exhaled.

Without pause she took another draw, and they each did in turn, blowing the white smoke up above their heads, forming a thick white cloud above and around. They swayed their feet, slowly moving clockwise in unison in a circle. Another draw, smoke above their heads, sway, step, sway, step. Gran's eyes rolled back; her face went dark. She began to speak.

"Spider spirit, Ancient Weaver of Magic
Mother of Women's Myriad Mysteries
Goddess of secrets and intuition
Send forth your bonds to weave a web!
Bless us with your Divine Essence
Weave for us a veil; shield us from distress.
Lend us your strength.
Block the way for those who wish us harm."

The smoke turned into wee white ethereal spiders, scarcely perceptible to the eye. They rained down on the three women, covering their bodies with bites and then gathering to spin a web formed by the blood of three generations of Culebra.

Cricket's mind wandered. Why did Gran see the court as such a threat? Habina seemed fine—content even. What could have gone so wrong that her family would put up a barrier and shield her and her sisters from the truth. In all her musings she never came close to imagining that the summer court was walkable from her home.

The ritual continued steadily, the smoke rose, the women walked, the spiders wove their delicate weave, a magical barrier. Cricket did her best to ignore the screaming welts forming all over her body.

Control. Patience. Draw. Exhale. Step. Focus.

Bash was out of her sight, but she could feel the healing power of the ancestral protectors as they worked on him.

Gran's voice had become so low, it was barely audible as she continued to chant.

Cricket kept her eyes on Habina's shoulder, directly in front of her; she focused on the rhythm of her steps in time with their movement. Her raised hand went from cold to tingling. All the blood had drained from it as it held tight in the air with Gran and Habina. She could feel Gran's grief circling around them, a heavy blanket she knew well, but Habina was feeling it for the first time. The weight of it pulled at all their souls.

Control. Patience. Draw. Exhale. Step. Focus.

The web came into Cricket's peripheral vision; the outline appeared complete. She guessed they were halfway through the spell. White spiders continued to rain down on them. The spiders crawled into their folds and crevices. Cricket could feel them in her ears, between her shoulder blades, under her arms, all over her feet.

Control. Patience. Draw. Exhale. Step. Focus.

Her mind wandered to her sisters, willing them to be safe and protected. Their faces swam in her mind.

Control. Patience. Draw. Exhale. Step. Focus.

She anchored her awareness to the solid floor beneath her feet. She couldn't feel the spiders on her body anymore. Her arm muscles were beginning to cramp; waves of nausea washed over her. Her head pounded as her breath became shallow. White lights began to float through her vision; depth perception eluded her.

Gran proclaimed, "And so it is," and Habina and Cricket echoed her words in agreement.

They released their grips, and Cricket fell to the floor. She was filled with joy that it had ended, tears flowing down her face. She crawled over to Bash, who seemed a bit better than before but was still pale from what had happened.

"Cricket." His voice came out hoarse.

"Are you okay?" she asked.

"You look like you have chicken pox," he joked, giving her a slow grin.

She nodded while pawing at his shoulder. His clothes were ripped and stained where the arrow had been, but there was no trace of the wound. The flesh was just a bit pinker than the rest of his tanned skin.

"I'm so glad you're all right. I'm sorry!"

"There's nothing to be sorry about," he reassured her.

"Nice group of stone dogs you have hanging out in your basement. Can we add them to the list of things to talk about later?"

She ran her hand across his forehead: no fever. He was taking this very well. She was starting to wonder if his secrets might rival hers.

"What? You don't have stone dogs that leap to life in your basement?" She grinned.

Gran's voice boomed like thunder. "Cricket has some serious explaining to do."

Cricket bit her lip, hoping Gran wouldn't scold her in front of everyone. But she guessed, all things considered, that really was too much to hope for.

"But first, Habina." Gran's voice broke.

Gran grabbed Habina fiercely, burying her face into Cricket's aunt's neck. Gran's sobs shook both women. The dam broke; it was all coming out, and Bash and Cricket were stuck in the corner of the room, unable to escape the splash. Cricket curled up into a tiny ball at the foot of the chair. Bash gently set his hand on her shoulder. She had never seen Gran vulnerable; it was terrifying.

"Why?" Gran wailed. "Why? Why? You follow *her* now? You know what she's done."

Habina held her till all the crying was out of her. "I will explain, if you are ready to listen," she said quietly, her face expressionless.

Gran let go of her and backed up, silently examining her from head to toe. The physical distance seemed to help Gran regain control of herself.

"I wasn't dead but would have died. One of the healers chose to save me."

"Better to be dead than a pawn in *her* games," Gran spat.

"You can't be serious!" Cricket exclaimed, taken aback by the severe look on Gran's face.

"Oh, but I am. You have no idea what pain the courts have caused our family through the generations." She whirled around on Habina. "And to think, my own daughter, a traitor. What will your sisters think when they find out?"

"How could you think I turned my back on my family?" Habina growled. Her almond eyes widened, and her mouth went slack, showing her long, needlelike fangs. Gran flinched, repelling a shudder. "By becoming a leading member of the summer court, I've gained *her* trust. I know where he is. I've been trying to find a way to get him back." Habina's voice softened. "I do more good on the other side of that wall than you do wasting away on this side. I make a real difference there." She pointed at the hardened spider web. "I didn't choose this path; it chose me. I rose to the challenge." Her scarlet cape swirled around her as she paced viciously through the space like a caged panther.

Habina straightened her back, put her hand on the hilt of her sword. "Sometimes our way is not what we had hoped. But we can decide to find, if not happiness, at least purpose."

Gran seemed to be weighing Habina's words, then switched her attention to Cricket. "I see you are no longer covering your hand." If Gran couldn't control Habina, she could at least control the conversation.

Cricket took a deep breath. How much trouble was she in? "In the last batch of items, I found an old diary that belonged to Sir Francis Drake; he cursed me with the Black Spot."

She droned on with all the details as Gran stood stone-faced, revealing nothing. Cricket knew she was jabbering, falling all over her words, but Gran's silence was making her nervous.

Habina threw her head back in manic laughter. Tears flowed down her porcelain-white face. "That—that is the craziest thing I have ever heard. Never when I grounded the energy of items did I have it out with a . . . pirate!" She continued laughing.

Cricket didn't see the humor in the situation. "Well, I think I would prefer risking pirate encounters to running around underground in that GenCon getup. What you do is the craziest thing I have ever heard," she retorted.

Bash jumped in. "Hey, I think GenCon tickets are on sale for next year already. You guys want to go? I've got a cousin—"

Habina and Cricket stared at him. Bash smiled and shrugged, obviously embarrassed.

Gran shook her head, clearly not understanding what they were talking about. "Where is the diary?"

"Safe," Cricket replied, pointing at the top of the fireplace, the crystal skull still sitting atop it.

"Who is . . . ?" Zadie's voice trailed off.

Babs and Zadie were descending the steps. They were both dripping wet, and Zadie had a slight green tint to her skin. Cricket hated to even guess what they had been through.

"Yes, it's your aunt Habina back from the grave," Gran said.

Babs and Zadie froze.

"Girls, come give me a wet hug." Habina opened her arms. "I promise not to bite."

Zadie walked slowly toward Habina while Babs ran over to Cricket, the giant wolf at her heels. She sat on the ground, grasped at Cricket's hand, and started to turn it over and around. A smile spread across her face as she realized all the damage was gone.

"Whoa—that's one big dog!" Cricket exclaimed.

Gran's face went white.

"You two all right?" Cricket asked.

"A lot better than you; we don't have chicken pox," Zadie exclaimed.

Bash grinned at Zadie and chuckled. "I made the same joke!"

"And what about you, ghostbuster?" Babs interjected, looking toward Bash.

Bash stretched his arm behind him. "No worse for wear. Did you fix your"—Bash coughed, not wanting to out Babs in font of everyone—"issue?"

Babs glanced at the sealed entryway to the tunnels. "All taken care of, thanks," she mumbled in response.

"Glad to hear it. So, anyone else feeling pizza and binge-watching a fantasy series?" asked Bash.

"After a much-needed rest," Cricket replied.

Gran's brows knit together as she eyed Bash. "Young man, I trust that anything you've learned about our family will stay with you. We are very private about our . . . lives."

"Your secrets are safe with me," he said sincerely.

"Gran, he has a few secrets of his own; you have nothing to worry about," Babs said.

Gran nodded.

Cricket felt a hand at her elbow. She turned, and there was Habina. They walked to the corner of the room for privacy.

Habina lifted Cricket's hand and examined the magical markings that wrapped around her forearm, they glimmered even in the low light of the basement. "We need to talk," she said in a low murmur. "Ambrosias won't leave you alone."

"What do you mean? He doesn't even know who I am."

"Yes, he does know you." Habina gently leaned against the fireplace. "When you touched the water, all your memories, all of your thoughts, poured through. Everything you know, everything moment was shared. You are connected."

"He said I called to him?"

"You did, through the portal. It must have been unconscious on your end, but it was in you, nonetheless. Then he answered, and you were publicly chosen, in front of both the summer and the winter court, in the Queen's Hall. That made it as official as any ceremony."

"That place was the Queen's Hall?" Cricket felt silly thinking it was a temple. "Well, we just did the spell. The tunnel is sealed off. He can't get to me."

"That?" Habina threw her head back and laughed. "That would never hold against a prince of winter. But he's not going to walk into the Sub."

"What do you mean?"

"You're *linked*."

"So?"

Habina's jaws loosened. Light from the fireplace reflected off her glistening fangs. "As you have opened to him, he will open to you." Amusement crossed her face. "You'll find out. If I were to guess, the experience should be—*pleasant*."

Cricket looked over at Bash. "I have enough *pleasant* in my life."

Habina followed her gaze. "I find you can never have enough—*pleasant*. But my appetite is insatiable." She licked her lips.

Cricket had spent years yearning for Habina to be here to teach her. Now that she was standing right in front of her, she felt hesitant.

The woman sanding by her side was nothing like the person she remembered from her youth. This person was wild and feral. She exuded danger and dark experiences. She was all hard, jagged edges. Cricket searched the woman's face for any hint of softness and came up wanting. Was that the price of giving yourself over to the faerie realm? But Habina was full blooded. Perhaps that was why she was affected by the court so.

"What if I don't want to be *linked*?" Cricket bit her lower lip.

Habina ran her fingers over the marks on her arm. "It's done. There's no going back." She scanned the room. "But I am the only one who knows. Your sisters weren't in the room. No one else needs to know."

"Bash was there."

"Sure, he was there, but he doesn't understand."

"I don't understand. You don't think I should tell Gran?"

"There's no need to tell her, or your mom, till we know what the bigger game is."

"I don't know. I should have told Gran about the curse. She took it well, but I am sure I am in a world of trouble—"

"Your intuition was right to keep her out of that fight.

You saw what it was like down there. The least in either court is more powerful than her. She's lived in the human world too long." Habina gave a huff. "Give me some time to get some intel. There is a reason Prince Ambrosias answered your call. And a reason he made such a spectacle of it."

"Well, I guess that makes sense." Cricket looked over at her sisters. "You'll tell me everything you find out, right?"

Habina placed her hand over the prince's marking. "I will tell you everything, and we will tell our family — when the time is right."

CHAPTER 21

ZADIE

She watched the sun rise. Orange and purple slithered across the sky, mirrored on the surface of the water. The clouds hung low and spread wide with just a little breeze. Did the Mer come up to watch the sunrise? She would miss it, living deep under the water. And the moon, she would miss the moon. She was being silly. Of course, she could come to the surface after the full change. Why was she feeling so melodramatic? It wasn't like it was happening anytime soon.

Her wet hair smelled of lavender and lay loosely about her shoulders; warm water soaked through her thin silk robe. The night's rest had done her good. Her aches were gone, coral sting all but gone as well, thanks to the water sprite. Beneath her bare feet she could feel *Yara* and *Dulcinea* happily chattering away. She cradled her thick cream-colored porcelain cup between her hands. Steam rose from her morning coffee. She felt Tom coming up behind her. His heavy footsteps swayed the boat ever so slightly. It was a comforting movement. One that always brought a smile to her face.

"Beautiful sunrise," Tom's baritone voice whispered in her ear. His arm encircled her waist, pulling the full length of her body into him.

She snuggled in, sliding one hand up and down his arm lazily, feeling the softness of his terrycloth robe. "Did you grab some coffee?"

He raised a matching mug to hers into her vision.

It didn't get better than this. The smell of coffee mixed with Tom's sandalwood aftershave enjoyed on a crisp morning during the sunrise. All felt right. They stood there, swaying with the boat, breathing in the morning while most of the world still slept.

"I have something for you." Zadie's voice caught in her throat. Why was she so emotional today? She turned around, walked over to the navigation center, and pulled out the envelope with the title to *Yara* and all the paperwork that went with it.

"Come with me to the bow." She grabbed his hand, and they walked to the front of the boat. "Look over," she said with a sheepish grin.

Tom looked puzzled.

"Go ahead." She continued to smile.

"Two mastheads? I don't understand."

"Look closely — you know *Yara*. Look at the other one. The one to the right."

He leaned all the way over the railing. He hung there for quite some time.

"I'll be damned! How did you manage to do that?"

"Total newbie trade secret. But you were right about where she was. I could have never found her without you," she said with complete gratitude.

"The coral?"

"Terrible. But I was able to keep *Yara* safe."

"How is *Dulcinea* not waterlogged?"

"Magic, of course." She shrugged.

"Of course." He shook his head, not believing a word she said. "So, the dive was off the record?"

"Yep, a secret."

"Middle of the night?"

"Of course."

"Reckless! The balls on you." He smiled.

She'd known he would be proud of her. She handed him the envelope.

"What is this?"

"It's the title and papers to *Yara*, and the paperwork that shows that if anything should happen to me, she and her boat slip are deeded to you."

"Don't be silly . . ."

"Tom, you know what this ship means to me. I'm responsible for her. You are the only person I trust to take care of her if something happens to me. Keep the papers and promise me that if something happens, you will keep her on the sea. Always on the sea. Do you understand?" She felt a hot tear fall down her cheek.

He came in and hugged her tight. "Don't be upset, love. Of course, I would take care of your ship like it was my own. There, it's all right now. No need to think about sad things. It's too beautiful of a day." He turned her around to face the sun. "Give that sun a look; it's a perfect day. It's already all the way up. We are lollygagging the day away."

His arms wrapped around her middle. She felt *Yara* and *Dulcinea* accept him, even if he couldn't feel them yet. She breathed a sigh of relief. It was going to be okay. When she did leave to go be with Maj and all the Mers, *Yara* and *Dulcinea* would be well taken care of. Hopefully that wouldn't be for a long time. Hopefully she would get many more sunrises like this, with Tom.

"Let's go for a sail," Zadie suggested. "The weather doesn't get better than this." Watching him work the ropes was a beautiful sight.

"Sure, are you up for some deep-sea fishing? I can grab all my gear; we can be ready to go in less than a half hour."

She set her coffee mug down on the railing and turned around to face him. His hands glided down, cupping her bum, rubbing in small circles. "I could be persuaded." She smiled wickedly and kissed his chest where his robe hung open.

He pulled her up against him as she wrapped her legs around his waist, her arms encircling his neck. "You seem more interested in an encore to this morning than catching fish." He chuckled.

"Maybe I want to land myself the big fish." She kissed him deeply; she could feel his fingers digging into her flesh. Sparks of pleasure ran through her body. His desire was always deeper in the morning. "Fishing, encore, I leave the choice to you." She breathed, a sigh escaping her lips as her back arched involuntarily as his hands played her body like an instrument.

"I choose both," he whispered into her neck, causing goosebumps to rise as she rocked her body against him. He moved his hands to hold her waist, letting her legs lower to the ground.

"You're right, why can't we have it all?" She ran her hands slowly down his chest, his stomach, while stepping away from him. Her robe had come undone and lay open wide, showing him her desire. She shrugged and let the robe slide down her body, forming a silky puddle on the floor. "Let's have it all."

CHAPTER 22

BABS

The shadows grew long in the woods. The sun was beginning to set, and soon, the moon would be above her head. Babs made her way through the woods, passing through the realms with her own magic to the entrance of the queen of summer's cave.

Gwylm's voice had been a constant in her mind since the catacombs. It had taken her a while to understand him, beyond just his name, but now they walked together in silence. Babs needed time to process all the events that had happened.

Who knew Cricket's job of grounding the energy from items could be so dangerous? It made sense that if you were going back and forth in time, you could interfere, alter, or, in this case, just plain screw up. They had come at it in arrogance and ignorance. They'd always assumed if they were together, the power of three sisters united, nothing could hurt them. That, they had found out, was an erroneous assumption.

How strange life was. Had she and her sisters not screwed up with Drake, she would have never tried to talk to Liande and would never have encountered the summer queen. The family wouldn't have found out Aunt Habina was still alive. Or was life set? If this sequence of events hadn't happened, would fate have found another way to get her here? To this point right now? Were they all just pawns on a chessboard?

She smiled at Gwylm, grateful for the quiet of the evening. Their footsteps echoed around her in the vastness of the cave.

"Ready yourself, they come." Gwylm's voice entered her mind. She nodded and softened her gaze and began to chant from her heart as she kneeled before an altar flanked by torches and candles.

> *"Lady of Flame, Horned One,*
> *Come to me.*
> *Bestow upon me your sacred magic.*
> *Great Queen,*
> *Mother of Wolves, Magnificent Ruler,*
> *Come to me.*
> *My body is of Earth, my heart awakened.*
> *Great Queen,*
> *I make myself an offering to you.*
> *Come to me."*

Babs swayed in small circles as she repeated the chant over and over, like a leaf blown in the wind. She was being moved by spirit and letting go of all that was not now. She felt light and free, comfortable in her own skin. Out of the shadow of the cave she sensed movement. The queen, in crimson robes with a star on her crown, came from the darkness, staring at her. A procession of women trailed behind, clad in much the same way, their hair arranged in ornate braids, wearing the same headdress as their leader, each accompanied by a large wolf. Out of the corner of her eye, she spotted Habina. The women formed a circle surrounding Babs.

"Lady of Flame, Mother of Wolves has heard your plea." The queen's voice cracked like thunder through the clearing. "Do you wish to serve the summer court, train to face the challenge, and embrace your fae side completely?"

Babs's mind wandered back to her vision given by queen. It was Babs clothed in crimson, with these women at her side, reuniting her mother with her father. A thought that before she dared not even hope for. The thought of failure was too painful. But now, a flame of hope had been ignited within her, and she felt the warmth of the tinniest bit of hope. "I do."

"Gwylm has called to you, and you have answered. Do you swear to be faithful and honorable to your bond?"

Directly in front of her, Gwylm sat proud, head raised tall. Babs was amazed by the kindness and openness in the pools of Gwylm's eyes. "I do."

All the fae of summer court surrounded her. "The old left behind," the queen murmured.

Knives cut at Babs's clothes. Warm, thin fingers roamed all over her body, pulling off her socks and shoes, cutting off her pants. She stood nude, the orange light warming her soft, vulnerable flesh. A bowl was passed from one woman to another; each murmured something, touched the surface of the liquid, then drew a spiral on their chest. They touched the liquid again and passed the bowl on. The bowl reached the queen.

"I anoint you with blessings of protection and acceptance; may you be found worthy to be numbered as one of us, a spoke in the wheel of turning," the queen said while raising the bowl above Babs's head.

Warm oil ran in rivers down Babs's hair, over her face, snaking its way around her curves, puddling in her crevices, leaving sensual, silky trails.

A crimson robe was pulled over her head, covering her flesh. Someone began brushing out her hair. The front was pulled back to form tiny braids that fell down the back of her neck. She looked just like them.

"The initiation begins. For twelve moons, you will be prepared by Verity, who will train you alongside Gwylm. You will earn the robe granted to you and become worthy of your place amongst us. Your name will be written in the annals. May your deeds be worthy of song and praise."

"And so it is," they all said.

The women and their wolves began to silently walk deeper into the cave.

One woman, as pale as the moon, grabbed at her arm. "I'm Verity," she whispered, not breaking the seriousness of the moment.

Babs took in her youthful gait. Her eyes shone like emeralds even in the dark evening. Mischievousness played at the corners of her mouth. "Gwylm and I are the ones who will walk the path with you. We have the honor of teaching you the way. Knowledge is like the stars; there is more to find than what can be seen. History is many millennia older than you have been led to believe. The old texts, the old songs, will be written on your heart. Tonight, you rest. Tomorrow, it begins. Follow me. I will take you home."

CHAPTER 23
CRICKET

Settling against Bash's chest, Cricket snuggled under the cozy blanket while swinging lazily in the hammock, looking up at the stars. The night sky seemed so vast over the black void of the ocean. It was a calm, windless night. All that could be heard was the slow creak of the hammock rope.

"More hot chocolate? I can run in the house and grab some," Bash offered.

They'd spent the last hour watching the end of a baseball game with Bash's dad before washing up the dishes and ending the evening on the back deck surrounded by dune grasses. The cozy seaside cottage was complete with its own wind chimes and wild roses. A wooden walkway led from their abode right down to the beach.

"Nope, I don't want to move a muscle. I'm overstuffed with pizza and oversugared with chocolate. I can't remember the last time I felt this sated," she said, nuzzling into him closer.

"I should have stopped two pieces before I did. I feel round," Bash replied.

She laughed. "There is nothing round about you." She placed her hand on his stomach; the cotton of his tee was super-worn and soft.

He leaned in and kissed her, long and lovingly.

"I feel like we are on a different planet. It's hard to believe this calm and tranquil spot is only twenty minutes from Old Town." She breathed in deeply and sighed.

"Oh, trust me, you would get bored fast out here." He laced his fingers through hers. "Especially you. You live a life of one crazy adventure after another."

"Bash, this is actual heaven. You can walk to the grocery store, sushi, and even a great pizza place. After doing that, you get to come back here. Here! Look at those stars. They are so much brighter here than in town."

"Well, come look at them anytime." He gently brushed his lips against hers. "I've always thought you were special, Cricket. But I would have never guessed a *faerie*."

"Would you really have believed me had you not seen it all for yourself?"

He was quiet for a moment. "I would like to think I would have. I wish I'd told you sooner about, well, me. Then maybe you would have told me about you."

Things would have been so much different if they had gone that route. She ran her fingers along his arm. "I thought you talked to yourself. You do it all the time!" She considered his conversation in the pirate museum with his buddy Ryan. "Seeing ghosts isn't a secret for you? Ryan knows, doesn't he?"

He pursed his lips. "Want to walk on the beach?"

"Sure," she responded as they sat up in unison.

Their bare feet padded across the wood planks, Cricket savoring the unfamiliar cool damp feel. They walked the long length in comfortable silence, fingers interlaced. He led her along the small solar-lantern-lit path down the stairs to the sandy beach. It was low tide, and only a few couples walked hand in hand, all spaced out like a well-planted garden.

"When I was four, I was asleep in my bed and woke up to see my grandma standing beside me. She told me she loved me and that she was very happy, and that I shouldn't be sad." He paused, kicking lightly at the sand as they stopped walking. "I ran to my parents' bedroom and told them what happened. They said I had a vivid dream and to go back to sleep. The next day, they got the call that Grandma had passed in her sleep. This creeped my parents out, so I kept it to myself whenever I saw something . . . odd."

"That must have been hard," she said.

"I felt like I was doing something wrong, but I didn't know how to make it go away." They began to walk again.

"Did you want it to?" she asked, keeping up with his stride.

"Absolutely, till Ryan. He figured out what was going on with me and thought it was cool. We watched all the ghostbusters TV shows, and when we were older, went on ghost tours here together. He's into ghost busting. He made it fun, kind of like how I assume you are with your whole family," Bash said.

"Yeah, I guess I took it for granted that I could always call up my sisters. Being half fae isn't exactly unique. It's just complicated."

They turned around and followed their footprints back to his cottage.

"So do you, uh, ghost bust?" she asked.

"I can, kind of. I can see them, but sometimes their energy is more . . . loud than mine. I can keep them from influencing me, or keep them from affecting people in the moment, but I can't always make them go away."

"It must be hard, seeing ghosts and living in the most haunted city in the States," she said.

"I figure there is a reason for everything. I live here for a reason; I have this ability for a reason. Hopefully I can do some good with it."

"Like 'literally chasing down death and taking an arrow for me' kind of good with it?" she teased.

"Exactly like that." He chuckled.

"Oh." Cricket reached around her neck to give him back the crucifix.

"Keep it, I like knowing you have it."

"If you're sure." She smiled. "Do you see any ghosts right now?"

He exaggeratedly looked around. "Nope, the beach is all clear. But I can tell you . . ."

"Let me guess, a woman in white walks the ocean at night, looking for her lost sailor love?" she joked.

"I don't know what she is looking for, but yep. She walks the ocean at night, and she's not the only one."

She shivered at the thought of being stuck in a loop of longing, constantly searching the ocean shore for the person you loved. She wrapped her arm around Bash. "So, now do I know everything there is to know about you, Bash Wellington?"

He stopped and cupped her face in his hands. "Not by a long shot," he said and pressed his lips against hers. "So, while we have all the cards on the table—" Bash rubbed his lips together. "The whole being *chosen* by that big guy?"

"Right." Cricket kicked at the sand at her feet. "Habina talked to me a little about it. She's going to poke around and see what that is all about."

"Okay. How do you feel about the, ah—event?" He lifted her arm and rubbed at the scroll work reflecting the moonlight down her arm. "Is this permanent?"

"I think so. I don't know, really, what happened or if it's permanent." She rolled her shoulder back and dropped her arm, taking a few paces back. "To be totally honest, I did feel a connection to him. Like, a recognition or a knowing. I just don't understand it."

"I see." Bash paced back and forth and ran his fingers through his hair. "Whatever you need, I am here. You don't have to hide it from me. Okay?" He closed the distance between them in two big strides, wrapping his arms tightly around her. "We've wasted enough time." He kissed her deeply. "Be with me, Cricket." His voice came out ragged. "Choose me."

She pressed her palms against his chest, gently pushing him away, taking a step backward to meet his gaze.

"Why, Bash, are you asking me to be your girlfriend?"

Her expression softened as she realized how simple this seemed, compared to everything that had just transpired. All she needed to do was embrace life on a day-to-day basis. She could make small decisions and appreciate the little things instead of worrying about plotting out her whole future.

"One condition." She smirked.

Bash's eyebrows shot up.

"Let me ghost bust with you and Ryan."

He laughed. "I am sure that can be arranged. Teach me about the faerie court?"

She grabbed at his shirt and teased his bottom lip with hers. "I'm not sure how much I'm allowed to."

"Hmmm." He ran tiny kisses down the nape of her neck. "Then just tell me about you. I want to know everything about you." He nuzzled into the side of her neck, and she shivered in delight.

"I don't want to put you in any more danger." Cricket's voice was but a whisper.

"Avoiding winter's freezing arrows." He traced tiny circles along her collarbone with his fingers. "Sounds like a good plan." She ran her hands along his sides lovingly. "At least team summer seems level-headed."

"Let's hope so, now that Babs is tangled up with them. Life just got more interesting," she said while softly pressing her lips against his ear.

"When you live it right, it always does."

ACKNOWLEDGMENTS

I extend my thanks to the Florida Star Fiction Writers for their invaluable insight and steady support. Your contributions came to be crucial in my writing journey. Also, a big thank-you to my husband for his encouragement and belief in my work, which have been essential to bringing this book to fruition.

CHRISSY CHICORY

invites you into her mesmerizing urban fantasy world with *Unabashedly Chosen*, the inaugural tale in the Culebra Chronicles. A graduate of Bradley University with a bachelor's in science, and an associate's in library science from Illinois Central College, Chrissy weaves her artistic vision and literary passion into her storytelling. Having been an esteemed member of the Florida Star Fiction Writers for three years, she deeply values the kinship and inspiration shared among her fellow writers. In her leisure, Chrissy enjoys exploring the mysteries of beachside towns with her Cavalier King Charles spaniel and engaging in spirited discussions with her author friends over lunch.

WWW.CHRISSYCHICORY.COM

www.ingramcontent.com/pod-product-compliance
Lightning Source LLC
Chambersburg PA
CBHW030810020726
47499CB00006B/1858

9 781963 402049